CW01080682

WINGS OF CHERUBS

The Saga of the Rediscovery of

PISCO PUNCH

Old San Francisco's Mystery Drink

Guillermo Toro-Lira

Wings of Cherubs
The Saga of the Rediscovery of
Pisco Punch
Old San Francisco's Mystery Drink
© 2007, Guillermo L. Toro-Lira
www.wingsofcherubs.com

ISBN 978-1-4196-7320-7

Library of Congress Control Number: 2007905344
Publisher: BookSurge Publishing
North Charleston, South Carolina

Printed in the United States of America

Contents

Prologue 7

Introduction 9

A Fire-Defying Landmark 13

A Needle in a Haystack 19

Connecting the Dots 37

Setting the Rules 55

Secrets Revealed 81

Cultural Parties 91

Telephonic Revelations 131

An Eternal Goodbye 185

The End 191

Pisco Punch 193

Acknowledgments 197

Bibliography 199

Illustrations 209

Index 211

Addendum 223

To my father, to my mother, to Brenda, to my sons which are the engine that gives the impulse to move forward, especially to Martin who teaches me everyday the courage to win, even when life puts obstacles in the way: I always follow your path son, your footprints show me the way.

Prologue

Ceviche. Guinea pig. Corn-and-potato cream soup. Impossibly large fava beans. Lamb sautéed with wildberries in its own juice. Cuisine from Peru is a singular blend of European, Andean and Asian influences that mirrors a culture unlike any other in the Americas. And what better way to wet your whistle than with the ne plus ultra of Peruvian drinks, a Pisco Sour.

Pisco Sour, you say? But isn't this a book about Pisco Punch? Yes it is, but let me explain. The former, invented in Lima during the 1920s by an ex-pat American barman, is an egg-white concoction not unlike America's Gin Fizz but made with the brandy of Peru's ubiquitous grape, the pisco. Pisco Punch, a clear drink also made with the brandy, is another matter. Its heyday was a century ago in San Francisco, but because the recipe was lost with the death of its inventor in 1926, the drink became extinct.

In this book, Guillermo Toro-Lira resurrects Pisco Punch with the creativity and zeal of a religious convert. His tale is part Sam Spade mystery, part Borges hallucination, part Michener novel, part scholarly history, part psychoanalysis, part diary, part comedy, and wholly original. Pisco Punch is the core protagonist in this broad, heartfelt, often leapfrogging account of how San Francisco came into being as a cosmopolitan American city and stayed that way. Mr. Toro-Lira gets beneath the skin of Mark Twain's drinking habits, Latin Americans rushing for gold, Junipero Serra's missions, Peruvian navigator Don Francisco de la Bodega y Quadra, pre-Columbian agriculture, and much more. His alluring maps, charts, photos and superimposed images fuse the past with the present and the familiar with the exotic. Then there's the mystery of the bartender...But enough! I don't want to give the story away!

As told by Mr. Toro-Lira, a Peruvian who has long resided near San Francisco, the presence of Peru was no small factor in the city's early history. Indeed, my own ancestor Domingo Ghirardelli, after leaving Italy in the 1830s, first prospered as a confectioner in Lima before moving his Peruvian wife and family to San Francisco, where he launched the chocolate business we know today in 1852.

I love San Francisco. This is not just for the obvious reasons of how beautiful and cosmopolitan it is, but because San Franciscans seem so marvelously pleasure-bound. They have the food, the wine, the user-friendly weather, the creative opera, the espresso cafés, and the "boutique" chocolates (and that's for starters). How natural and perfect, then, that a drink like Pisco Punch should arise and thrive in the City-by-the-Bay, a metropolis so intoxicating, to paraphrase a jazz song, that even people who don't indulge in alcohol feel a bit woozy there. The labor of love that follows bears witness to a great city, a great drink, and a great way to be. Long live pleasure.

Sidney Lawrence
Washington, DC

Introduction

I could never have imagined that after reaching middle age I would decide to write and publish without reservation and only try to present through the crystal of my eyes, the history of several cultures which are connected by a thread that pulls them with as much force as the famous cable cars that furrow across San Francisco. I introduce myself with the self-confidence that I get from this pisco glass, Peruvian brandy, brandy of Pisco, Italia, or whatever the persons who wrote about its virtues and its mysteries wished to call it.

Because I am a Peruvian who has resided in the great Bay Area of San Francisco, California, for many years and being an incorrigible fan of pisco for many more, it is very easy to understand my obsession when I discovered the existence of Pisco Punch, an emblem drink of this city of old, and which made it famous in the business, intellectual, and political circles and theatrical high societies at the end of the 19th century and beginning of the 20th. The discovery was filled with mysteries that joined the characters with stories which made them extremely amusing. The feelings that were triggered attracted me intensely. Moreover I noticed that the recipe of the drink, which had inspired many great writers and important societies of those days, had obscurely been lost. It had remained in the past engraved in its creator's soul,

Duncan Nicol, who died in 1926 taking the secret with him to his grave.

Revealing the magical mystery that the Pisco Punch entailed took me five years of caring research. I plunged myself heart, nose and brains into libraries, books, archives, microfilms, city directories, and periodicals. I visited museums, missions and ghost towns, trying to find the answers to the same questions that stalked my mind since the beginning of this journey. Unbelievably, every answer would only tie the story into knots and the last straw was that the books that were published about Pisco Punch committed the same mistakes as the first one did. The subject had to be treated using tweezers, because this book knocks down all of the previous theories on the Pisco Punch recipes. These authors which I truly respect, unfortunately stumbled over unforgivable errors considering their stature as researchers.

This entertaining historical novel based on true documents, clears the myths and introduces, as an exclusive, the real recipe of Duncan Nicol's Pisco Punch as well as the history of the Bank Exchange, the world renowned bar which was referred to as Pisco John's bar. All historical events have bibliographic sustenance and references to the sources so that the reader can corroborate the events and my conclusions, if desired.

I hope you enjoy reading this book as much as I did when I wrote it. The secret has been revealed, use it wisely. I invite anyone that wishes to follow me to take a little time, hold a glass of pisco in your hands, after pondering it and appreciating its aroma drown your spirit and praise your soul with this elixir, ambrosia from the Gods and Peruvian privilege spread around the world. Salud!

San Francisco's "Bonanza Kings" walking hastily towards Duncan Nicols's Bank Exchange to drink Pisco Punch. Illustration of the early 20th century.

A Fire-Defying Landmark

As soon as I arrived at home, the first thing I did after taking off my shoes was to pour myself a small glass of pisco: an unquestionable tradition that I celebrate with disciplined solemnity each evening after work. While contemplating the drops going down slowly and gracefully adorning the glass, suddenly that delicate scent of sweet fruit, of a green prairie, of *mosto verde*, approached me by assault urging me to drink. Picked up the glass and drank the elixir in one gulp. I felt its elegant and magnificent power, I fell on the arm-chair ruminating the flavor that my mouth was tasting. Then served one more glass and lit a cigarette. I have to quit, I thought. I always say the same thing. There will be another opportunity. I picked up an ashtray, put it on the little table beside me and threw myself on the sofa. Shit! What is this?! *A Fire-Defying Landmark?*

It was a small publication, written by Pauline Jacobson in 1912. But where did it come from? How interesting! I thought. Then I sat down comfortably, laid back and raised the sofa's feet support, took my glass of pisco and began to browse through the booklet. The story was simply seductive, it dealt with the Bank Exchange, a very famous saloon in the city of San Francisco and of how it had survived undamaged the earthquake and the fire that knocked the city down in 1906, turning it into a pile of rubbish, like Pompeii or Nero's Rome. Certainly interesting, and in a way shocking, that information didn't cause me either the interest, nor the impact, that was caused by the drink that was prepared there, whose components were kept as a confessional secret in the conscience of a town's priest.[1]

An unspeakable drink and pernicious for the sobriety, delicious and embracing, before which the worse of the atheists would give thanks to God three times, with blows to the sinner's chest!

The story kept getting more interesting, so I got up, cleaned my glasses with a tissue that Brenda had left on the small table where I put the ash tray and continued. I almost fell down when I read that the emblem drink of that bar was called Pisco Punch, elaborated with "pisco, a Peruvian grape brandy."

I jumped like a hare from the sofa, and immediately went to my library. I have to organize it... There will be another opportunity.

Whenever I see an interesting book or what seems to be, I buy it. Years back, while looking for an engineering book, I was attracted by *The Barbary Coast* of Herbert Asbury. Now that I think about it, I believe it was in such a bold way for it to be a mere coincidence: there was something I had to know, and that it wanted to tell me.

1. The Bank Exchange saloon was located in the southeast corner of the Montgomery Block, a neighbor to the Hotaling Building, constructed in 1866 and occupied by A.P. Hotaling & Co, where the largest warehouse of liquor of the West Coast of the United States was located. These constructions survived the earthquake and fire of 1906, partly because the U.S. Navy decided to install a one mile long hose to pump water from the fisherman's wharf located over Telegraph Hill. This fact inspired the famous doggerel of Charles Field:

"If, as they say / God spanked the town for being over frisky / Why did he burn the churches down / and save Hotaling's whisky?"

March 28, 1992
E Clampus Vitus

I had never given it importance until today. I found it! A whole page dedicated to the Bank Exchange, Duncan Nicol and his Pisco Punch, a drink of world-wide fame that raised spirits and inspired hearts! There was no one who boasted of fame that had not tried the secret concoction, the inspirer of hypothesis and treaties signed and affirmed by the more reputed thinkers and intellectuals of the time, of which Rudyard Kipling heads the list, exposing his theory of the secret brotherhood, that enclosed the preparation of the appraised drink, conformed by Nicol and a mute barman.

With respect to the secret ingredients, Kipling said he was sure, it was "shavings of cherub's wings."

Immediately I closed the book, took a deep breath and decided I wanted to taste that Pisco Punch. But, according to Asbury, the recipe had died with Nicol. Was such a tragedy possible,? How can somebody be so selfish and deprive the world of such an experience? Somebody that drinks pisco can not be that evil!

I savored another sip of pisco, returned to the sofa and started to meditate. One feels so comfortable here. There should be a device that brings everything that I want to my hands, so I would not need to stand up again, how nice and warm...

The Montgomery Block and the Bank Exchange Saloon in the corner, behind the carriage in 1854.

Bottom, left: San Francisco's downtown a few minutes after the 1906 fire had started and the earthquake ended. Middle: Same view as the previous photo, after the disaster. The Montgomery Block is shown to the left, at the distance. Right: Montgomery Street in ruins. The Montgomery Block and the Bank Exchange are shown unscathed. The Hotaling Bldg., partly shown to the left, was also undamaged.

–Hey, hey, hey! Do you want to sleep with a glass of pisco in your hand? What kind of person are you? The well to do people do not sleep with a glass of pisco in the hand, they take it with them. Let me taste what you have...

–Yes of course –I answered–. And got up confused.

While rubbing my eyes with my fists, I tried to find the reference, within my still sleepy brain, about the guy that was speaking to me, whom I swear to God, I had not seen before that night.

I approached the bar and slowly, while serving him a glass of pisco, I searched inside my head, trying to recognize one by one all of Brenda's friends and relatives, I did not want to be rude with the man.

I gave him the glass, he took it and shook my hand. Then I perceived a sensation of eternity: it was something dry and cold, with glimpses of antiquity. The squeeze was firm, from top to bottom, with a finger in the center of my wrist, like indicating some type of secret code, of brotherhood. I felt overwhelmed, while my tremulous hand moved away from that so frozen and inexplicable. The man looked directly into my eyes, at the same time as he tasted the concoction with gestures of a connoisseur, and then, a single thought echoed inside my head: Pisco John.

DUNCAN NICOL

COMPLIMENTS OF
THE BANK EXCHANGE

2

A Fire-Defying Landmark

Still one link in the downtown district with the present changing age of iron and the days of gold in the Bank Exchange saloon, on the ground floor of the Montgomery Block at the corner of Washington and Montgomery streets. Untouched, the Bank Exchange remains today as when its swinging doors first opened in 1853. Everything came around the Horn—the marble flagging which the feet tread today; the same enormous, solid mahogany table from which the free lunch is served, the same bar of solid mahogany, its edges rubbed smooth by the elbows of innumerable drinkers of the past, and upon whose counter the dice rattled at twenty-dollar gold pieces a throw; the same mirrors; the same mahogany glass racks; the same engravings of scenes of the French Revolution, mildewed with age, yet by connoisseurs reckoned worth $1,500 today—the same prints in the backroom of the House of Lords and the House of Commons.

The Montgomery Block was built by the wisdom of six great men. Six times between December 24, 1849, to June, 1851.

3

the thousands to farm her fertile lands. Nor was the Comstock Lode discovered which converted Bush Hill into the Nob Hill of palatial residences; which erected in Happy Valley the Palace Hotel, famed the world over for its court and cuisine; which transcended in the solid business blocks owned by the wealthy mining operators the greatest glory of 1853, the Montgomery Block.

Dwarfed now is that block into insignificance by the steel-structural sky-scrapers built in the wisdom of the seventh fire. Sleepy even at noon is the once active corner. At spasmodic intervals an antiquated car crawls past the Bank Exchange, waking the stillness by the noisy jerk of its painful travel over the worn track. By night it is as deserted as a village byway. The popular gentleman's cocktail route swings now between the Palace and St. Francis bars.

The Bank Exchange is a gentleman's saloon still. Duncan will have no rough element. Recently he warned a millionaire who was spending money freely, but had grown abusive, he wanted none of his money if he couldn't keep a cool tongue in his head. The same quality of 1853 holds with the liquors and wine, although since the fire, the price on straight drinks has been reduced to a bit. Thirty year old brandy is to be had, and Duncan's Pisco punch is famed as in the old days. Pisco is a Peruvian brandy made from the grape

which grows in the high Andes of South America. It is clear as spring water in color and appears harmless as a lady's drink. One authority claims one punch "will make a gnat fight an elephant." Others maintain it floats them in the region of bliss of hasheesh and absinthe.

The secret of Duncan's success in mixed drinks, the prosperous retired little barber who shaved every one of them in the old days confides in whispered admiration. "E-v-e-r-y one of them is mixed the same. I had nine of them punches and e-v-e-r-y one of them was mixed the same. If you came in here for THIRTY-FIVE years e-v-e-r-y one would be mixed the same. Look! Watch him!"

Duncan, obviously, clad in a handsomely frogged spotless white linen coat, his eye-glasses hung behind one ear like a book-keeper his pen, his white hair cropped close, his smooth-shaven face pink with health and intent upon his work, with hands trembling with the years, yet measuring with the nicety of an apothecary, was standing behind his shining bar with tall vases filled with roses from his garden mixing several ingredients in a thin cut glass.

"See," coached the ex-barber. "He is squeezing a f-r-e-s-h lemon. In the bars uptown they have the lemon juice already prepared, which leaves a bitter taste after drinking. And Duncan n-e-v-e-r uses any of them effervescent waters" with a contemptuous intonation for the cheaper art

10

11

A Fire-Defying Landmark, Pauline Jacobson, San Francisco, 1912.

San Francisco at the present time with the original coast delineated.

A Needle in a Haystack

S uddenly, the sound of bells jingled uninvited. The entrance door opened. It was Brenda.

–Guillermo?! Ah, hello love, you are there. What are you doing? Why that face? Did you just wake up? Listen, Karen Verushka called. She invited us to her Thanksgiving dinner. Yes, I know it's not coming for a while, but...

I looked through her, then I saw her, but when I returned to look at the man at the bar, he was no longer there, he had disappeared.

–Guillermo? Did you have a bad dream? Don't worry, because I have the right thing for you, I happened to pass by the grocery store and I found this little jewel, it is prosciutto mixed with asiago cheese. So? Do you want me to serve it to you? Wait while I leave these bags in the kitchen. We must think of what we are going to take to Karen's party, last year we... –Brenda continued saying.

I felt completely disoriented, didn't know what was happening, so I took Brenda by the arm, sat her next to me and said:

–There is something I must do, Bren. Don't ask me why, but I must find Pisco Punch.

–What it is? Is it like a Pisco Sour or something?

–Something like that, but it's not the same. San Francisco was some time ago famous not only for their steep streets and cable cars, but for a prodigious drink that lifted its name to glory.

–But, love, I believe San Francisco does not have its own drink.

–But it had it, and it was as important or more than all the tourist attractions, including the sunset on the Golden Gate. Imagine, Robert O'Brien refers to it in his book *This is San Francisco*, published in 1948, that the drink had magical components, because it "was like lemonade but came back with the kick of a roped steer." [2] That legendary drink was created at the end of nineteenth century, it was called Pisco Punch. Its creator was a man nicknamed Pisco John, who served it in a bar called the Bank Exchange.

–Pisco Punch? In the United States? You mean a drink with pisco? –Brenda asked me surprised.

–Yes, Peruvian pisco.

–But in those days?

–Remember, California was a Spanish colony and one of the men that first mapped its coasts was a Peruvian. Furthermore, Bodega Bay takes its name for Francisco de la Bodega y Quadra, a Limean explorer who discovered it while looking for the entrance to San Francisco Bay. The relation between Peru and California was somewhat close. Look, during the Gold Rush, the Forty-niners, which were the miners that arrived in 1849, were to a large extent Peruvian. The point is that the pisco was a part of the history of this part of the United States, and still more, the Pisco Punch.

–Then, San Francisco had a native drink?! –she exclaimed, excitedly. Brenda has always been enthusiastic about the history of cocktails, and San Francisco, a place where there are more bars than days in seven years, not having its own drink, as Rome has its Negroni, always surprised her.

–Of course, so much, that to go to the Bank Exchange and have a Pisco Punch was part of the forced itinerary

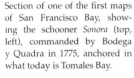

2. In 1973, Bronson changes the word "lemonade" for "nectar" and "roped steer" to "Missouri mule." (Bronson, 1973)

Section of one of the first maps of San Francisco Bay, showing the schooner *Sonora* (top, left), commanded by Bodega y Quadra in 1775, anchored in what today is Tomales Bay.

of the tourists of the time. You could not leave San Francisco without having tasted Pisco Punch. But the story ended as a Verdi opera, in tragedy, because of the Volstead Act of 1919 –that proclaimed the prohibition of the sale of alcohol in the United States– ended with the Bank Exchange, the Pisco Punch and the glory days of pisco in San Francisco.

Duncan Nicol, the owner of the Bank Exchange and the creator of the drink, died in 1926. This happened six years after his bar was closed by the prohibition and apparently the recipe died with him too. Look I found all the information in these books.

–You should clean-up that library!... –Brenda said but then she apologized–. Sorry, continue.

–Well, the sure thing is that Pisco Punch is still alive in the collective subconscious of all genuine San Franciscans.

–But, then, if it no longer exists, what are we going to do? Are you sure that Duncan Nicol never gave the recipe to anybody?

–The recipe was a secret according to Herbert Asbury and Pauline Jacobson, who was the only person who interviewed him at length. That was one of the reasons for its success, something like Coca Cola. Look, according to O'Brien, Nicol used to say: "Not even Mr. Volstead can take the secret away from me" when people asked him for his recipe.

–I don't know what we are going to do –Brenda said puzzled.

–Neither do I –I answered–, but I need to go to the place where the Bank Exchange stood, in the intersection of Montgomery and Washington, in San Francisco, of course.

–Guillermo, in that place now stands the Transamerica Pyramid. Also, the streets have changed –Brenda indicated, pointing out the difficulty of the situation.

–I know it, honey, but I need to go. Something tells

Limean navigator Don Francisco de la Bodega y Quadra, explorer of Bodega and Tomales Bay and co-discoverer of the entrance to San Francisco Bay, in 1775.

Illustration of passengers of the ship *Niantic*, that weighs anchor from the Peruvian port of Paita in 1849, bringing one of the first American gold rushers to San Francisco.

The base of the present day Transamerica Pyramid building, between Montgomery and Washington streets, location of the Bank Exchange.

me there's the haystack where I am going to sting myself with the needle. You mentioned Thanksgiving dinner at Karen's house. But isn't it too soon?

–Yes, but we must be thinking of what we are going to bring. It must be something spectacular. This year is our turn to cause commotion –she said waving her hands and jingling her bracelets.

–We have enough time to think about that. Now lets go to the Bank Exchange.

At last, we arrived in San Francisco. We parked the car and started walking. At the corner of Washington and Montgomery, I could already feel it. My heart started pumping with such strength that I thought it was going to explode. Suddenly, I felt like I stumbled over somebody...

–Eh man be careful, watch your step!

–Excuse me –I said instinctively, as I turned my head to see a man with an awkward appearance.

–What are you looking at?! –he asked.

–It's your clothes, and the streets... What happened? –I said in a low voice as if I were speaking to myself.

–Hey, have you had a Pisco Punch, or what? My clothes are very trendy, but I am afraid I could not say the same of yours. You are a foreigner, right?

–Yes, yes... But have you heard of Pisco Punch?

Corner of the famous intersection of Montgomery and Washington streets.

–Of course. Who doesn't know it, they serve it right here in the Bank Exchange. Excuse me I have not introduced myself, Oliver Stidger, manager of the Montgomery Block –he took his hat off, and saluted ceremoniously.

–Guillermo de la Moscorra, a pleasure –I answered, having no hat to take off.

–Eh! You look puzzled. Come, let me buy you a drink. You have an interesting accent, do you come from far away?

–Yes –I answered without knowing what else to say.

–I assumed that, come with me –he said in a friendly manner leading me by the arm.

While arriving at the bar, I saw a mature man with a calm aspect, aloof glance and a pleasant smile exiting the door.

The Montgomery Block, in 1856. The Bank Exchange and its awning, shown in the left corner.

–Come in –he said.

I recognized immediately, he was Pisco John.

–Duncan Nicol –he introduced himself– welcome to the Bank Exchange; I was on my way out, but please come in. So you already met my good friend Stidger? Good, come in I know what you are look-ing for. Lannes take care of these two gentlemen, but do your utmost for this young man, who seems to come from far away –then turning to me he whis-pered in my ear–: the house recommends Pisco Punch.

Nicol gave Stidger a friendly good-bye, and extended his hand while looking deeply into my eyes. I answered with a strong handshake that forged a promise in time, simultaneous to that sign that paralyzed my pulse, when his imposing finger touched my wrist.

I took a long look at the place. It was extremely cozy and quite elegant. The marble floor tiles kept pace with the rhythm of the distinguished gentle-

Duncan Nicol at the Bank Exchange bar in the 1910s.

men's steps who, when entering, left their hats and their raincoats on the mahogany hangers that decorated the entrance and walk by the oil paintings that framed the wall of the place, where it seemed that the cream of the crop of the intellectual society of San Francisco got together every day.

Stidger and I sat at the bar and John Lannes, who was the administrator, handed me a glass with an amber colored liquid, with a piece of pineapple inside, and a quite pleasant aspect, seemingly inoffensive, I would dare to say. It looked like a lady's drink to me.

–Take it easy, my friend –Stidger said with honest concern-, this drink is deceptive. It seems harmless, but in reality it is like the scimitar of Harroun with an edge so fine that after a slash, a man could walk on unaware that his head had been severed from his body until his knees gave way and he fell to the ground dead.[3]

–Well, it seems to me, excuse me for butting into the conversation... –the administrator interrupted.

–Go ahead Lannes, since you are the one that knows the drink better than anybody.

–That's not true, Mr. Stidger, I simply serve it, Nicol prepares the mix downstairs and brings everything ready.

–You have disappointed me, Lannes, I thought you also kept the secret.

–Unfortunately, no. But I have the pleasure of drinking it whenever I want to feel like a super human that could face smallpox, all fevers known to the faculty, and the Asiatic cholera, combined, if need be.[4]

–Then let me have the pleasure of tasting such grace –I said excited.

The flavor was very pleasant, enhanced the

3. Words of Oliver Perry Stidger, manager of the Montgomery Block at the beginning of 20th century.
(Bronson, 1973)

Scimitar is a curved sword of Arab or Persian origin. Harroun al-Rashid (766–809) was the fifth caliph of the Abasi dynasty of Bagdad.

Stidger was instrumental in convincing the fire chief of San Francisco not to blow-up the Montgomery Block during the 1906 fire. Although the Navy was already very involved in saving that area, the fire chief considered the action necessary to prevent the expansion of the fire towards other zones of the city. The wise and irrefutable argument Stidger used, was that there was too much liquor stored in the area and that the explosion could be dangerously excessive.

4. Words of a miner when he drinks pisco in 1872.
(T.W. Knox, 1886)

It was also said that Pisco Punch "could make a gnat fight an elephant" and that "it floats them in the region of bliss of hasheesh and absinthe."
(Jacobson, 1912)

senses and went down as smooth as a velvet, caressing the throat and sheltering it, strong and firm at the same time. I felt fullness, it was like a light pat on the back by a strong hand. Its strength and its gentleness were shameful accomplices of a delicious prank.

After some time, I could not say how long, I was faced upon glory. I learned the meaning of pondering; but a fellow arrived, he sat himself at my side and while he analyzed me with the cunning of an old wolf, but still being very young in appearance, said to me:

–They damn the wind, and they damn the dust, and they give all their attention to damning them well... But it is human nature to find fault – to overlook that which is pleasant to the eye, and seek after that which is distasteful to it. You take a stranger here and show him the magnificent picture of Samson and Delilah, and what is the first object he notices? – Samson's fine face and flaming eye? or the noble beauty of his form? or the lovely, half-nude Delilah? or the muscular Philistine behind Samson, who is furtively admiring her charms? or the perfectly counterfeited folds of the rich drapery below her knees? or the symmetry and truth to the nature of Samson's left foot? No, sir, the first thing that catches his eye is the scissors on the floor at Delilah's feet, and the first thing he says: them scissors is too modern –there weren't no scissors like that in them days! [5]

It's true, I thought; and then an endless stream of thoughts and hypotheses created in my mind poured like shooting stars inside my brain, I felt I had the answer for all existentialist problems that afflicted the world since man questioned the purpose of life. So my young friend and I dedicated ourselves to reconstruct all the theories that until

5. Words written by Mark Twain referring to the Bank Exchange, place he visited very frequently when he lived in San Francisco. (Mark Twain, 1864)

that moment governed human thought, not even Plato was saved from our intellectual audit.

–A couple of piscos and you feel you own the truth eh? –a man who I have not seen before and who was very entertained with our talk said.

Although thinking about it better, no one was here just minutes before. The situation had turned strange, although the place looked the same in appearance, all the people around me were different. It seemed I went back in time, and the drink I had in my hand, which was half full, since the other half was pleasantly refreshing my brain, was not Pisco Punch. It was a punch, certainly of pisco, very tasty too, but it was not Pisco Punch.

Samuel Clemens, Mark Twain. Photo taken just a short time after he resided in San Francisco.

–John Torrence! What a pleasure to see you! You certainly know how to appreciate a good conversation. This man –my young speaker told me, without taking his eyes away from Torrence– is one of the most visionary people that I have ever known in the world. He foresees all good things, that's why he is the forerunner and defender of the delicious liquor we are drinking here: Health to the *perulero* brandy!

–Take it easy –Torrence insisted–, because this drink is enjoyed sip by sip, and although a nectar of the Gods that seems the work of the hands of Eirene, it is pretty strong, it is powerful and you, Clemens, should know that better than anybody –he said pointing at Samuel Clemens–. Well, gentlemen, you have been warned. Now enjoy it at your fullest; I must leave you, duty calls, going to my theater because the show must go on.

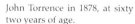

John Torrence in 1878, at sixty two years of age.

But Torrence stayed where he was, and continued talking.

–Nevertheless, how could the show continue if the responsible man keeps reminiscing his old times at the Bank Exchange. Don't pay attention to what I say! It is that sometimes my heart fills with nostalgia when I remember the times when the bar belonged to me. It was my life, and to plan every evening or to invent a drink motivated me as much back then as it does now producing a play or building a stage where so many famous stars perform, which are as many as all the throats that tasted pisco from my hand. But now it's the young people's turn and young Parker is taking very good care of the place. In addition I can not return, in spite of the melancholy I feel, because today my heart and head belong to the stage. As a matter of fact, Clemens, when will you return to tell stories at the theater? We were making numbers with Maguire and you are very good for the ticket office, you filled the house. Lets talk business later, Ok? Have the next round to my health and on my account.

Suddenly, a middle-aged man with a flair of importance, approached us. He was part of the group that was seated next to the billiard table.

–Eh! You are the one that lectured at Maguire's Opera House –he said to Clemens, and then speaking to everybody added–: Hey! This is Samuel Clemens, Mark Twain, the journalist that is now a writer, the one that appeared in Maguire's theater![6] –and emphasized–: You are good boy, you are going to go far, let me invite you... what are you drinking? Pisco, is that right, of course, a brilliant mind, what other thing.... So you are writing about Tom Sawyer[7] eh? Let me know later why you chose him –and he told the barman–: Boy!, serve the young man one drink with pisco –then he noticed me and asked–: and this one is also a writer? Serve this young man too, in case he is not a writer so that he becomes one –he also told the barman.

The man left laughing, he had that luxuriant laughter that shakes all the body, not only the face.

6. On October 2nd of 1866, Maguire's Opera House becomes scene of one of the greatest events in the history of American literature. Samuel Clemens, popularly known by the pseudonym of Mark Twain, rents the place and offers a lecture about his experiences during his recent trip to Hawaii. Twain had begun his writing career in 1850, in Missouri, at a young age as a reporter of a newspaper owned by his brother. Twain emigrates to San Francisco in 1864, and while being a reporter of the *Sacramento Union* he travels to Hawaii where he remains a few months. The lecture by Twain is a resounding success when in the front of an audience of hundreds of spectators, he recites a very humorous mixture of cultural information and sarcasm.

7. Mark Twain, in addition to being an assiduous visitor of the Bank Exchange during his stay in San Francisco, he also visited a Turkish bath located in the cellar of the Montgomery Block, that was frequently attended by a fireman called Tom Sawyer. Some years after the publishing of the epic work *The Adventures of Tom Sawyer*, the fireman of San Francisco names his new bar "Ales & Spirits: The Original Tom Sawyer."

Maguire's Opera House, located across the street from the Bank Exchange and place where Mark Twain's career takes off in 1866.

With each step he took you could hear the sound of a cane following the cadence of his walk, he was a big man whose black cloth suit, perfectly fit and better mannered, denoted a bulky banking account.

While we enjoyed our complimentary drinks, I saw Torrence return towards us.

–Ok, Torrence, I am going to go to your theater, however I am spinning a better idea: I am going to write about you! –Clemens mentioned amused.

–Be quiet, man, don't be foolish. What could you say about me? –Torrence asked intrigued.

–A lot, although not much. You are an interesting personage, father of the bars and precursor of the theater that acts illustrious, while being illiterate; but no, will not write about you, but about your name: I like it so much as the one of Sawyer: Tom Sawyer, John Torrence both sound like protagonists, but don't believe that the stories I am writing, in which surely Sawyer will have a leading role, will have even half a penny about his real life.

–That's what I said: the man is a fireman, but other than that he doesn't have any blessing... And speaking of blessings, where are you from? I have never seen you before –Torrence asked me.

–I am Peruvian –I answered.

Torrence made an expression that strongly caught my attention, he then approached me with a very formal gesture as though paying homage. He extended his hand and gave me a strong squeeze.

–Very well man! Then you know about good pisco.

–Of course –I assured him with pride.

–I had an obsession with pisco since the first drink I took. A sip was enough for me to know that it would definitely be a part of my life, as well as the theater. They are my two great passions. Both are elements of exquisite elegance, they glorify the senses and grant joy to the world. But then, you must know Mr. Larco.

I knew who Nicholas Larco was; I had read about him in an article written by Andrew Canepa, some time ago. Larco had arrived in Peru from Liguria, Italy, along with his family in the 1830s and emigrated to San Francisco in the midst of the Gold Rush of 1849. He was enticed to come by Domingo Ghirardelli,[8] his good friend and neighbor in Peru, who told him of the wonderful possibilities of a great future in San Francisco because, as any good *perulero,* they knew that gold was not the only thing that could shine in a city that was growing as fast as foam, and whose demographic explosion was taking geometric proportions.

8. Domingo Ghirardelli, an Italian chocolate maker on Mercaderes Street in Lima, arrived from Peru to San Francisco persuaded by his neighbor and friend James Lick on February 24, 1849, on board of the Peruvian ship *Mazeppa.* Married to the Peruvian Carmen Alvarado-Pimentel, Ghirardelli opened his first store and candy factory on July 18, 1852, a later version of which will become a landmark of the city of San Francisco. Ghirardelli had 9 children, four born in Lima and five in San Francisco. (Dominga, his oldest daughter was in fact daughter of his wife's first marriage to a Frenchman named Martin who died at sea).

(S. Lawrence, 2002)

The Italo-Peruvian Ghirardelli-Alvarado family in San Francisco, in the 1860s.

Announcement published on the front page of the *Alta California* newspaper of San Francisco, in March of 1849, showing shipments of pisco and Italia type pisco, coming from Peruvian ships and for sale at the corner of Washington and Kearney streets, one block away from the future place of the Bank Exchange.

9. The University of San Marcos in Lima dates from 1551, and represented an important catalyst of the intellectual and social movement of the new continent. It is the oldest university of South America and the second oldest of the American continent after the Universidad Autonoma of Santo Domingo which was founded in 1538 in the Dominican Republic.

10. Californio was the term used to name the non-Indian inhabitants of Alta California (present day California). Any "people of reason" bred, and later born and bred, in California were considered Californios. The term Californio was used by Spain since the 1700s in Old California, (present day Baja California, Mexico) and became popular in Alta California during the first half of the 1800s after the independence from Spain.

Oil painting of the Peruvian-Californio Mariano Malarin. (Leonardo Barbieri, 1850s)

Ghirardelli was in turn convinced to come to California by James Lick, and Lick was enticed by Mariano Malarin, when he was studying Law in Peru, because his father, Juan Malarin, a Peruvian resident of Monterey, back then the capital of California, had sent him to study at the University of San Marcos of Lima,[9] so the future could smile at him when English speaking people take California as a land of their own.

Mariano Malarin and James Lick met during one of Lick's extensive afternoon reading sessions which he did, from time to time, at the library of the university. Mariano was a very enterprising and intelligent young man, and when he met Lick he was surprised to find out about his interest in the ancestral history of Peru, the history of the Incas and their gold. The connection was almost immediate, and although Malarin already lost his knowledge of the English language which he had learned in California by insistence of his father, who as a good pioneer envisioned the changes to come, they understood each other well because Lick's knowledge of Spanish was quite good. Juan Malarin returned to Peru only to visit his son, because since he had left Peru for the Californias and became himself a Californio, a lineage of elite men, of people of reason,[10] he did not think of returning even to taste his so longed drink of pineapple *chicha* with pisco, who he ceremoniously used to take every day at eleven in the morning with his neighbors in Lima (to drink *las once*). And if he returned, it was only to inform his son of the latest news and the scent of the times to change that arrived from the north.

As any old fox used to smell good opportunities, Lick had his nose raised and pricked-up ears. He also accepted the notion that Alta California would eventually become part of the Union, and that sounded like cash in his ears. That he liked, because Lick was obsessed with money after his father-in-law-to-be told him loud and clear to stay away from his daughter, because he would never allow an indigent to be a member of his family. Lick swore to return with more money than anyone, and this is the reason why he left Pennsylvania to look for his fortune. So after hearing the news that Juan Malarin brought, he put all his things in order so he could sail as soon as possible to California; but he still had eleven orders for delivering pianos pending. During his eleven year stay in Lima, Lick devoted himself to manufacturing pianos of excellent quality. In addition, he had made himself a reputation of being a correct and honorable man, for that reason the Limean high society, so closed and elitist, considered him a member of their circle, at a time when foreigners without lineage were not so well regarded and were mainly ignored. His departure was not going to serve as an occasion to ruin his reputation, he had to leave Peru ending his story there in the most satisfactory way. He finished the eleven pianos in eighteen months and sailed to San Francisco with a chest full of Peruvian gold doubloons and six hundred pounds of chocolate, from the factory of his close friend Domingo Ghirardelli.

Monument bust of James Lick.
(Martha M. Mullin, 1996)

House of the Ghirardelli family at the present time. The Transamerica Pyramid at the distance.

The office of Nicholas Larco at the present time, located a few feet from the Ghirardelli's. Both structures also resisted intact the 1906 disaster.

Ghirardelli Chocolate Factory at the end of the 1910s and one of the main tourist attractions in present day San Francisco. The building shown in this photo was constructed by Domingo Ghirardelli Jr, born in Lima in 1849.

Connecting the Dots

A peculiar and familiar sound echoed in my ears as Brenda pointed at a plaque located inside the Transamerica Pyramid. Every movement of her hands increased the sound level of the jingles of the tiny charms that hung from her bracelets, raising the volume above the maximum permitted by any astral trip.

–Guillermo, look at what is written on this plaque, this was the exact site of the Montgomery Block –I heard her say, as I returned back in time.

–That's right honey, we are standing right at the door of what was the center of the universe, the Bank Exchange. What a wonderful place, I need to return!

–When were you there? –she asked sounding disturbed.

–A while ago... Don't pay attention to what I say –I replied, realizing how absurd my answer was.

–Everything has changed a great deal since that time, just by glancing at the buildings someone can easily figure it out –she continued.

–Wasn't it around here where Samuel Brannan started the Gold Rush? –I asked curiously.

–Yes, that's right. We are standing where history was made. Over there was the print shop of his newspaper, and take a look over there, just a short distance away is the first house that James Lick bought after arriving from Peru with Peruvian gold. Did you know it was the

Commemorative plaque of the Montgomery Block.

11. The name of present day Gold Street, Ca. 1849, which led directly towards the back of James Lick's first San Francisco house (corner of Montgomery and Jackson Streets), was due to the gold hidden by Lick in the area.
(Richards, 2002)

It must be noted that James Lick bought that land in February of 1848. Later he acquired many other lots. Lick buys his last lot on April 22nd, just a few days before the beginning of the Gold Rush.
(Byrne, 1924)

12. Samuel Brannan runs the streets of San Francisco with a small quinine bottle full of gold dust on May 12, 1848.
(Holliday, 1999)

first significant gold transaction in the history of San Francisco? [11]

–These two places are very close, eh? How convenient –I said letting my imagination fly away.

–Gold, Gold, Gold! From the American River! –a voice shouted alone on the streets. [12]

–But, what is going on? –I asked.

–Don't you see, man! It is Samuel Brannan with a bottle of gold dust in his hand which he says it was found in a Sacramento river. It's true that gold pours from the rivers of the valley! Follow me, lets go and see!

–Eh, come here! –someone running on the street shouted–, Brannan has found gold! Lets go to the office of the *California Star*, where we can find the real proof!

Present view of Gold Street, located adjacent to the land that James Lick first bought in San Francisco. The property had an Adobe house with the only cellar in the city.

The office of the newspaper was crowded. Inside, Brannan showed off with a big smile the fruit of minimal work, since according to him, he found gold all on his own. A bit later, when all the racket had ended, Brannan left the office, straightened his suit and walked away, without haste nor hardship, down the street that led to the sea coast. I followed him until we arrived at a house located on the corner of Montgomery and Jackson streets, a block away from the Montgomery Block. He entered the dwelling acting as if he owned the place. He walked through the thresholds of exquisitely carved wood, the lack of furniture gave no indication of the presence of any human being inhabiting the place, he then walked down the cold and lifeless stairway that led to the cellar. The place was quite dismal and somewhat dark, with only one old candelabrum of singular beauty, carved in silver, illuminating a work table and a tool chest used for building pianos. Seated next to a bottle of pisco was James Lick.

Samuel Brannan in 1855.

Montgomery Street in the heat of the Gold Rush. Some years before, Samuel Brannan ran through this street initiating the Gold Rush. Notice the *pisquitos* –small clay jars where pisco type Italia was transported–, in the center, at the feet of the man facing Washington Street.

James Lick portrait.

–How did it go? –Lick asked without flinching, as he started to fill the glass.

–Everything is ready, my friend, our future is being served on a gold platter –Brannan answered.

–We have served it ourselves, my dear Brannan, we certainly have. I expect the headlines to travel immediately to the East Coast.

–Everything has been planned accordingly, don't worry. To our health! –Brannan concluded, and drank his glass of pisco in a single gulp.

–Guillermo? –I heard Brenda's voice calling, wondering if I was awake.

–Ah? Brenda? Yes, what's going on?

–That's what I want to know. Five dollars for your thoughts –Brenda challenged.

–They are a bit more expensive –I joked.

–What are you talking about? –she asked.

–Do you remember the story of James Lick?

–Yes, why?

–Do you realize that all the land that Lick bought for a bargain soon increased in value after the phenomenon of the Gold Rush. Meanwhile Brannan focused his ef-

Samuel Brannan's house and site of the *California Star* newspaper.

forts on opening a pair of general supply stores, in which he stocked all the mining supplies he could find around, and later published the discovery of great amounts of gold in the rivers of Sacramento in his newspaper.

–Do you think they had some type of conspiracy or plan? –Brenda asked suspiciously.

–I don't know –I responded lost in thought–. I only know that Brannan appeared in a photo as being one of the bearers of Lick's coffin. They had a close friendship, not everyone gets to carry his friend's coffin.

–It is true, did we see that picture when we visited Lick's observatory? –Brenda tried to remember.

–No, I think it was in Rosemary Lick's book –I answered.

–Lick's life story sounds incredible to me. First, he left Pennsylvania without a penny to his name, traveled through parts of South America making money here and there until he finds out about the boom of the guano fertilizer and the economic prosperity of Peru, and travels there, amasses a large capital and returns after foreseeing business opportunities in the new state of the United States –Brenda said connecting the dots.

–Brenda, Lick did not improvise: as soon as he heard the news of the first gold discovered in California in 1842 he begins researching about the Incas and the gold of Peru at the library of the University of San Marcos. Later, when he heard from Juan Malarin that California could be part of the Union, he decides to move back. Then he writes to Ghirardelli encouraging him to leave Peru and to come to California in 1849. He tells him there will be overpopulation and that the service business would be very lucrative. He knew what was coming.

–That man was really able to make so much money! –Brenda exclaimed.

–But look at the legacy he had left us. The Lick Observatory was the most powerful in the world until some years ago. The fifth moon of Jupiter was discovered there and just a few years ago, the first extra-solar planetary systems that exist in our galaxy.

—Is it true that he built it as his mausoleum? I don't believe it! Is that true Guillermo? —she asked skeptically.

—Yes, it is true! This man was pretty eccentric. Look at the mansion that he built for the love of his life, whom he never saw again, when he had enough money under his arm and returned to visit her for the first and only time, she was very well married...

—Just a moment, what about his son? When he left her she was pregnant. His future father in law didn't even consider the baby and banished him from her life. What an evil man: destroyed a love story in exchange for money —Brenda said.

—Step by step, step by step. The mansion that he built was amazing, in a wonderful location, the dream of any mortal, it was very beautiful, but it did not have a single piece of furniture in it. He left it like that so she could furnish it to her taste, but since she never moved there, the man lived in an empty place and slept on top of his piano!

—It's hard to believe.

—He also built a mill in front of the mansion, a mahogany mill. It was very expensive, and the only reason

Present day view of James Lick Observatory.

James Lick's mansion as seen today.

View of James Lick's mill at the present time. Originally it was a luxurious mill totally covered with mahogany.

that he built it was because his father in law to be had one too. He was obsessed.

–But what about his son? –Brenda insisted.

–Lick took his son to live with him for a while, but it seems that they did not get along and the relationship ended badly. Therefore he did not leave anything to him in his will at the time of his death, all his assets were donated. The son was able to recover eight hundred thousand dollars by suing the State, but got nothing else.

–And what about the observatory? Is it true that he built it only to be buried there? –Brenda asked.

–Yes. It happens that Lick was a great believer in astrology, in the influence of the cosmos. The Egyptian religion caught a lot of his attention, to the point that he stubbornly insisted on building a pyramid in San Francisco's downtown to serve him as his after–life dwelling, crypt, tomb or whatever you wish to call it.

–Really? What an unusual individual! –Brenda smiled.

–Yes indeed. That idea scared many. They had to find a way to persuade Lick to stop such an absurd plan. For their good luck, and that of history, a young astronomer who was lecturing in the city told him on an occasion: "Mr. Lick, if I had the money that you have, I would build an observatory, the largest in the world."

–Then Lick probably thought that in a way he could have power over the stars and the universe in general –Brenda completed.

–That's right, thus Lick's remains rest at the base of the telescope.

–What a shame he never saw it completed.

–But, regardless, he knew what he was doing. As well as when he donated enormous amounts of money to asylums for the homeless and the mentally ill, or when he left his entire fortune to the State for the benefit of the helpless. He was, as the book says, a

The main telescope. James Lick's remains are located at its base.

"Generous Miser." Anyway, should we return to Montgomery Street for a while?

–Ok –Brenda said–, but this wind is going to blow me away, why did I have to forget my coat?

–Here, wear mine –I said to her while I took my coat off and put it over her shoulders–. If you want you can go by Chinatown or by Portsmouth Square.

–Lets go together, please, I love all of this. It's pure history –she told me with that expression on her face that I find impossible to say no to.

So we went to Chinatown together. When entering Portsmouth Square it was impressive to see the Chinese seated like in a school recess, lumped together in generational groups, playing cards and hurling to the ground the cigarette butts of just smoked cigarettes, which had become a carpet of ash and tar, upholstered with yellow tips of still lighted cigarettes dropping with winding smoke and sparks.

–These Chinese are very heavy smokers. This is why the Peruvians probably came up with the expression "you smoke as much as a Chinese businessman in bankruptcy." That's a good one! –Brenda commented smiling.

–It is true, they smoke more than I do, I don't feel that bad anymore. Look, this is a little piece of China! And to think that it was here where Captain Montgomery raised the United States flag for the first time...

–Gentlemen, gentlemen, we have fulfilled our duty: This city in now part of the United States of America!

–Very well, Captain Montgomery! Lets go and celebrate!

–Yes, lets go! –a companion said.

–Good afternoon! Is there somebody working at this tavern? –Montgomery said entering the bar.

Present view of Portsmouth Square, the old downtown of San Francisco. The plaque that commemorates the place where Captain Montgomery raised the flag of the U.S. for the first time, in 1846, is shown to the right, above the park bench.

–What are you going to have? –the barman asked.

–Give us the specialty of the house. What is your name?! –the captain requested.

–John Brown, sir! –the barman responded martially.

–At ease, man, that is not necessary! Only serve us right, and that is enough for us!

–Whatever you say sir! I'll bring the specialty of the house on the double. Sir! –Brown said, and in an instant he put the glasses down in front of the newly arrived.

–Eh, Brown, what is this? It is very good for heaven sake! What exotic concoction have you served us? –the captain asked pleasingly impressed.

–It's a punch made with pisco, sir!

–Is it real pisco, or that counterfeit pisco made in Fort Sutter?! –rebuked the captain.

Porstmouth Square in 1854. Kearney Street is shown to the right and Washington Street at a distance. In 1849, pisco was sold on the corner of those two streets.

–It's pisco brought directly from Peru, sir! –the barkeeper assured the captain while he drank.

–It is good, Brown, so, from now on you will see us here frequently! –the captain said while he raised the glass finishing the drink.

–Alright, sir! My Captain, sir! [13]

–Guillermo, I will go bankrupt if I keep offering you money for your thoughts. Are you alright? –Brenda said bringing me back to reality.

–Yes, I just had a revelation, which I am sure I'll be able to deal with later. At least for now I know pisco was well known in these lands since long ago, but Brown... That person intrigues me. Now let me go to the Bank Exchange for a while.

–What are you talking about, Guillermo! You are starting to worry me. The Bank Exchange does not exist any more, honey. I think the cold weather is affecting you –my wife said to me tenderly. The truth is it was very cold indeed, but I was in another place and time.

13. In 1845, a person named Hutchings, who worked as a cook in a hotel in Sacramento, visited Fort Sutter and wrote in his memoirs that there was "a type of pisco made using the wild grapes of the region." Fort Sutter, the first construction of the city of Sacramento, present capital of California, had a liquor distillery which manufactured a brandy similar to pisco. (Leslie, 1859)

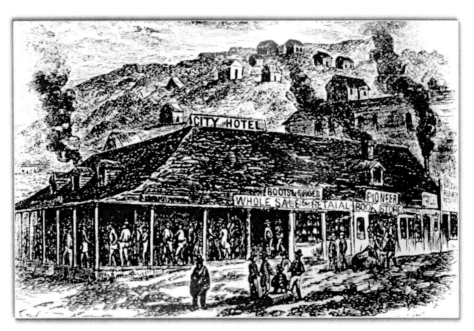

The City Hotel, managed by John H. Brown at the end of the 1840s. Notice the person dressed with a Peruvian poncho in the foreground.

–I meant to say the Transamerica Pyramid. I need to return there to resolve an issue –I rectified.

–How about if I just stay around here searching for information while yo go back to Washington and Montgomery and to your reminiscences of the past –Brenda proposed.

–Ok, honey, when you finish, look for me at the Bank Exchange, I meant, at the Pyramid... –I almost messed it up again.

–Hey, you are back! What happened to you? Are you Ok? Let me introduce you to my good friend Victor Morris –Lannes said to me while he introduced me to his friend.

–My pleasure, I am Guillermo de la Moscorra –I greeted him amiably, not paying him too much attention, it was Nicol that I wanted to see, I asked–: Well, Lannes, has Mr. Nicol arrived?

–Who Pisco John? –Lannes answered– No, he

will come back a bit later, he left with his wife. He had to help her with some chores, because she is blind.

–I believe that he married her so that she could not find his secret recipe of Pisco Punch! ha ha ha –Morris said joking.

–Imagine, his trusted assistant of confidence is deaf-mute –Lannes protested.

–Then, the rumor is true about the blind wife and a deaf-mute assistant? I thought they were tall tales, legends of lore. Now I see that it was not the case –I said, incredulously.

–Yes, but the two things are not related at all. He hired the assistant deliberately, but Mary was blind because God wanted it. In addition, she was blind from a very young age, she must be used to living like that.

–Ok good! That's enough. Now, tell me –Morris approached me, cutting into the conversation–. Lannes tells me that you come from Peru, so you must be very familiar with pisco. You know, I'm intrigued by that liquor.

–Ok, but in fact there is not much to say. It is distilled must, which is fermented grape juice. It is only grape, nothing else, that's the secret. It has been made in Peru since the 17th century, approximately. There is a will dated from 1613 of a fellow nicknamed *El Griego* (The Greek), in which he left his survivors thirty jars plus a barrel of pisco, in addition to a still and two *puntayas*, all distillation instruments. This document defines the minimum age of the liquor.[14]

–So the damn pisco is older than San Francisco! –Lannes interrupted.

–Be quiet man! Let him talk. I find what you are telling me very interesting. I knew about Peru only from its Inca gold and guano fertilizer; but well,

14. The oldest historical document about the production of grape *aguardiente* (a type of brandy) in the Americas, goes back to the year 1613. It is a handwritten testament in the will of Pedro Manuel *El Griego*, a settler of the villa of Ica and a producer of grape brandy, in which he describes a series of equipment used in the production of pisco.
(Huertas, 1988)

15. Contrary to California, there was no native grape in Peru before the arrival of the Spanish Conquistadors. The grape species *Vitus californica* is native to California. The grape introduced by the Conquistadors, and the ones planted by the padres of the California missions since 1770, was the species *Vitus vinifera*, the same species planted in South America more than two centuries before. The species *Vitus labrusca* is native to the east coast of the United States and it is presently called Catawba.

about this liquor, I didn't even know it was from there. Now, tell me something, the grape used in making pisco is not of American origin, right? At least not the one that they use in Peru, because we have here in California a wild grape native to this part of the continent, but there is no such thing there or is there? –Morris continued asking.[15]

–No, the grape, according to Spanish history, arrived in Peru from the Canary Islands, ordered by a certain Marquis Caravantes, in 1551. The Spanish Conquistadors were already desperate to bring a little of their native land to the new world, I imagine nostalgia was killing them. In addition the wine that was brought from Spain turned into vinegar after undergoing those long and humid sailing trips, with lots of wind and swaying. It must have been horrible! –I said.

–What about the pisco?, Guillermo, how do they make pisco? –Morris asked again.

–Now the real issue comes up. The Peruvian wine turned out to be so good and it was so much cheaper, that it started to displace the one that was imported from Spain. Almost immediately thereafter, the Spanish wine producers started to complain out loud when they saw their profits on their way down. Then King Phillip II prohibited the production of wine in all the Viceroyalty of Peru. And what did the audacious Peruvian men do to counteract that order? They produced pisco –I said enchanted to tell that history.

–You see, my dear Lannes, now you know the history of the secret ingredient in your boss' drink. Since you profit so much from it, at least you should know its origin. Don't you think so? Well, it is getting late and I have to leave. Here, keep the change. Where are you staying, Guillermo? –he asked me after he paid his bill.

–I don't know. I just arrived –I answered in a desperate attempt not to break the moment or wake up from my dream.

Suddenly the jingle of bells caressed my head, while a fragile and sweet hand took me by the arm. I thought that it was a good way to return.

–Should we leave now? –Brenda asked me–, we must hurry up if you want to find the library open. It is going to take a long time to do the research that you need, you know.

That strong dry wind that felt as if it was coming from an air conditioner, which caresses and strikes, sometimes upset the long and red curls that framed Brenda's face. Her hand held onto me strongly while we crossed Montgomery street on our way to the library, but when I stepped over a small track that marked the old coast before the city gained land at the expense of a cove... I heard voices.

–Damn! I'm getting wet –I said without believing what was happening.

–Hey you, are you crazy or what's your problem?! –a guy screamed at me from the other side.

–Leave him alone, Captain, for sure he must be a drunk –said the man who accompanied him.

–But he can drown! –he insisted–. Hey! What do you want? –he asked me waving his arms signaling to move out of the away.

–Sorry I didn't realize it, excuse me; but, who are you and what are you doing? –I asked them, breathing slowly and carefully looking around.

–We are working on a very important job –said the man who the other called Captain–, for we are trying to sink this wood raft. But if you insist on jumping into the sea and interrupting our work we are never going to finish. Get out of there! –he said

16. The Montgomery Block was constructed by the lawyer and captain Henry W. Halleck in 1853. Later in his life, Halleck was a General in the Union Army during the Civil War of the 1860s.
(Shutes, 1937)

and extended his hand to pull me out.

–Yes, pardon my interruption –I apologized while jumping out of the water–, but what's on your mind with the raft.

–We are going to use it as the foundation of a monumental work, the most impressive construction that San Francisco has ever seen, and which will take the name of Montgomery Block. By the way, I am Captain Henry Halleck.[16]

–My pleasure, Guillermo de la Moscorra –I introduced myself, making the same ceremonious gesture as my interlocutor, attempting not to be out of sync for those times. At least, not too much.

–You are not from around here, eh? -Halleck asked me–. I can tell from your clothes and the way you speak. This is my partner –he introduced us– we are constructing this place gaining a little space from the sea, which already has enough and we need the land. Your pants are wet, you may catch a cold. Well –he said removing his hat– we are leav-

Alley between Jackson and Washington streets. The old coast line is shown with the wavy line figures imprinted in the asphalt.

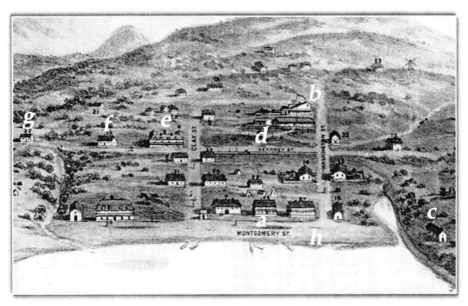

Illustration of 1846 of the city of San Francisco showing the coast at the time. a: Montgomery Street, where Samuel Brannan ran with a small bottle full of gold dust. b: Brannan's house and office of the *California Star,* and leased from Stephen Smith. c: James Lick's house, which had the only cellar in the city. In the future, the offices of Nicholas Larco and Domingo Ghirardelli will be located a short distance away. d: Portsmouth Square, where the flag of the U.S. is raised for the first time. e: John Brown's City Hotel and bar. f: John Vioget's house. g: Robert Ridley's house. h: Site of the future location of the Montgomery Block and the Bank Exchange.

ing. It was a pleasure meeting you, and next time watch your step.

–Where are you going? –I asked.

–We are done for the day, friend, now it's our turn to go to Bob Ridley's bar. Maybe you should come with us, he serves a very nutritious milk punch, which they say cures everything –the captain informed me.

–Is it medicinal? –I asked, expecting to find a clue.

–That's what the legend says; and also that it comes from the prescription of an old wise Peruvian lady, who manages to cure scurvy and other fevers using mixes of pisco and lime. I don't know what's in it, but it tastes glorious, and while it keeps me happy and healthy: it is very welcomed.

–Well then, I'll go with you –and I joined this group of healthy parishioners, in search of the tonic of joy.

–Hey Bob! –Captain Halleck said to the man at the bar–. I am bringing you a foreigner. I found him swimming around by my raft, and I think he is in dire need of one of your punches.

Brenda's voice pulled me out of Ridley's bar. This time it was not so delicate.

–Guillermo? Hurry up! –she pulled my hand strongly, as if she was pulling me out of a ditch.

–Honey, did I tell you before that you are my contact with reality? –I asked her smiling.

–I believe so, you are a day dreamer, you were stuck in the middle of the street, if we were back two centuries ago you could have drowned. Look at these signs on the street, they mark the boundary of the coast at that time. You are standing where the sea was.

–Yes, I know –I said to her thinking back to the fact that I did not try Ridley's punch.

–You are incorrigible! There is no way we will make it to the library on time –Brenda said looking at her watch.

–You will always take care of me, right? –I said laughing– Lets go back home, you are right, we ran out of time.

Setting the Rules

At night we went to dine at the bar where I met Brenda, all our friends were there. While telling them what I have discovered about Pisco Punch, the barman, who already knew my likes and dislikes very well, served me a glass of pisco from a bottle I had given him days before. Then, we treated all our friends to a round of shots.

Bob and Michael were more than excited with my story, because stories told in bars are the most incredible and outlandish that exist on the face of the Earth. I always thought that if someone here had decided to compile all the stories that were told every night since we have known each other, we could have compiled a saga as hallucinating as George Lucas' Star Wars. Obviously I made it clear that everything I was telling about Pisco Punch, Duncan Nicol and the Bank Exchange, was true. But many of them doubted me, I don't blame them, I would have done the same thing if I were in their place.

The comments and jokes about my incredible story took over the night, Pisco Punch and the Bank Exchange were the main topics of conversation which were woven into the most unexpected stories, all created at the spur of the moment with the only purpose of a good laugh. We were all having a good time that night and I did not let go of my glass of pisco...

–So you want a piece of the story, eh? –I heard somebody behind me say.

–Duncan Nicol! –I said very surprised although I had been looking for him–. But I... Yes, really yes, I want a piece, although I do not know exactly what to expect.

–Yes you do. That's the reason why you are here. That's why you speak so much about Pisco Punch.

–You looked for me –I thought out loud, as I was backing out of any of the responsibility.

–That's not the subject. But since you are putting it that way I'll tell you that I never do anything without a reason. And anyway, you answered my call –he added taking a drink from the glass of pisco I had in my hand.

–I'm all in –I replied with certainty–, I am honestly interested in the subject. I want you to give me the recipe of Pisco Punch.

–No, sir, I never imagined something like that from you. You are not that way. A slacker? What a pity –Nicol said sounding defeated, as if I had let him down.

–I don't understand –I said, without really understanding what he wanted from me.

–If you want the recipe, you'll have to look for it –he rebuked–. You were given the grace to travel across time and space, to intervene or just to snoop around. I think you should know that by now.

–But, what is all this about? –I said to him realizing what was happening. It was clear, the visions and the revelations were part of the game; I had been given a gift.

–Hey! –he clarified, looking deep into my eyes–, this issue is not that simple. It cost me God hands and his angels to get public recognition and fame. I worked very hard to reach what I had proposed myself. By 1890, Pisco Punch was, by far, the drink of highest demand in all San Francisco.[17] Many people tried to imitate it, but nobody could even reach as far as my knees. This is serious, son, it is an important legacy, and if you keep your faith things will work out. Nothing you get for free is really worth it.

–Perfect. I am on board, so I'll keep sailing ahead –I answered feeling proud of my decision.

–That's it, jump aboard, because so far the winds are blowing your way, you are on the right track. Jump aboard –he repeated before going out of sight.

17. Asbury stated that Nicol invented Pisco Punch and, mistakenly, that it was the most popular drink of San Francisco in the 1870s. (Asbury, 1933)

Monterey, was the first word that came to my mind, and repeated itself incessantly.

–Monterey!

–What are you talking about Guillermo –Bob asked sounding worried.

–Nothing in particular, I think. Don't listen to me, Bob –reassuring him that everything was Ok and taking his hands off my shoulders.

–You look pretty bad, buddy. I think it's time for you to go back home. Brenda! Here's a package for you –he laughed, and joked raising his glass of beer once more to have a drink.

–Bob? Is Monterey's old Customs House still a museum?

–It sure is! What is happening to you? –he looked perplexed, as if hoping to receive a secret from me.

–Do you know if it is open tomorrow? –I asked him, without paying attention to the concerned expression of his face.

–I don't know. I understand it closes on Wednesdays, so tomorrow it should be open. At least that's what I think. What do you want? What's the problem? –he continued asking curiously.

–It's nothing, my friend, don't worry. Brenda! Honey, we have to go, it's late and tomorrow we have work to do very early.

–Early? –Brenda shouted at me from her seat.

–Yes, love, we are going to the Customs House in Monterey –I replied almost whispering, so only she could understand our plan.

We started our trip the next day, at dawn, as Brenda exclaimed while still yawning, after four coffees and two aspirins, we arrived in Monterrey which Americans gracefully spell it "Monterey" and pronounce it as written, instead of using the double "r" as it was in the original Spanish language and pronouncing it with the dramatic, rolling "rr" from the times that the port was the capital of California for Spain and for Mexico.

The first thing I noticed after entering the customs house, was a cargo that came from Peru owned by John Begg & Co., an English company with headquarters in Lima, and a large and diverse amount of other cargo that

Customs House of Monterey, at the present time.

arrived here from all over the world. There was also an export cargo exhibit showing several hides and some barrels of tallow. I cautiously stretched my hand and touched the white cylindric containers where the name John Begg & Co. was printed in Gothic letters. Suddenly, I saw something that took me out of sync...

Reconstruction of the Customs House of Monterey. Notice the cargo of John Begg & Co. to the right.

There was a man with a white and dense beard seated behind a desk, he had a well combed mustache and a somewhat untidy uniform faded by wear and tear and the wind of the sea. Sideways on his head he was wearing a simple and small hat that seemed to be on the verge of falling off, revealing his thinning hair and the leathery furrows of his forehead, tanned by a sun that does not surrender when salt is its best pal. His eyes were shiny and quarrelsome, fierce companions of men of the sea.

The man only looked over his eyeglasses, which he removed frequently to clean with a handkerchief

Illustration of the port and the Customs House of Monterey, in 1854.

that was white a long time ago. When I approached him he was writing on old sheets of paper the cargo of the vessels that anchored in the port before they were allowed to travel to other California regions.

–Who is the person responsible for this cargo?! –he shouted with a military voice.

–I am! Hartnell, William. Of the merchant ship *Huascar*, commanded by Captain José Maria Oyagüe. The shipment belongs to the Macala and Arnel House in the city of Lima.[18] Port of origin, Callao –responded somebody that was standing across the room.

–Lets see –the man said, cleaned his eyeglasses and put them at the end of his nose.

Then, the old sailor settled in his seat and using a well inked quill began to write in his book, while singing each word aloud: during the 27th day of the month of May of the year 1827 the merchant ship *Huascar* arrives from Callao, Peru, commanded by Captain Don José María Oyagüe...

Peru had a commercial presence in California a long time ago, the most important Houses of the city of Lima, for example the Cavenecia and the one of Juan José Cot & Miguel Pedrorena, exported products of excellent quality and basic necessities in exchange for hides and tallow. The later was used in the manufacturing of candles, an indispensable tool for the workers in the silver mines of the Peruvian Andes, where the demand was so high that all tallow production was barely sufficient to satisfy the illumination needs deep inside the entrails of gigantic and fertile caverns that lodged the highly appraised metal.

This commercial relationship between California and Peru started at the beginning of 19th century, when two events changed the course of history: the Napoleonic invasion of Spain and the Spanish

18. "Macala and Arnel" was the Spanish name of the company called McCulloch & Hartnell. Louis McCulloch (Don Luis Macala) was the Lima representative of John Begg & Co., a trading company based in Liverpool, England. William Hartnell (Don Guillermo Arnel) arrived in Lima during the dawn of the South American war of independence, in the 1820s. Soon after, the company negotiated with the friars of all the missions in Alta California an exclusive export contract for shipping all the tallow produced to Peru and all the hides to England. It must be emphasized that all the information John Begg & Co. was able to obtain about Alta California before Hartnell's first visit there in 1827, came from Don Jose Cavenecia, a Limean merchant sailor who traded with Alta California since the 1810s.
(S. Bryant, 1949) (R. Ryal, 2001) (J. Señán-L.Byrd, 1962)

Workers collecting and purifying tallow in California. Watercolor by W. Hutton, ca. 1848. Notice the Peruvian *chullo* hat worn by the personage in the front. These hats were called "vicuña hats" in California. (Barry & Patten, 1850) (W.H. Davis, 1889, 1929)

American wars of independence. During that time, the poorly supplied California faced the crude reality of seeing itself forgotten by the peninsular Spanish authorities, in addition to those of New Spain's Viceroyalty (Mexico), who were concentrating their strongest resources on more urgent problems, such as defeating the emancipation movement. Taking advantage of that historical context, the Viceroyalty of Peru decided to make an attempt to benefit from that market, thus significantly increasing its commerce with California, in addition to the desperate acceptance of contraband commerce provided by astute Yankees.

In 1776, the United States had become independent from Great Britain, which caused the closing of its doors to commerce with all the crown's territorial possessions. This reaction pushed the Yankees to discover new commercial routes that proved to be very beneficial in the future, such as California or China, to which they arrived sailing through Cape Horn and into the Pacific Ocean.

–Guillermo! Where were you? –Brenda's voice made the scene disappear–. It looks like you are sleeping with your eyes open. Should we ask the man if he has some information that can be useful to us?

–Excuse me, honey –I apologized–. Yes I was elsewhere. Well not elsewhere, but in another time... Don't listen to me. Thank you, Hartnell! –I waved towards the empty desk.

–Who? –Brenda, asked surprised.

–Hartnell, William Hartnell... Lets go and ask the person in charge of the museum if they have the archives from that time, the first half of the 19th century.

We departed after talking with the man in charge. The gentleman gave us the telephone number of Mrs. Godrel, who was in charge of the Casa Boronda –site of the archives of the Monterey Historical Society– and told us he was certain she would be able to help us. Then we had lunch at the fisherman's wharf, at an Italian restaurant where they served an exquisite menu of calamari with vegetables. We sat at a table at the border of the sea, calm, immense and powerful, and so full of history. Portolá, Bodega y Quadra, Quimper, all of them had arrived on this coast.

–Can you imagine Brenda? We are in the same place where the Portolá expedition made camp almost three hundred years ago –I said, watching the bay with awe and nostalgia.

–Yes, of course, to safeguard the North Pacific territories in the name of the Spanish Crown and out of the hands of the evil Russian Empire... It is preposterous! –Brenda exclaimed, imitating the Spanish accent of King Charles III–: the Russians want to usurp our Northern American territory, issue a decree immediately for creating missions and towns which could serve as human borders in those lands, so as to protect our patrimony from those foreign hands that so badly want to benefit with our own resources.

Map of the Americas from a French traveller's guide at the beginning of the 1700s. Notice California poorly delimited.

–Certainly, your excellence –I responded, playing the part of a Royal Advisor–, since the Danish Vitus Behring discovered the Straight of Behring in 1727, thus immortalizing his lineage at the service of the Russian Empire, their further advances of the aforesaid power has grossly stained our Western North American territories. Almost twenty years have passed since these thieves have done and undone our wealth, ignored by our Crown, who was focusing on the more colonized places of the Americas. If you allow me, Your Highness, and with all due respect, the wealth could be more abundant in those places, but it is necessary to take into account that the commerce of hides of marine animals, otters and other beasts, which abound in our northwestern coasts of our Americas, could be of extreme benefit to the Crown, since in China they pay fortunes for that merchandise used in the tailoring of very fine articles. Consequently, Your Majesty, it is our duty to avoid further advancement of the Russians, the scent of vodka dims our intentions, and the apparently inexhaustible resources of our Pacific North America could be exploited and made into very good benefits.

The court of the Spanish King Charles III.

–Let it be sent then –Brenda emphasized, with her arm raised as if issuing a royal order– a decree to the Marquis Françoise of the Croix, Viceroy of Mexico, to enlist his better men for an exploration and colonization expedition, without scrimping any effort, since the resources that are being stolen away from us are very well worth any enterprise.

We were very entertained with our historical charade until I got goose bumps thinking about the hardships and the dangers of exploring unknown territories and sailing into little known waters, without the aid of a GPS or a digital compass that could accurately tell your coordinates. In those days you had to trust your instincts, your skills and in the cartography designed by early navigators, who were so very much prone to error.

At that time, this place was like the end of the world. It was necessary to make a true act of faith and commend yourself to the guidance of God with the best of your spirits. In 1769, the Spanish military man Don Gaspar de la Portolá was chosen by the Viceroy Croix, to accomplish the urgent mission of the rediscovery and colonization of San Diego and the Bay of Pines in Monterey. They were first sighted in 1603 by the navigator Sebastián Vizcaíno. Portolá was accompanied by the Franciscan Friar Junípero Serra, who was given the authority of the founding of the missions to be used in the conversion of the native people to Christianity.

Reconstruction of a typical Spanish ship from the 16th century.

Portolá's land expedition was quite perilous, he underwent shortages and mishaps but was also able to fulfill his goal, surpassing all adversities.

Portolá arrived at the present day city of San Diego, where Friar Serra founded the first California mission: San Diego de Alcalá.

Portolá left Friar Serra behind in San Diego and continued his course due north in search of the legendary Bay of Pines, which he passed through without recogniz-

View of Monterey Bay (Bay of Pines) and its port. Illustration of 1842.

ing, partly because the old charts of Vizcaíno were not totally accurate and he was traveling by foot, until he arrived at the surroundings of the Port of the Kings, near present day San Francisco. When he realized his serious mistake, he was already far away. He decided to return to mend ways, but not before exploring the region across the mountains that are parallel to the coast. Suddenly, in front of their eyes appeared something that, until then, only seemed to be part of a mythological tale: the great bay of San Francisco, which for so many years had eluded discovery because of the frequent coastal fog that sheltered its entry.

Illustration of the Portolá expedition discovering San Francisco Bay in 1769.

After such a wondrous finding, Portolá decided to return to the Bay of Pines which he had mistakenly left behind. With a company on the brink of revolt, encouraged by hunger and thirst, Portolá gambled the last cards of his deck, offering his men just the glory of returning with the satisfaction of having fulfilled all the objectives of the mission, without leaving any goal half done, like losers do. His men accepted the challenge and the expedition painfully returned to the Bay of Pines, where Friar

Serra soon founded the second mission of California: San Carlos Borromeo del Rio Carmelo, which is located in the present city of Carmel.

–Bren, let's go to Carmel's mission! –I said excitedly.

–Ok. That was exactly what I was going to suggest –she answered.

Immediately we left for the mission. When we arrived at this place we felt like were part of a beautiful dream. Today the mission is a museum, but also contains a school. A kid must feel very lucky to be able to study in a place like this, because of all that history present behind its walls. But I bet that the story of a beheaded priest roaming its hallways at night also exists, as in any typical Catholic school.

The site was impressive, a green countryside surrounded by mountains framed between the sky and the sea, it was like a painting...

–Wow, what a beautiful place! –I said.

I imagined the mission when it was first completed, two hundred or so years ago, without electricity nor

Carmel Mission as it stands today.

cars... Bet it looked even nicer than it does now.

–What an insight the priests had for building their missions in such perfect locations! –I exclaimed while admiring the natural beauty.

–Sure, but don't forget that in those days the priests were the ones who had access to all the knowledge and were the ones teaching it, of course –Brenda replied.

We walked and explored the building, so old, that each wall I touched transported me to the past. It was like magic to be standing in the same place where so many lives had been risked for a good cause, to evangelize the end of the world and, of course, to take possession of somebody else's land in the name of the Spanish Crown... Oh well.

We went inside the church, it was a beauty (in the fullest extent of the word): the altar, the picture frames, everything was original and perfect, as well as the oil painting of Santa Rosa of Lima, the first saint of the Americas, born in Lima in 1576 and canonized in Rome in 1671, fifty four years after her early death.

That painting was commissioned by friar and pioneer Junipero Serra, first chaplain of the mission and founder of the mission system of Alta California, to the Mexican painter Jose Paez, in 1773.[19]

Oil painting of Santa Rosa of Lima located inside today's Carmel mission.

19. Information courtesy of sir Richard-Joséph Menn, Curator, Carmel Mission, in private correspondence with the author, in 2001.

Interior of Carmel Mission's Chapel.

Reconstruction of the first mass given by Friar Junipero Serra at the Bay of Pines (Monterey).

We walked into the main room, where Friar Serra had long conversations with naval explorers that arrived at the mission to find shelter, to convalesce from the terrible diseases caught on board ships during their long trips at sea and to commend themselves and pray to the Almighty. It was there where a meeting took place between Serra's successor, Friar Fermin Francisco Lasuen, the Alexander of the missions of Alta California, and Don Manuel Quimper Benitez del Pino, a Limean navigator at the service of the Spanish Crown, whose naval career started in 1770, and was later under the command of the not less famous Francisco de la Bodega y Quadra.

Quimper arrived on Monterey Bay on September 1, 1790, looking for shelter for his scurvy beaten crew and to repair his worn down ship. It was in this mission where he found, in the hands of the missionaries led by

Friar Lasuen, the necessary care he so badly needed. Quimper's stay was not ephemeral, it lasted almost two months, during which he and Lasuen established a fruitful friendship, in spite of the well-known antipathy that the chaplain had for all people in uniform.

–It was in that hall where Quimper and Friar Lasuen spent some time talking and exchanging ideas and stories, both had so much to tell –I told Brenda, while I approached the room getting a bit closer than allowed.

–Guillermo! You can not do that! All these things are museum pieces you are not allowed to touch them –Brenda scolded.

At the left side of the meeting hall, there was a small desk that belonged to Friar Serra, monitoring the surroundings. Then, there was a large wooden sofa at the head of the arrangement of the furniture, all of similar caliber. At the center, there was a small table above which hung a discreet crystal chandelier that held in its entrails several candles, made from tallow, and that fulfilled the task of illuminating the room's long conversations. It was in this place where all the important meetings of the mission took place and where the missionaries entertained foreigners who arrived here for different reasons and circumstances. Finally, I could not hold myself back and touched the table.

–In the name of my crew and my own, I thank you Padre Lasuen for giving us shelter and letting us convalesce from our evils. Have my assurance that His Majesty the King of Spain will repay you in full for all your help –the naval officer standing in front of the priest said ceremoniously.

–There is nothing to thank for, not at all, Commander Quimper, it is my duty to shelter my fellow man; even more if they are brave gentleman who risk their lives in such a sacrificial work, exploring the most inhospitable territories in the

Engraving of Carmel Mission made by the Malaspina's expedition of 1791, a year after Manuel Quimper's visit.

20. Nootka or *Nutka*, is an island located in the North Pacific coast of Canada, today called Vancouver Island. It was discovered and explored in 1774 by Juan Perez, a Spanish navigator. The Convention of Nootka of 1790 took place in that island, between Don Francisco de la Bodega y Quadra, representing the Spanish King and George Vancouver representing the United Kingdom, with the objective of negotiating the territorial possession boundaries between both countries. After a series of very friendly negotiations, but without being able to reach an agreement, both men decide to rename Nootka to Quadra and Vancouver Island. Soon after, the border line is agreed upon between England

name of God. Ah! We are well acquainted with the evils that those with a giving and adventurous spirit, like yours, suffer. We know them well and we fight them skillfully, we are faithful guards of the body's health although more so of the soul, you know it –the priest answered.

–Then I thank you an infinite amount of times over, you are a saint, Padre Lasuen.

–None of that, but tell me, if it is possible, what adventures have you had lately? –the friar asked the commander.

–In fact, our mission started with the mapping of the coasts of the North Pacific, when Don Francisco de la Bodega y Quadra sent me off in the *Princess Royal* as a member of an expedition composed of three ships. We weighed anchor off the port of San Blas in February of this year and sailed through the northwestern coast of the Americas until arriving at Nootka, where we anchored in April.[20] Immediately we were assigned the duty of exploring the strait of Juan de Fuca, named, as Your Paternity well knows, in honor of the mythological Greek explorer of the same name who, according to legend, sailed there in 1592. But we disembarked and made a detailed scientific survey of the archipelago. I hope I have not exhausted your patience with these accounts, Your Paternity.

–Proceed, with your tale honorable man, from these stories we feed our spirit, in addition to prayers and penances, of course. Allow me to confide in you a piece of information: it is a good Christian who shares the experiences brightened up with spirited waters, as long as they are of good quality and good natured. I have a treasure from Peru kept under seven keys, brought from the viceroyalty by Don José de Cañizares to the devout Padre Serra, which he unlocked only when celebrating important events... and it seems to me this is one, and a very good one.[21]

–But this is brandy of Pisco! And of very good quality, from the best grapes of the Ica Valley, please allow me to taste it. What a perfect companion while narrating our recent adventures! I am going to grant myself a license and I am going to trust your Paternity with a secret, it was with this grape distillation that I was able to sustain our tired crew in high spirits, to keep them going on, regardless of the vicissitudes and inclemency of the weather. Life at sea is difficult, and a little joy to the spirit is never out of the question.

–That is very certain, to your health! And continue with your story –the friar said, taking a drink of the crystalline elixir.

–I will summarize my tale, so it doesn't become tedious... in May we raised sails regaining our course and took possession of several bays in the name of the King of Spain, such as Port of Cordova, located at the north of the continent, Port of Bodega

and Spain (the present border between the U.S. and Canada) and the island becomes an English possession. With the passing of the years, its name is simplified to Vancouver Island, perhaps to avoid a tongue twister when pronouncing. (Cardenas, 1994) (Beerman, 1994)

21. Don José de Cañizares, a Spanish creole whose place of birth is unknown, was the first navigator that managed to enter San Francisco's Bay, mapping its coasts for the first time in 1775. He did so with a small crew paddling a boat, while his commander, Don Juan Manuel de Ayala, stayed convalescing of scurvy in the stateroom of his ship, the *San Carlos*, that was anchored just at the bay's entrance. In 1769, Cañizares had been a member of Portolá's expedition with Friar Junípero Serra, the founder of the San Diego and Carmel missions. During the course of his notable career, Cañizares sailed to Peru at least twice, first in 1776, bringing Don Jose Antonio Areche, the Spanish King's *Visitador General*; and the second time, at the beginning of the 1780s escorting the new Viceroy of Peru, Don Federico de Croix. Cañizares visited Junípero Serra for the last time in August of 1784 and was present during the friar's death. (Beebe, 2001) (Cardenas, 1994)

22. Manuel Quimper Benitez del Pino commanded the first European expedition that explored, disembarked and made detailed cartography of the archipelago located in the present limit of the U.S. and Canada, where the cities of Vancouver, Victoria and Seattle are located. During May of 1790, Quimper disembarked on several bays, named several places and took possession of the area in the name of the king of Spain. He named one of the bays Port of Cordova, present city of Victoria, the capital of British Columbia, Canada. He also named a site Port of Bodega y Quadra, renamed in 1792 by the English navigator George Vancouver as Discovery Bay, probably without being aware of the fact that the area had been previously explored. (Cardenas, 1994)

23. Chinook is a King salmon. The King salmon presented to Quimper by the Indians of the Elwha river, is one of the biggest ever recorded in that area. (Olympic P.A.N., 1994)

24. The Elwha river is in the Olympic peninsula, located at a relatively short distance to the west of the present city of Seattle, Washington.

25. A Presidio, was a Spanish military garrison. There were four in Alta California: San Diego, Santa Barbara, Monterey and San Francisco. The one in Monterey defended the official port from entrance to Alta

y Quadra, and similarly, other places.[22] The work was arduous and complicated. Not always were the natives friendly, the situation always required our utmost care; although there were very pleasing moments with some of the natives. There was one occasion where the Indians of the Olympic peninsula gave us as a gift a Chinook salmon [23] weighing 110 pounds, which was caught the same day in the Elwha River.[24] It's not difficult to imagine our hungry crew tasting such a fresh delicacy together with, and why not, that pisco brandy from Peru which is never in short supply on our ship, we always share it with good company, as we are doing today, Your Paternity.

Quimper enjoyed very much his stay at the Carmel Mission and the Presidio of Monterey[25] where, for the first time in his life, he attended a bull and bear fight, a traditional spectacle of Spanish California that lasted until the first half of the 19th century. But it was a year later, on February 11 of 1791, that Quimper imprinted his name in the annals of history when he discovered the bay of Pearl Harbor,[26] giving the world another reason to celebrate with the Peruvian brandy.

–It is amazing –I said to Brenda– how pisco has been present in so many important events in the history of California, uniting people with a single glass.

–Look, for centuries and centuries man's history has been tightly bound with liquor. Alcohol is an elixir that, when used wisely, liberates man from his inhibitions and complexes, enhancing thus his creative genius, that can propel him to take actions capable of enriching humanity.

–The great Peruvian thinker, Manuel Atanasio Fuentes, writes in his book *Elements of Personal Hygiene* of 1859, that "liquor, pisco in particular, is a warm stimulant, that quickly builds on the brain, and that the physi-

A bull and bear fight. The bear was chained to even the odds. This "sport" was popular in California until the mid 1800s. The Acho Plaza in Lima offered this spectacle for the first and only time in 1805. (Calmell, 1939)

ological effects of alcohol can be summarized in the acceleration of the blood's circulation, heat and swelling of the skin. These effects explain very well the following changes that occur in the organism: the face blushes, the eyes shine, all actions are performed with more energy, the muscular system is fortified, at the same time there is a pleasant sensation of well-being; the present surroundings are enjoyed, and the future is forgotten; courage increases, enhances the heart, the tongue gets untied, so to speak, and the intelligence shines. Later, weakness is experienced, and after the mercy of repairing sleep, calmness reappears."

–How about if we turn into scholars and go to a bar, there is one close by –Brenda suggested with excitement in her voice.

–Alright! Lets see if our mind clears, our spirits are raised and our hearts are enhanced. My treat –I answered without thinking about it twice.

As soon as we got there I asked for a shot of pisco and Brenda for a glass of cabernet, of course. But there was no pisco.

California and, together with the one at San Francisco, were the furthest northern human settlements Spain had ever managed to posses in the Americas. They were also the furthest away from Spain.

26. Eric Beerman, an American researcher living in Spain for many years, states that in 1791 Manuel Quimper explored the present bay of Pearl Harbor in Hawaii which he named "Ensenada de Quimper" or Quimper's Cove. He also states, that Quimper received presents from the king of the island, which are preserved at the present time at the Museum of America in Madrid. Beerman adds, that Quimper was the first one to make a detailed map of the islands of Hawaii, which is currently located in the Archives of Foreign Affairs of Madrid. (Beerman, 1994)

–What do you mean there is no pisco? –I asked the bartender incredulously–. You don't even know what it is? This is unbelievable!

–No sir, I don't have the slightest idea of what pisco is, and the bar menu doesn't show any drink with that liquor in it, nor in all the bars I know around here –the bartender assured me, surprised by my reaction to the lack of pisco in his drink menu. I was speechless.

–Oh, dear –Brenda said, with the same sadness in her voice as if telling a child that Santa Claus didn't exist–, how long have you lived here, have you ever heard of any bar that serves pisco? There is no more pisco in San Francisco. The times of the Bank Exchange were over long ago. We are in the year 2001, another century, and there are things that just die with the passage of time.

–But this cannot die! Pisco is part of the history of California, and Pisco Punch was the emblem drink of San Francisco –I turned to where the barman was and said to him–: Hey! Do you know which is San Francisco's own drink?

–I don't think it has one, sir –the young man replied, somewhat bothered–, but the Long Island Iced Tea is a spectacular drink. Of course, it is the drink of Long Island, but it's potent, and if you allow me to give you an advice, it's not for rookies.

–Hey! Where are you from? –I said to him looking into his eyes.

–I am from San Francisco, and my whole family is too, and we are proud of it, although we know we don't have a local drink. If you want we can invent one and apply for a patent, then we can become famous and create something that can give us an alcoholic identity –the likeable young man joked. Typical Yankee of these days: Caucasian, of amiable gestures, military stance, straight look and kind smile.

–What's your name?

–Matt –he answered smiling.

–Look, Matt... –I began.

–Would you like a beer? –he interrupted in a friendly tone.

–Sure, thanks: make it large and a very cold one. By the way, I want you to meet Brenda. Now I have some news for you, Matt, San Francisco had a drink of its own, it was the *creme-de-la-creme* of the drinks at the time. I am talking about the end of the 19th century. It was a punch that was classified as an ambrosia by the experts and by the ones that were not, to such an extreme that if you asked someone in a bar in London, Berlin or New York for a Pisco Punch, they'll immediately answer "intersection of Montgomery and Washington streets, San Francisco, America!" I am talking about the Bank Exchange and Duncan Nicol, better known as Pisco John.

–It's amazing! I had heard something about that, but I thought it was one of those legends, you know. But this is very good news –Matt exclaimed. His eyes were shinning–: Is what you are telling me the truth?

–It was a spectacular drink –I continued–, but I don't know if you may be able to try it someday, the recipe died with Nicol, its creator, who did not allow anybody to have access to it. The story goes that Nicol went to the cellar of his bar by himself to prepare the punch, sometimes his inevitably discreet assistant, who enjoyed his complete trust thanks to all his years of service and to a blessing of nature, he was deaf-mute, would follow him.

–But, there must have been some evidence. He must have left the recipe to somebody, its not possible to think that all doors are closed –Matt exclaimed, who without even noticing it, crossed the limits of conventionalism and became a new member of the order of "The Revelation of the Sacred Mystery of Pisco Punch."

–Man! Bring me another beer, that barley becomes handy when lacking good grape! –I told him excitedly.

–Ok, but this one is on the house, or rather, on the barman –Matt answered, obviously affected by my enthusiasm.

–No way, I pay for mine –I cordially said to him, then I hugged Brenda–: Honey, do you want another glass of wine?

–Definitively –Brenda answered without flinching.

Brenda gets as emotional as I do and also lives intensely through the search for facts and events that can fit in this puzzle, that has Pisco Punch as its nucleus and pisco itself as its bond, but she always prefers a glass of red wine among all other things. It is very hard to see her drink anything else that is not a cabernet. She drinks one glass when we go out anywhere, when she eats and when she doesn't, and one glass before going to sleep.

–Did you know that pisco was even served in Napoleon's court? –Brenda said, distilling historian dowries through the pores of her skin. She always becomes very proper when she mentions a new discovery or some novel data–. Pisco, my dears, was exhibited in the First Universal Exposition in Paris in 1867, the very same Napoleon III tasted the Muscat variety from the vines of Domingo Elias. And after praising it he served himself more, at least that's how the story goes. In addition, let me tell you Matt, this liquor should not be taken lightly, its alcoholic content is high, between 40 and 45 per cent; but in spite of that it's very pleasant, I like it, but I prefer to drink wine.

–Then, is it like brandy? –Matt sounded very interested.

–Certainly, the grape is distilled. The grape juice, or must, is fermented until it arrives at a specific point, before it turns into wine, then it is distilled at a certain temperature using special stills until it becomes pisco. Now you know –I told him with the simplicity of a pre-school teacher.

–There are several varieties of grapes and different processes, as you may know. Guillermo likes the "mosto verde" type better, which is made from green must; "green" meaning not matured or not completely fermented –indicated Brenda, like reinforcing the lesson.

–Yes, "in-matured" must, ha, ha, ha –I said joking.

We all laughed, enjoying the happiness of good conversation and joyful drinking.

–And, as I was telling you, in the mosto verde process there is a level of glucose that has not yet evaporated, the last flavor after tasting this pisco is of sweetness, very tasty. I also like that one very much –Brenda said.

–I want to taste it, if Pisco Punch doesn't exist anymore, pisco does. I only want to know what it's all about and experience what you are talking about for myself – Matt begged, while preparing a drink for a customer that had just arrived.

–We have a deal, then. The next time I come I'll bring a bottle for you to taste how good it is –and I turned saying to Brenda–: Honey, let's bring him a bottle, Ok?

–That's a great idea –Brenda answered raising her glass of wine.

–You know, Matt, Pisco Punch was a very expensive drink in its time, San Francisco was an expensive place –I said, regaining the conversation.

–As it is now –he added, while he dried a glass with a white linen cloth that he soon left hanging.

–Something like that, but at that time pisco and the Pisco Punch, in particular, were synonymous with power. It was as a passport to a social and intellectual circle that was closed to any person from down the block. Only the great personages of literature and politics had access to this drink. Pisco was always tied to the arts, the theater... Because it has some type of properties that raises the spirit...

–It really enhances it. Do you know the story of Chola Hunilla? –a stranger called out to me.

–No –I said, looking all around puzzled.

–It is the story of a woman who is saved from her tragic destiny thanks to pisco –the stranger's voice added.

–Really? How's that? –I replied cheerfully because of the drinks I had consumed.

My eyesight was a bit blurry, but after I focused my pupils I could have sworn that the man talking to me was Herman Melville, the author of *Moby Dick*. I don't know if there was one or two of them, but it was him certainly who was telling the story.

–It was my first visit to the Encantadas Islands, the Norfolk, to be more exact –he began to say, laying down his glass of pisco that he had brought with him. I do not know how nor why–. Two days had been spent ashore hunting turtles without luck. We were just in the act of getting under way, the uprooted anchor yet suspended, as the ship gradually turned her heel to leave the isle behind, when a seaman who heaved with me at the windlass suddenly directed my attention to something moving on land, not along the beach, but somewhat back, fluttering from a height. It was surprising that such small white object, so distant, which appeared to be a fluttering dove, could be seen by any person, since the rest of the crew, myself included, merely stood up to our spikes in heaving. My belted comrade leaped atop the windlass, with might, his raised eye bent in cheery animation. Being high, lifted above all others, was the reason he perceived the handkerchief, otherwise imperceptible; and this elevation of his eye was owing to the elevation of his spirits; and this again to a dram of Peruvian pisco, secretly administered to him that morning by our mulatto steward. Now, certainly,

Herman Melville, author of *Moby Dick* and of a short tale where he narrates how pisco brandy saves a soul.

pisco does a deal of mischief in the world; yet seeing that, in the present case, it was the means, though indirect, of rescuing a human being from the most dreadful fate; must we not also admit that sometimes pisco does a deal of good? We returned to the island and we found Hunilla, a poor Chola woman from the port of Paita. She had arrived on the other side of the island three years ago, hunting turtles with her brother Truxill and her new husband Felipe, a full blooded Spaniard. Both men had died, drowned while fishing in a poorly constructed raft, in front of Hunilla's frustrated eyes because she did not know how to swim. She had waited for months in vain for the French sailor who brought them from Paita, and promised to take them back sixteen weeks later. Perhaps the French captain sank at sea, or perhaps he considered that the "half in turtle oil and other half in silver" deal, was not worth the effort of coming back. Be that as it may, the poor Chola Hunilla remained alone on the island for three long years. And if that day she had not decided to climb to the top of the island, to see the other side for the first time, which for her unfortunate ignorance was very frequented by ships, she would have never seen us. When she saw us and realized we were on the verge of weighing anchor, she frantically ran down the mountain, stumbling and waving her white handkerchief, the same object that our sailor whose spirits were so much lifted by pisco saw.[27]

–Is that true? –I asked Melville, I was touched and proud.

–Of course, man! And the story is still longer, don't think that it ends there. I will tell you another day. Or better yet, you do the research. Do you know where you can find the real facts that were the basis of the most impressive stories and legends

27. Herman Melville, author of *Moby Dick*, writes these words in a story in 1854, after visiting the Enchanted Islands, today known as the Galapagos Islands, when he was a member of an American whaling ship in 1841. (Melville, 1854)

The Norfolk Island, to which Melville makes reference in the story, may be the present day Floreana Island.

of the past? In newspapers of that era. There you have first hand sources, the data, and who knows what other surprises. Search –he told me, as though guiding my thoughts.

–Hey, Guillermo, did you fly to the moon or something? –Matt asked me, while he watched surprised.

–No, sorry Matt, I was, only... forget it –I answered trying to play it off, and trying to listen to my thoughts that repeated the final words of Melville's conversation–Brenda, we should go now, tomorrow we must get up early, at what time does the San Francisco Library open?

–At eight o'clock in the morning –Matt answered.

–And at what time does it close?

–At eight PM –Brenda said.

–Thanks for everything Matt. Next time I'll bring you that bottle of pisco that I mentioned. Here, take what I owe you and keep the change.

–What's going on, Guillermo? –Brenda asked, somewhat disturbed.

–Nothing, love... In fact yes, we must search in newspapers of Nicol's era.

–Ouch, Guillermo! That is going to be a very tough job –Brenda complained.

–Well, then, that's one more reason why we must go –I said to Brenda and said goodbye to Matt–. Thanks, Matt, we'll see you soon.

Brenda also said goodbye. A bell inside the bar began to toll, somebody must have left a good tip. I think it was me.

Secrets Revealed

This place is impressive, it's a melting pot of very different types of people, one can easily blend into this mass of different social classes and not be able to recognize the difference between a Prince and a Pauper. How can one tell if that long and white bearded man with an untidy stance is just a nobody or a reputed physicist or a famous painter? Inside San Francisco's Public Library we are all equal, just as we'll be standing in front of the eyes of God, during the final judgment day. Well, there are always some exceptions. Then suddenly, Brenda took me away from my thoughts...

–Ready! The bathroom is crazy, although for a public library it's very modern and functional. I mean, it's very clean, everything is in its place and lacks nothing, but so many homeless people, one may think they are Hippies right out of the Sixties!

–Oh, honey, you took so long that I thought you had drowned.

–Don't start –Brenda pushed me, laughing.

I love Brenda when she laughs, she does so with so much sincerity and self assurance that for a moment it gives me the impression that life is not difficult to deal with at all.

–Lets go to the elevator –I said–. We have to go to the fifth floor, according to the information posted on the wall, we may find what we are looking for there.

San Francisco Public Library.

While we were inside the elevator we joined a very interesting and diverse group of people, I could have written a sociological thesis at that very instant if my head hadn't been immersed in the Pisco Punch ordeal.

Happily, Brenda is a warrior and she can confront any type of experience to its limit, like this one. She seems fragile because she is small, just like Junipero Serra was, small in size but a giant in spirit.

–Guillermo, what should I be looking for? –she asked in front of the monitor.

–Anything that mentions the word "pisco." Choose the newspaper microfilms. Today we'll search from 1900 on until time permits, Ok? –I said to Brenda, as if asking for her approval.

–Ok, but wouldn't it be better to start from the date the Bank Exchange opened its doors? –she asked.

–No, because I am interested in knowing what was written about Pisco Punch and Duncan Nicol during their times of glory. I have a hunch that we are going to find interesting stories after 1900.

–Fine with me –she answered. Brenda began her search in silence. After a while, she called me excitedly.

–Look! I can't believe it. Guillermo you have to take a look at this –she was almost whispering.

–What, what is it?! –I stopped my own search and moved my chair close to her monitor, trying to be as discreet as possible.

–All of these thousands of hours of searching have not been in vain! –she said in that muffled shout that can only be heard in a library.

–Don't exaggerate, only three and a half hours have passed, not thousands.

–Whatever. Look at what this reporter wrote in 1959 in her newspaper column, she's talking about Duncan Nicol and the Bank Exchange, she tells about the glory days of the bar and mentions that Nicol, or Pisco John, had built a special lounge for the ladies that wanted to come to the place. This way women could enjoy Pisco Punch as much as men. It's some type of compilation of nostalgic reminiscences from those who had direct accounts from the Bank Exchange and Duncan Nicol.

–You are terrific! It's unbelievable! We must search in all of this writer's columns to see what else we can find –I whispered.

–Here it is! Look at the letter this man wrote to her two weeks later in relation to the Bank Exchange article. He signs E. J. P. and writes that he was a personal friend of Nicol, and that after prohibition they got together at least once to prepare Pisco Punch. He also says that he has the real recipe, which Nicol entrusted to him from his deathbed, but that out of respect for the memory of his good friend he cannot allow it to be published, but that he is going to send it to her. Obviously he will not send the correct one because there is an ingredient that cannot be disclosed, which in any case it is very difficult or almost impossible to obtain in San Francisco, and by including it or not, will not alter the drink's flavor in any transcendental way.

–Oh my God, Brenda! That man had the recipe, we must look for him –I said excitedly.

–How can we do that, Guillermo? Look at the date of the article –she said looking at me as if I was crazy.

–No, honey –I replied, trying to justify what I had just said–. We are going to look for him in the city directories of the time.

–Ok –she answered not very convinced–, then we should also look for the reporter, or the descendants of both.

–That's right, honey, she had the real recipe because this man gave it to her, although missing one ingredient she truly had it!

–Ok, I'm going to search for these people –and she went to gather the city directory microfilms from that era. In the meantime, I continued reading the newspaper article where we got the information from.

–Bren, look at what this man named Stephen V. Chiuda writes in the following column: he says that his father –V. Chiuda, who rests in peace–, was a fruit and vegetable distributor, that supplied Mr. Nicol with limes imported from Acapulco, Mexico, and that once he himself delivered a box to the Bank Exchange, where, he adds, Pisco John rewarded him with one of his champagne cocktails.[28]

Reproduction of a section of the column of M. Robbins, where E.J.P. writes that he has the original recipe of Duncan Nicol's Pisco Punch.

"The formula for the punch DID NOT DIE with Mr. Nicol. But out of my great respect for him I do not believe that this recipe, which he treasured so much, should be published.

"However, I am enclosing a formula which, although not an exact facsimile of the original (the main ingredients are not now available in San Francisco anyway) is so close no one today could tell the difference."

This we have in our hot little hands.

–At least now we know Pisco Punch is made with limes. But, did you notice what was Nicol's nickname, Guillermo? Pisco John, why?

–I don't know, they always called him that. We must find out why.

So we kept searching trying to decipher this labyrinth that was unveiling before our eyes with such clarity as though we were looking through the mist of Niagara Falls. I needed to know how pisco got to these shores and what was the inspiration for the punch recipe.

That night we returned home pretty exhausted, after spending eight hours in the San Francisco Library. I knew Brenda needed a rest and a well deserved prize so I asked her:

–Honey, I think we deserve a good celebration. What do you think?

Allegory published in the 1850s noting that "modern palates" prefer sugar and lime in the punches of the day.

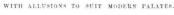

"SUGAR ON YOUR LIME."

A PATHETIC BALLAD.

WITH ALLUSIONS TO SUIT MODERN PALATES.

As though a water-spout had burst,
The Captain took a quid and curst,
And, having braced him for the worst,
Cried, "Speak, you gibbering mime!
Is there a sudden overflow?"
The steward faintly answered, "No;
But here's a woman down below
Want sugar on her lime!"

...

They had not been at sea a week
When spars and planks began to creak,
And soon the store-room sprung a leak.
Then reigned a jolly time;
Hot punches flew the vessel 'round,
And "tods" and whiskey skinx abound,
Gin-slings a certain cure are found,
With sugar on the lime.

...

For sweets become a lady's lip,
And what's the world? a floating ship,
We passengers - with whom to sip
Gin-punch is not a crime:-
We've all our failings - each his sin,
Instead of sugar, lets read "tin,"
And, 'twill be found that each, like Gwin,
Likes "Sugar on his lime!" (Point.)

–I agree, but at home, I am way too tired to go out. Why don't we invite Matt, the bartender whom we promised the bottle of pisco to, so he can try it?

–Great idea! Lets invite your friend Ariel and also Bob and Michael.

After arriving at home we called our friends and got everything together, including pisco and Pisco Sour, for which luckily, we always have ready all the ingredients for its preparation. I wanted to see what type of reaction would typical American people have to a drink such as Pisco Sour. If it had the effects as reported by the guests at the Bank Exchange, or close to it, then we will know that Pisco Punch must have been somewhat like Pisco Sour. We must take into account that the sour was invented in Peru decades later than San Francisco's punch, and as a pending matter, that its creator was an American barman named Victor Morris, who emigrated to Peru during the roaring twenties as a consequence of the prohibition's Volstead Act.

–Hey! Guillermo, we finally meet again. To tell you the truth I have been looking for you since our conversation at the Bank Exchange. I was thinking about what you told me. So they drink pisco in great quantities in Peru, eh? Humm. I am very interested in this, because pisco is a pretty versatile liquor, it can be mixed with many agents, it blends very well with other components without losing its properties. Even so, it doesn't prevail nor does it overshadow. I am sure several of the existing drink menus and punches can be adapted with much success just by exchanging the base liquor with pisco. There is a drink which especially comes to mind and I could bet without any fear of losing, that it will be spectacular by just replacing the gin with pisco.

–Victor Morris? How did you find me? –I asked surprised.

–No, my good friend, you found me –he answered calmly.

–I was just thinking about you. You are a bartender, right? –this was my opportunity to follow my search.

–Not yet, but I am investing much of my time and energy in learning all bartending secrets. Meanwhile, I manage with just being a sales clerk and I am saving as much money as I can until I save all the capital I'll need. I am looking for the perfect opportunity and the right place, really –he confessed to me excitedly.

–Why do you want to spend so much time and money learning bartending? What's so exciting about it?

–Well, Guillermo, bartending confines a very rich world, almost magic. You have no idea all that can be obtained with the right knowledge, you can make a stray cat look like the most beautiful rabbit, and turn a toad into a prince. Which means that if you know how to combine the proper spells with the precise skills, you can perform magic in the mind of unknowing people. To do this there is a secret, a rule of mixing drinks that is law, like those of Newton's: the calculation of the measures of the ingredients must be exact, there can not be any type of concession. Other things are just extra. Three bartenders of the same school, using the same recipe and ingredients, can produce three different flavors from the same drink. It's because each ingredient has its time, its measurement and its place. A little earlier or a little later can make the difference.

–Guillermo, open the door, our guests have arrived, –I heard Brenda say from the kitchen, waking me up from the trance I had fallen into.

The party began with a simple hello and ended with a cheerful goodbye. The results were impressive and worthy of a thesis. Although Matt apologized for not being able to come, because he had something urgent to do at the last minute, the other guests came on time, and from the moment they stepped in, I bombarded them with pisco in every way I could think of preparing it. Each guest's sensation and commentary was registered in the research, which delivered the following conclusion: pisco is a liquor that pleases the palate of any guest. Everyone at a different level, according to the alcoholic culture of the particular individual, but it's the same for a woman as for a man, this liquor has the faculty of loosening up the tongue. During that night, I discovered the best kept secrets of all my guests. Some probably regretted later the lightness of their unconscious when they undressed their privacy and conferred in such a public way and without shame. Brenda and I were amused with our experiment. By the way, since I didn't drink much because I was taking notes, I served myself a small glass of pisco, hoping for a good night sleep.

–I am impressed, Guillermo –a voice which I recognized immediately said, as I turned my head.

–Duncan Nicol! I wasn't expecting you –although the truth is I was waiting for him all the time.

–I like your findings, they are going full steam ahead, in theory and in practice. They are correct and it is important that you have a bit of fun with all this, the idea is not to let yourself burn out with work, one has to enjoy it, if not, the job doesn't come out right, and I need you to be inspired.

–I found your friend E.J.P. –I said to him with a proud smile on my face.

–Yes, I know, but don't even think for one second that it will be easy to find the rest. Remember, the man is more or less my age, lets see how you'll manage to communicate with him. The only thing that I can say is that you are doing a good job. Don't get confused.

–I am going to try.

–I'll leave you before your favorite jingles scare me away –he joked as he disappeared.

What an incredible man I thought, he was on top of everything.

Cultural Parties

After I woke up, I felt a very strong urge to have a cup of coffee and to smoke a cigarette. I am not on the right track if I wanted to quit smoking, I said to myself. Without thinking about it twice, I jumped out of the bed, walked towards the room where I had my pack of cigarettes and I threw it into the garbage. I couldn't believe I finally did it, I was proud of myself. That day I decided that I'll take a one week sabbatical from work. My obsession for discovering the truth and to put together all the bits and pieces of history roaming inside my head, fighting to provide coherent information, were damaging my nerves but still, I would not start smoking again.

That day Brenda's sister arrived from Miami with her husband. They were on their way to Vancouver to get on a cruise celebrating their 25th wedding anniversary. We decided to have lunch together, but since they are from Uruguay and I am from Peru, we decided to go to a Mexican restaurant. As soon as we arrived we ordered drinks, everyone bought a round and nobody complained since we seldom get together and we can never find something better to do than to celebrate drinking in each other's company. In the midst of the cheering –for this and for that– I interrupted that carnival of clinking glasses, and with my most sincere feeling of amusement I asked:

–Could it be possible that we don't know of a more effective way of communication than when drinking alcohol?

–Look –Debbie said to me, with that Uruguayan accent that Brenda has almost completely lost–: if you trace steps back and replay history, all cultures have used liquor as a basic communication factor between individuals and even with the gods. Just look at the religious ceremonies.

–Of course Guillermo! –Eduardo shouted cheerfully–: and you being an Inca must know that better than anybody, your ancestors were great elbow raising drinkers with all those strange concoctions they prepared.

–You are both right –I told them –this is an ancestral thing, even the priests drink. And by the way, the strange concoction you are referring to, was a maceration of corn which they called *aka* or *chicha*, and it was used not only during celebrations, it was a drink used commonly, in place of water.

–What are you talking about, Guillermo? Do you mean everybody in the Inca empire was drunk all the time –Debbie exclaimed, looking at me with that glance of extreme doubt she always shows when somebody is talking nonsense.

–I did not make this up –I assured them both quickly–. According to the chronicles of Pedro Cieza de Leon, Inca Roca decreed the public consumption of *chicha* in the 14th century.

One of the most important Andean culture technologies was preventive medicine, and that law was decreed to prevent diseases. They ordered people to drink *chicha* instead of water, because, at that time, they discovered that the drinking water was contaminated because as it made its way down the mountains it passed by rich sources of minerals and metallic substances that were harming the health of the town. *Chicha* not only eased the thirst of the people, but it was also a very powerful nutrient, it was very good food. The one drunk daily was *chicha* made that day, without fermenting; its effects were very significant because it provided energy. People didn't get drunk with this *chicha*, and if they took it in excess for some reason, like a special celebration or a festivity for example, the only thing that happened was that they felt full of energy, they could dance and celebrate for so many days without getting tired. There were other special types of *chichas* that were used for very important occasions. These were processed and kept buried under ground for 30 or 40 years. These were the ones that could knock anybody down. Anyway, in the Andean civilization, people were very moderate and lived in balance with the cosmos. There was an abundance of nature and a great respect for it.

Illustration of the Inca Roca by Guaman Poma de Ayala, ca. 1600.

–That was the reason why the Spanish could not keep pace with the Incas, and for good reason! I didn't know that. Man! The Spanish that stepped on these lands for the first time were indeed no saints, they were first class drinkers, moreover, they were tough people, or am I mistaken?

–There it is, my friends, a very important point –I said to them– the Andean man was very strong, he had a very good physical build and very good nutrition. The people

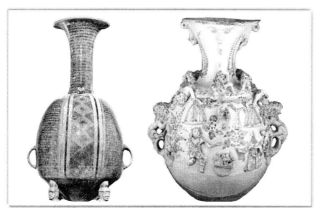

Illustration of an Inca earthenware vessel (left) and a Spanish colonial wine jar (right). Note the Inca influence in the Spanish jar.

who arrived from Europe, were fed badly and of the lowest cultural level. There is a nutritional table of Andean food, made by Santiago Antúnez de Mayolo, who, using the old writings in the Spanish chronicles, developed an approximate list of what was consumed by one person everyday day. Then he compares the list with the ones of other societies of the world and in all, the Andean surpasses by ample advantage the level and quality of nutrition. There is more, in some world communities phosphorus does not appear at all, whereas in the Andean culture it surpassed two thousand milligrams a day. Can you imagine what their mental development was?

–Just a question, Guillermo –Debbie asked, shaking her glass of wine around on the table before taking a large gulp–: Why do you call it Andean civilization? Were the coastal areas and the forests excluded from that civilization? Wasn't the Inca civilization a total civilization?

–It was called Andean civilization, –I responded–, because it had a constant, a structural base from which they developed all their achievements. There was an original thought, which is in all the manifestations of their civilization, whether on the coast, mountain range or forest. It takes different forms in some places but the essence, the base, is the same one, it is just necessary to notice their symbolism, it reflects a continuity.

–That culture, –Brenda added, after requesting to speak by raising her glass,– was pretty advanced, they had total control of all the fields on which man could develop, and they showed it in every thing they did. No object, structure, construction, painting, weaving or celebration, was for no reason, everything had its meaning, it had a reason. It was like a big puzzle.

–Using astronomy –she continued– they managed to gather a pretty good understanding of nature. Each construction, building or city, was built in a strategic observation site, which was used as a measurement system, as a registry of events and as a solar clock. They had very well educated people living in these places which were prepared to observe stellar events and to anticipate facts. It worked liked this: At the moment when a constellation appeared or a star was positioned in a certain way and that indicated the beginning of the sowing or the harvest season for a particular food, or the period of fertility and development of a certain species, they precisely located on the soil the place of coincidence with that astronomical event and made a construction there to record the exact date. They were very careful with the observation of the sky, a tradition that continues today in the present day Andean communities.

– Ah! Then that was the way they interpreted the Sun God, and celebrated their religious festivities. What were they called? Inti Raimy, or something like that?

–In the Andean civilization, compadre, the festivities were the ways of implanting knowledge to the population. It was an extremely wise organization, they did not adore anybody. They interpreted what the celestial positions said to them, and thanked the Earth and the stars for their generosity and information; but believing in gods, it is not true. They had venerable personages and words with the meaning of Creation, but their festivities coincided with the repetition of an astronomical event that indicated the beginning of some agricultural or cattle activity. The way the knowledge was exactly recorded was with the type of clothes that were used, the type of music that was played and the dances that were danced. Even so, they were conscientious, no event repeated exactly, thus they were prepared for variations.

–How come? Weren't the Incas considered children of the Sun God? –Debbie questioned somewhat confused.

–The Incas were men of lineage –Brenda said– and prepared to govern. The subject of the thirteen Incas has to do with an astronomical structure, as the organization

A view of the night sky from the Southern Hemisphere. The Southern Cross, delineated to the left, was one of the constellations used by the Andean man to predict the appropriate times for planting and harvesting. During the course of the year the extreme angles of the cross approximate the summer and winter solstices.
(Photo NASA)

of Jesus and the twelve apostles or King Arthur and the twelve knights of the round table, all added to thirteen.

–There is a chronicle written by a lawyer named Montecinos in 1644, –I added– that was based on Blas Valera's writings of the 16th century, now lost, where he mentions there were 120 sovereigns from four dynasties, as in the legend of the Ayllar brothers. In this chronicle, not only were the names mentioned but their ages too, the period of regency and the age at death of each sovereign, but it also makes reference to geological and stellar events that happened during their reigns.

–And were all these registered in their buildings? That is, were these as hieroglyphics? –Debbie asked.

–They also expressed it through quipus –Brenda noted– which was their handwriting method.

–But wasn't it true they did not know writing, and that quipus was only an accounting system? –Eduardo asked impressed.

–The quipu was the most precise of several systems of writing and storage of data that the Andean civilization had, –I responded trying not to create too much confusion–. According to the historian Mario Osorio, the procedure was the following: the *Amautas* were the ones in charge of collecting, processing and transmitting all information to the *Quipucamalloc*. These people registered it in detail using quipus, with knots of different sizes, colors, thicknesses, et cetera. All this data was passed to another human group called *Arawi*, who finally took the knowledge to the rest of the population where it was then transmitted from parents to their children. But in addition, they were in charge of refreshing and updating the knowledge as required. They were so careful with all the recorded information, that if a *Quipucamalloc* altered a number or a concept, he was killed on the spot. There was no place for mistakes. Compare it with the intense attention with which scientists launch a satellite into space, if their calculations fail

Ilustration of a *Quipucamalloc*, right, communicating with the Inca, left, by Ayala, ca. 1600.

just half a percent, the objective can be missed; equally with this society, they had goals of human importance and when varying a piece of data, it also changed their objective. To an equal level of importance. On the other hand, the Andean symbology was another system of writing and storage of information where each symbol contained in itself, essential and unmodifiable data, which added with others, it extended the message.

—Furthermore —Brenda said— in a recent research made by Osorio's team, in which one of the members is a doctor of obstetrics, on a tapestry they found an illustration showing a drawing in the form of a *chacana*, a stepped cross that describes cycles: next to other elements, there is an accurate description of the stages of the human development from the time of conception. It clearly showed, according to Osorio and the obstetrician, who was overwhelmed by the meticulous information shown, each cycle from the time the fetus is conceived, to when it received consciousness, forming a complete and detailed account of the preparation when ready to leave the mother's womb.

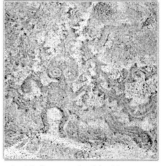

Aerial photograph of the Nazca plains showing an anthropomorphic design representing a fetus with its umbilical cord, 60 feet wide by 30 in height. (Eduardo Herrán Producciones, 1985)

—Che, that's incredible! —Eduardo said moving his head and using that Uruguayan word of attention—. Sure they must have had a very advanced knowledge of medicine, if not, how could they have dared to perform cranial surgery. Can you imagine? Opening another human being's head, che!

—That's right, compadre. In addition, the instruments they used for cranial trepanations were highly sophisticated, if you take a look at the cranial incisions you will clearly notice they were made by a circular saw-like apparatus that turned at high speeds providing a perfect cut. And for perforations they used drills to make orifices that outline the edges on which later they made the cuts.

—These people were masters... How did you say they called them? Andean? Good for these Andeans, Incas. Very skillful people! Cheers!

—Hey! One moment, Guillermo. Are you saying these men knew about the wheel? Because if you are talking about a tool that turned, you are inferring that they must have had a complete knowledge of the wheel. Or am I mistaken? —Debbie pointed out without breathing, remarkably surprised with this information— Then for heaven's sake, why didn't they use it, eh?

—They clearly had the knowledge —I said—, and yes, they did use it. If you analyze the forms of their graphical ideology, you will realize a complete concept of the wheel and in the drawings, there is movement. Take into account that when something turns it produces the expansion and contraction of the elements contained in the circular movement: the exteriors dilate and those towards the center are contracted. According to the work of Osorio, the wheel was applied in many fields: in their iconography, in the concepts of creation, in the textile area, to name just a few; but for transportation they did not need it, the abrupt Andean geography did not allow the use of the wheel; still now it is impossible to cross a mountain range with something that has wheels. In addition, they did not have beasts of burden, not even on the coast, it was useless. In fact they saw it as an obstacle to their development, because the use of a wheel meant destruction of nature, since it squashes fields on its way. Without using the wheel they transported much more cargo than in any other society. There is a study of Santiago Antúnez de Mayolo from the beginning of the 20th century, that indicated that the volume of minerals that were transported by llama from Peru to the Rio de la Plata in only one year, was so much that using all the trucks and trains available at the time of the study would not be enough to match it. It was a civilization, I am telling you, that was years ahead of the civilizations that prevailed at that time.

—But then it was not a relatively recent civilization, as it is believed, eh? —Debbie asked very interested.

–There is proof –I responded– that it was a very ancient and a very advanced society, it appears, by looking at their registries, that the Andean society existed and was in total control of its territory since long ago. There are traces of an earthquake of tremendous proportions which can be seen in the buildings of *Tiahuanaco*: huge megalithic pieces broken, impossible for the hand of a human being to move, it must have been a tremendous force of nature. On the other hand, the large lithic blocks whereupon the fortress of *Saccsaywaman* was constructed are very fragile pieces and of great volume, some weigh up to 300 tons. Some are limestone, and if one pays close attention, it is possible to see fossils of shells and other aquatic animals buried in them. The quarries where those stones were taken from were found only 37 miles from *Saccsaywaman*. This stone must have been formed in a type of delta, in an ocean, because the shells and small aquatic animals are the ones that generate that material. This means that 37 miles away from *Saccsaywaman* there was a very large current of water. Can you imagine how much time it must have taken to create that formation? But that's another point. Well, that cataclysm caused their organization to be completely destroyed. It took a long time for nature to re-stabilize, meanwhile some populations continued with the old traditions while others did not, these were barbarians, very dangerous people. The legend of the Ayllar brothers comes from that time. Several chronicles registered the legend, in which each brother was a representative of a dynasty or organization that came together at the time of a cosmic reading, to begin the reorganization of the territory and the restoration of balance. This legend is very important because through the name of each personage and his origin, several data can be deciphered which could be used to interpret: the essence of their food, musical structures, colors, calendars, etc.

–My God! A toast to the Ayllar brothers, che!

−Cheers! −we all said with a smile.

−And that's nothing −Brenda added with excitement− there are records that these men traveled through the world, they were excellent navigators. There are theories and studies that they reached Egypt,[29] Polynesia,[30] and many other places.

−But then, with all that knowledge, how come the Spaniards could surprise and defeat them.

−The Spaniards −I answered− did not enter the empire suddenly and with force, no. They waited for the permission of the sovereign, the Inca. Diplomatic exchanges and gifts were given, until finally an appointment was agreed upon. They were guided by native people in order to get to the Inca, who was in Cajamarca. Pedro Pizarro writes in his chronicles that there were sections of the road in which had these guides wanted to kill them, they could have done it with little effort. Even today a Peruvian finds it difficult to cross the Andes ranges on foot, and adding *soroche* or altitude sickness, imagine what it was like for these people, who not only arrived from overseas but walked carrying heavy metal armor. In order to enter in Cajamarca, they had to leave the horses behind because their horseshoes would slip on those steep stone roads.

−But then, these Spaniards were traitors!

−Something like that, compadre, they tricked the Inca, then they imposed their customs, their own religion on the people; they built churches on top of the *huacas* or sacred buildings, trying to erase any indication of culture, while accusing them of idolatry and several other things.

−But they brought wine. It was a joke! −Debbie said apologizing while we all laughed loud.

−A few years after the conquest −I continued− the Spaniards realized that alcohol was an impressive business, the wine and sherry shipments were more sought after by the residents of the Indias than even the gold of

29. In 1992, a German scientist discovered evidence of plants of American and Andean origin (tobacco and cocaine) in samples of Egyptian mummies. This has caused a great deal of debate on the modern theories of the trans-oceanic communication between civilizations of antiquity.
(Balababova et. al., 1992)

30. In 1947, Thor Heyerdahl sailed from the port of the Callao, Peru, to Polynesia in a raft made of Andean totora to prove the legend that the Inca Tupac Yupanqui once sailed to Easter island and possibly to Mangareva. In 1992, they made a discovery in the Pyramids of Túcume, located in northern Peru, of an adobe carving that clearly shows two sea vessels that appear to be very appropriate for navigation over long distances.
(Thor Heyerdahl, et. al., 1995)

the Incas. In addition the native people quickly acquired a taste for the exquisite flavor of the Moorish liquor. Shortly before decade of the 1550s, they brought grape-vines which they planted in the region under the sacred pretext that priests labeled *chicha* to be a heretic drink and impossible to use in their religious ceremonies as an alternative to wine.

–Obviously –Debbie said somewhat seriously– it was inadmissible for Christians, if wine represents the blood of Christ, how to change it for *chicha*?

–And, sure, the Indianos (which was the name of the Spaniard residents of the Indias) who never lack reasons to get drunk, received the news with great joy; there were never enough hands to start the planting of grape-vines on their lands– Brenda added.

–So the Indianos were hard drinkers, eh? Take a mo-ment and see if you can keep up with me– Eduardo chal-lenged me while he served me a drink.

–It's not only a matter of head, my beloved fanatic of the *Candombe* dance, it's about attitude, and now I am in a defying mood. Two rounds of shots for men and women, to see who can keep up with whom. In addition, it is better to be a known drunk than an anonymous al-coholic.

–Never anonymous! –Debbie shouted, laughing.

–Che, tell me, is it true that you are going to write a book? Love, did you know Guillermo is writing a book?

–A book? About what? –Debbie asked.

–Don't look at me honey, I only told them that maybe you were going to write a book. I never said it was for sure. But you know what? I think it is an excellent idea. You should do it –Brenda insisted.

–Its a research about the history of pisco in San Francisco. In fact I am following the track of the Pisco Punch.

–I always asked myself, where does the name pisco come from, Guillermo. What does it mean, buddy?

31. "*BOTIJA Perulera* [earthenware jar from Peru]: it has a height of one vara [33 inches] and a half, and one half in average diameter in its greater width; it's shape is conical inverse; it contains 23 1/2 regular bottles, and in it they ship wine, aguardiente, olives, and other things to the Kingdoms of Tierrafirme, Guatemala, and New Spain. When they disembark these earthenware pitchers, the slaves places them perpendicular to their heads using a linen cloth bun where it fits at the end, and are jumping and dancing with them, without losing balance."
[Textual translation]
(Alcedo, 1789)

Pisko, Andean vessel used to ferment and store *chicha*.

—In reality, pisco is a type of bird and originates from the Inca quechua word *pisko*. But the liquor takes its name from the clay jars where it was stored, which were called piskos and because it was made in the valley of Pisco, a place founded by the Spaniards using the same name of the natives that lived there, who called themselves piskos, because they lived in a region where birds where abundant.

—Lets see —Brenda explained more clearly,—: Pisko is a type of bird, and the name is shared by the natives of the region, the valley, the river and the semi-conical containers that they made.

—That's right, Honey. Those containers were made of clay and served for *chicha* to ferment. Its shape was specially designed for ease of transportation on the back of a llama, the beast of burden of the empire. When the Spaniards arrived, they also took the jars and called it *botija perulera*.[31]

—Also, the container was coated with bees wax that sealed it from the inside to prevent the escape of liquid and gas during transport —Brenda said enthusiastically. Brenda loves Peruvian history, and I think she knows it better than I do. When I realized it, she had monopolized the conversation, and if she ever looked at me, it was only to offer me a toast. She presented herself as the most knowledgeable, and continued, although I had already lost the thread of the conversation.

—...and by 1572 wine production from the Ica valley reached 20 thousand botijas or piskos a year. One of the first documented historical descriptions of wine of Ica, which was distributed from the port of Pisco, dates from the expedition of Don Pedro Sarmiento and Gamboa where he anchored on his way to explore the Magellan Strait. He writes in his memoirs something like this: "By request of the sailors and the officials we entered Pisco on Saturday October 17, 1579, where we bought two hundred *botijas* of local wine at a cost of four pesos and a half each which totaled nine hundred pesos." During the late 16th century, –Brenda continued– wine commerce from the port of Pisco, was already very considerable, it was pretty rare that when a ship anchored on its coasts it would not stock up with a large amount of the drink. After all, what a better way to raise the moral of a self-sacrificing crew. It was Sarmiento's greatest secret for avoiding mutinies.

–And for everything else, little sister, but if you don't drink your wine we are going to start a riot right here.

–So here it goes then. Cheers to you! –Brenda toasted very animated.

–Honey, to tell you the truth, I must clarify something. You are right by saying that the valley of Ica, near where the port of Pisco is located, was one of the most well suited places for growing grapes [32] and later one of most flourishing, but the first wine making attempts were made in the valleys of Arequipa and Moquegua.

–Arequipa and Moquegua?

–Of course! During the first half of the 16th century the valleys of Tiabaya and Socabaya had obtained productive vines, and by 1560 at least seventeen families of Arequipan *Encomenderos* already had very large estates with productive vineyards. For example, one was the estate of Miguel Cornejo, who was one of the first beneficiaries of the distribution of land, and the gold and silver treasure that the Inca Atahualpa offered Pizarro in 1533, in a vain attempt to recover his freedom.[33]

32. The modern theories in the science of the wine making and in general about the growing of grapes, indicate that for them to grow in greater amounts and in the most continuous way, the climate of the area, although having to be very sunny, does not need to be excessively benign. At certain times, the grape vines need to be taken to their limit of survival. Paradoxically, this causes the triggering of a self protection mechanism which causes the grape to become more robust and to grow better quality and in larger quantities (information courtesy of Robert Mondavi Winery, Napa, California, 2001). The lack of rain in the desert coast of Peru and its limited irrigation, has caused the grape of Ica to have optimal climatic conditions for several hundred of years.

33. Miguel Cornejo was a member of the artillery forces of Pizarro. (Keith A. Davies, 1984) (Manuel A. Fuentes, 1858)

Callao's customs tax for *Piscos de aguardiente,* full and empty. (Cisneros, 1898)

llar..............	"40	"10	Cada uno
Palos de balsa.........	2 00	"40	Cada uno
Piñas y sandías.	0 01	"01	Por cada cinco
Piscos de aguardiente llenos..............	"06	"06	Por cada cinco
Idem idem vacíos.....	"04	"04	Por cada cinco

34. *Pir Ua*: "They thought and they said that the world, the sky and the earth, and the sun and the moon, were created by a greater being than they themselves, which they called *Illa Tecce*, which means eternal light. The modern people added another name, *Uira cocha*, which means great God of *Pirua*, that is, to who *Pir Ua*, the first settler of these lands adored, and from whom all the land and empire took the name of *Pir Ua*, which corruptly they now call Peru or Piru." (Blas Valera, 1596)

In the general language of the Andean civilization called runasimi, the word "Pir Ua" means: the deposit of all the things. (Mario Osorio, 2002)

Illustration of the 1860s of a *chichera* woman serving *chicha* in a *botija perulera* (Peruvian earthenware pitcher) or *pisko*, in the bullring of Acho of Lima.

–What wretches, these Spaniards, they exploited them to an extreme. And they traitorously killed your Inca, che! Don't you feel resentment for that?

–No Eduardo, why keep resentments, much water has passed under the bridge. Furthermore, the arrival of the Spaniards and everything that historical time brought, for good or for bad, gave rise to what is now Peru . Look, we are a mixture, Peru is neither Spanish nor Inca, it is a blend of two cultures, and Peruvians are now neither Spanish nor oppressed, we are just Peruvian.

–Peru as a nation –Brenda replied– because as a name, it has a different meaning. The name came from the royal *runasimi* Inca language, it meant: The Deposit of all Things.[34]

–Ok, people, lets not turn rhetorical, che! Guillermo please continue, you stopped when telling the part of the distribution of goods. I'm getting into this history thing, when I return home I'll start to investigate a bit about Uruguay's and then we will face again in a duel.

–We have a deal! Well, I was talking about the estate of Cornejo which had received a large territory in the Tiabaya valley and had an *encomienda* of more than seven hundred Indians. Pay attention to the fact that, in 1569, he had twenty thousand productive grapevines. That means, my dear friends, it was one of oldest wineries of Peru; but most importantly, and for everyone to know once and for all, this date is thirty years older than the Mexico date, which erroneously appears as being the oldest winery in the Americas. So, now you know.

–And what happened to it? Why didn't it prosper? –Eduardo asked intrigued.

–It prospered. The wine production of Arequipa was tremendous, it produced more than one hundred thousand two gallon *botijas* a year in 1580. The wine was mainly distributed in Cuzco, to the Potosi silver mines and to the coasts of Chile, which were facing a bloody war against the Araucano Indians.

–That was the reason why they could not produce a significant amount of wine of their own –Brenda commented.

–Indeed, they were fighting for the territories that belonged to the most aggressive Indians of the continent –Debbie added.

–For that reason the coasts of Chile depended on Arequipa's wine for many years, but as all good things must end, it didn't last forever... –I answered.

–Che! This sounds like a sad bolero. What do you mean all good things don't last forever, buddy?!

–That's what happened with Arequipa's wine. By the end of 16th century, its climatic story ends because of a new commercial route that opened through the port of Arica, ending the commercial monopoly of Arequipa with the rich silver mines of Potosi. A great commercial opportunity for the wine of Pisco and Nazca was created.[35] But that's not everything, in fact it's not that im-

35. The discovery of mercury mines of Huancavelica caused the establishment of the commercial route Huancavelica-Potosi through the ports of Pisco and Arica. Mercury, an indispensable material used to amalgamate silver ore, was earlier brought from the mines of Almaden in Spain or from Mexico. Eventually, the mercury of Huancavelica gets to supply almost all the mines in the Spanish colonies.
(Keith A. Davies, 1984, José Coroleu, 1895)

Old colonial map of the *Corregimiento* of Arequipa, place of the first significant economy based on wine production that developed in the Americas.

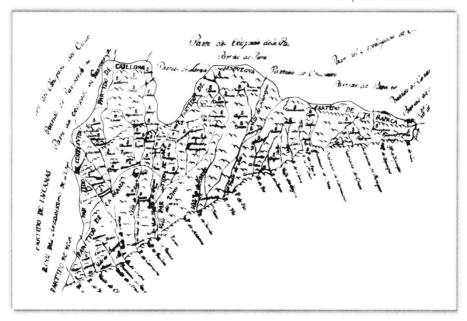

Satellite view of Huaynaputina volcano where the greatest volcanic eruption in the history of the Andes took place between February 19 and March 6 of 1600. It destroyed completely the urban and agrarian economy in an area between 125 and 300 miles. (Photo NASA)

Satellite view of the valleys of Chincha, Pisco, Ica and Nazca. Pisco was created for the first time here in the 1600s. (Photo NASA)

portant, the mortal blow was given by the volcano Huaynaputina on the 18th of February of 1600, ending all of it with a golden touch.

–No! This is not a bolero, buddy, this is a tango. Wow!

–That's it, brother, the blue skies of Arequipa turned black and the fertile earth and vineyards were covered with ash. More than two feet of sand and ash, compadre. Can you imagine what happened to these people! All vineyards were completely destroyed, as well as their whole life, man.

–What a shame, che! But that's about wine, what else do you know about pisco?

–The oldest data about pisco was discovered by a Peruvian historian named... What was his name Guillermo?

–Mr. Lorenzo Huertas, dear, he found a will written by a Pedro Manuel *El Griego,* who was a settler in the Ica valley and it is presumed was a pisco producer. It is one of oldest, because the document is dated in 1613, that is, almost sixty years after the arrival of the first grape.

–How did they know he was producing pisco, eh?

–Because of the will, man. That document describes assets of his property that scream: I am a producer of pisco!

–But what type of assets could "shout out" that?

–"Thirty large vurney earthenware jars full of aguardiente (brandy), plus a barrel full of aguardiente with a capacity of thirty small botijas of this aguardiente. Plus a large copper boiler for making aguardiente, with its pipe cover and another one in good shape that is smaller than the first." Literally. I know it by heart, hermanita –Brenda said, after reciting the will that shocked her from the first time she read it from beginning to end, surely because of the ancient and precarious Castilian Spanish that was used.

–It is clear to verify the authenticity of the will, which

coincides perfectly with the fact that in the 17th century pisco was very well known in Spain. At least that's what I had learned, even I being Uruguayan knows it, eh?

–That's true, in addition, the Viceroy of Peru was the most important of the Spanish Crown. Lima was, for more than one hundred and fifty years the capital of South America, with total jurisdiction of all the viceroyalty including Panama, excepting Venezuela and the territory of Brazil, which belonged to Portugal. The other Spanish viceroyalty in the Americas was the Viceroyalty of New Spain which included Mexico, Louisiana, Florida, Central America, the Caribbean, Venezuela and the present American states of Texas, New Mexico, Colorado, Nevada and California. Remember, the latter territories were not colonized until the end of 18th century.

–Is it true that the Spaniards paid special attention to the Viceroy of Peru and went as far as hand picking the citizens that were allowed to emigrate to Lima? Was that crazy or what?

–Compadre, it was a special privilege to arrive in the city of the Kings, not a punishment as it was in other places of the Americas. In addition, it was during the first one hundred years of its foundation that Lima, also named The Kings, arose to an economic and cultural vanguard. It became a bastion for mining, at the same time as the first history and geography books of the Americas were published. Peru was a power back then. [36]

–For that reason it is logical to understand why Peruvians did so well during San Francisco's Gold Rush, they handled the job of mining with expertise, they knew how to work it out, not like other foreigners who had no idea of what it was all about. They thought they were going to pick up gold from rivers and mountains, just as gathering pebbles down a stroll on the beach –Debbie asserted while raising her hand and moving her forefinger in a circular motion. Infallible indication of one more round of drinks.

36. In 1567, the Jesuit order arrived in Peru and they founded schools and introduced the printing press. In 1577, they printed a catechism in Juli, Puno, the first book published in the Americas.
(Robert Appleton, 1910)

Lima produced several world re-known writers, such as the poet Diego Martinez de Ribera, who was even praised by Miguel de Cervantes; Luis de Góngora and Argote, and Juan of Valle and Caviedes, among others.
(J. Monaghan, 1973)

With respect to the wealth of Peru in the 17th century, perhaps the best description can be given by Mugaburu, when he writes in his diary of 1640-1694, that some streets of Lima were in one occasion covered with silver bars to celebrate the entrance of a new viceroy.
(Joséphe de Mugaburu, 1640-1694)

Old illustration of Lima or City of the Kings, the capital of Spanish South America for more than 150 years.

–Guillermo, do you remember the story of the two Frenchmen who arrived with their wives, all dressed up, with the idea of just furrowing down the Sacramento river to pick up the gold using special portable rafts brought from Europe? They didn't want to get wet! –Brenda said laughing.

–I can't believe you! –Debbie exclaimed with tears of laughter in her eyes.

–Sure, you could find just about everything –I said while trying to speak without having outbursts of laughter–, Brenda do you remember the story of the Chinese people that bought a bankrupt saloon?

–That's a good one. These Chinese buy a bar at triple its price, everybody made fun of them thinking they had taken them for idiots, but as soon as they had ownership of the bar they tore it apart completely and removed the wooden floor. And much to everybody's surprise they discovered that in the soil underneath the floor was a fortune in gold dust, which over time had fallen through the cracks when patrons paid their bills and gambling bets, in those days all payments were made in bits, which is a pinch of gold dust. They also found other objects of value, surely lost by bar regulars in a drunken state.

These Chinese "mined" everything in the bar soil and returned home very happy men, with a lot of gold in their bags and without having to work hard on the mountains as all those who initially laughed at them.

–Is that true? –Debbie, who never stopped laughing, asked.

–Absolutely –I answered.

–What I can't believe is that we have spent more than three hours talking about Arequipas, piscos and the Chinese and Guillermo is still working on the same glass since we arrived.

–No! That is not true, but I would prefer to drink a glass of good pisco. Let's go back to our house and continue our chat there.

–No, Guillermo, thank you very much. Your invitation is very tempting, but remember we must get back to the hotel early tonight because they are going to pick us up for the cruise early in the morning.

–Well, don't worry! And don't look at me like that, I promise we'll celebrate our next anniversary on a cruise too.

–I am only looking at you like that because you have completely forgotten the get together we have tonight with your Peruvian friends.

–Oh! That's right. It left my mind completely. And we can not fail them again, they have invited us many times before and we have never been able to go. Thanks honey for reminding me. That would have been very rude –I said, then we said our good byes and drove straight to the party.

We were a little late to the reunion, it was a typical celebration of Peruvians in San Francisco, with pisco, dishes of *Carapulcra*, and *Marinera* and *Tondero* dances. Everything was decorated for the occasion and a large Peruvian flag was prominently upholstered to the wall of the room, its unique coat of arms looking more majestic than ever.

–Guillermo, what type of tree is in the Peruvian coat of arms? –Brenda asked, while she took a good look at the place and especially the way it was decorated.

–It is the Peruvian bark tree, an endemic species from Peru –I answered smiling. I thought everybody knew about the Peruvian bark, because of its quinine.

–And what is the merit of this little tree which gives it a place in the coat of arms of your nation, like a symbol, the species native to Peru abound, such as the potato, corn, cocoa, and many others, you have one of the greatest botanical diversities in the world.

–The Peruvian bark tree is a symbol for the Peruvians because it saved thousands of lives from the claws of malaria and of other similar diseases. The Peruvian bark is a medicinal tree; from its bark an alkaloid called quinine is extracted which was one of first medicines in the western world, and it takes the scientific name of chinchona or cinchona because, thanks to the medicinal properties of quinine, the wife of the Peruvian viceroy, the Count of Chinchon was cured almost miraculously after suffering from very high fevers produced by an acute case of malaria. After this event the fame of this tree spread through all Europe, becoming one of the greater medicinal achievements of the time.

–But what is going on here? Have you all gone mad, you are insane, how do you pretend this heretic concoction can cure the fevers of the Countess of Chinchon, one must only do what is proven and accepted. Nobody has ever been bold enough to contradict Galen, and according to what he indicates in these cases, bleeding and emulsifying should be enough, we must leave the rest to the hands of God.

–*Hombre!* I don't give a rat's ass about Galen and all his treaties, my woman is dying and I no longer want to continue torturing her. If these men can assure me of the effectiveness of that concoction then we'll try it, we should exhaust all the possibilities.

–But that is not a possibility, Count of Chinchon, for the love of God, come to reason!

–*Joder!* And what other choice do thou offer me. I have seen what these indigenous plants can do for the natives. Let them try it and lets see what happens, and may God's will assist us.

–Excuse me Your Mercy, but using pagan methods is against the will of God.

–Against the will of God is to let a Christian die without exhausting all possibilities! So go ahead!

–My Viceroy, I know that I do not have the right to direct myself to Your Mercy, I am only an Indian, but please let me suggest to you to dissolve the bark concoction in brandy of Pisco to disguise its bitter taste.

–Be quiet! insolent Indian! I am making an effort not to send you to the Inquisition to be burned alive for heresy.

–Leave him alone! You foolish doctor! My ears are receptive to the wise advice of these people, in whom I am placing my last hopes. Do what this man suggests immediately. Add some of the perulero brandy to the concoction!!!

–Whatever you say, Your Excellence.

–Your Honor! the Lady Countess came to her senses!

–It's unbelievable! My Love, you have returned to life! How is it possible that the native wisdom could defy Galen himself? This must be known in the Peninsula immediately!

–Guillermo! Please don't leave me with half of the information –Brenda requested taking me away from my revealing lethargy.

CHAPITRE VI.

Du Kinquina.

17th century French illustration of the Peruvian bark tree (quina), a revolutionary medicine in the 1630s.

–Sure! That's it –I said to her without knowing if she understood what I was referring to–, look: in 1630, according to the chronicles of Agustine Padre Antonio de Calancha, Peruvian bark was extensively used. Later they mixed it with pisco and it was one of the most popular drinks of Peru, this trend survived in Lima until the end of the 19th century.[37]

–Then, these type of drinks were already used in Peru centuries ago. Is that what you mean? Are you talking about the root of the Pisco Punch, or am I mistaken?

–Yes, but lets continue with the conversation later and smile because here comes Mrs. Reinteria with a *tamalito*. They are excellent, I had three already.

–What is the *tamalito* made of, Guillermo?

–Yes you can eat it, it's only processed corn –I whispered to her.

–Good, she wanted to stuff me with a *Cabrito con frijoles* and I almost died –Brenda commented in the same breath.

–There she comes, just smile and show a happy face. I am going to serve myself another drink.

–Where were you, boy! How did you like the drinks that you did not try? First you arrive here soaking wet, after taking a quick dip at my friend Halleck's work site, then you suddenly disappear and the next thing I know, you are here, standing right in front of us with those strange clothes and a strange way of speaking.

–I am sorry –I said coming back from my hallucinated state, trying to clarify the things that were occurring to me and realized that I was being confronted with some kind of space-time jigsaw puzzle, each event that was being revealed to me had something to do with another occurring someplace else. Weird. So I sat up and continued, as not to upset the balance –I've had a minor mishap, but now I

37. "Bitters," drinks containing Peruvian bark, coca leaves and pisco, were very well accepted by the wealthy class in the Lima of the 1880s.
(Benvenutto, 1932)

would like to try one of your nutritious and famous punches of pisco, Mr. Ridley.

–Ok then, taste one, and I hope you like it –Ridley grumbled and approached me with a glass already prepared, and by looking at his expression I could tell it was the drink I didn't try the first time.

–It's really good –I praised savoring each sip– but where did you get the recipe from?

–Why are you asking? What do you have in mind, boy? I want to warn you that this is the only tavern that works in these territories and I own it. I bought it from Vioget who was the first barman who set foot on Yerba Buena. John Vioget, my good Swiss friend. Before arriving in California he was a sailor years ago.

–Vioget arrived in 1837 –Captain Halleck interrupted–, and after receiving a land grant from the Mexican government he became the first surveyor of the city. He drew up the first streets and his establishment was the only bar, billiards saloon and meeting place of this city.

–Don't you forget –Ridley continued– his place was also the center for public administration of this port.[38] Vioget is a modest man, somewhat serious, but definitively fascinating and a great conversationalist, it is impossible to become bored with him; one could listen to him for hours.

–He is a self-taught scholar –Halleck added– eager to find the answers to all the questions, for that reason, he manages to inspire, in those who listen to him, phrases and expressions that nobody had ever thought to articulate. What I never got to understand is why he never let go of his old Californio clothes.[39]

–How interesting! –I said to them, trying to get more information.

–Well –Ridley continued–, What more can I say,

38. "El Paraje de la Yerba Buena" (The Place of the Yerba Buena –an aromatic herb from the mint family) or Yerba Buena, was the original name of the port which was changed to San Francisco in 1847.

39. The description of the character and the clothing worn by Vioget by Barry & Patten. (Barry & Patten, 1850)

pisco, which is an exotic liquor, was on his bar's drink list, which I later inherited.

–But how did you get it? –I asked, trying to keep my composure so that my heart would not skip a beat when they gave me the answer.

–On some occasions ships with important cargos arrive directly from Peru –Ridley answered– the registries should be in...

–Where! Where!

–Where what Guillermo? –Brenda asked trying to calm me down–, I believe that's all for today, we have had enough to drink.

–No, Brenda, you don't understand, I must search for the shipments of the boats that arrived at Yerba Buena, which is San Francisco today, from the beginning of the nineteenth century. I believe that tomorrow we must return to the library –I said anxiously and impatiently.

–That's good, but I can only go with you in the morning because I start work at four in the afternoon. Calm down, whatever you are looking for you will find. Being impatient will lead you nowhere –Brenda assured me, holding my face between her two hands in a motherly fashion.

–OK –I agreed, breathing deeply and feeling peaceful when holding Brenda's hand–, lets go back home, I am dead tired.

–First we should say goodbye, don't you think? –she exclaimed tenderly.

–I'm not sure, what if Mrs. Reinteria insists that we eat the whole enchilada?

–Don't be a clown, lets go and say goodbye.

On the following day I woke up very excited, I wanted to get to the library as soon as possible, to search in the archives for the information I needed. Brenda already was in the shower, so I prepared a strong cup of coffee and bit into the cheese that my mother sent

Brenda from Peru. It was an Andean cheese that Brenda hoarded like gold, but the temptation was greater than my will.

Before arriving at the library, we ran into a group of boys aligned in formation wearing white T-shirts and dark, brown sunglasses playing drums that hung from their necks. It was a very pleasant show, so we dedicated a few minutes of our time to lift our spirits with a bit of street art that was pretty good.

Entering the library and settling ourselves at will was easier this time. We already felt like the place was our second home. We each went separate ways to save time.

–Here it is, Bren! –I shouted as softly as one can inside libraries–. The first documented import of pisco occurs in July of 1830 by Captain Henry Fitch who brings it to San Diego on the ship *Leonora*. The second one, and perhaps the most important one, was on the ship *Daniel O'Connell* which arrives at Yerba Buena in 1839 with a large shipment of pisco.[40] Did you know that the only bar in the city belonged to a certain Jacques Vioget?

40. The English ship *Daniel O'Connell*, commanded by Andres Murcilla, arrived in San Francisco at the beginning of 1839, from Paita, Peru, with Peruvian cargo, having on board a considerable amount of "pisco or italia, a fine delicate liquor manufactured in a place called Pisco." Also on board were vicuña (a member of the llama family) hats and ponchos. The ship returned to Peru in the spring of 1840 with a large cargo of tallow.
(W.H. Davis, 1889, 1929)
The ship *Leonora*, arrived in San Diego with "great quantities of sugar and *piscos de aguardiente de Ica* [pisco brandy]" which were loaded in the port of Callao, Peru.
(A. Odgen, 1981) (Dictation of Mrs. Capt. Henry D. Fitch, 1875, Bancroft Library, UC Berkeley)

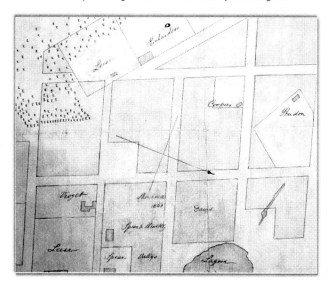

The first map of the city of Yerba Buena (San Francisco). Drawn by Jean Jacques Vioget at the end of the 1830s. This map was hanging in his bar, the first one of San Francisco, and shown with the name of "Vioget" on the map.

Newspaper advertisement of 1848 in which John Vioget announces the sale of cargo of the Peruvian ship *Veloz*, showing Peruvian bark (or quina tree bark).

Reproduction of the first panoramic drawing of the port of Yerba Buena (San Francisco) drawn by J. Vioget from the east side of the bay, in 1837. The first constructions of San Francisco are shown at the distance. Vioget's saloon is one of them. To the left is shown a small boat full of hides of cattle ready to export. To the right, possibly the Peruvian brigantine *Delmira*. (*Sunset Magazine*, 1915) (Joséph A. Baird, 1961)

–And where does the pisco end up at? In the only bar in town, Vioget's, obviously. You are a genius, Guillermo. Then, he is the core of the matter, he's the one we must concentrate on. But where do you come up with the clues?

–Would you believe me if I told you spirits revealed them to me?

–Don't make up stories! Listen to this, Vioget travels to Peru in 1838, a year before the arrival of the *O'Connell*, as captain of the *Delmira* which had Don Miguel de Pedrorena as supercargo.

–Pedrorena? Brenda, do you know who Pedrorena was? He was one of the ones that signed the first Constitution of the State of California after joining the Union. He was a resident of Lima, isn't that amazing!

–We must go to the Casa Boronda, Guillermo. I guarantee we will find invaluable information about Vioget's era there.

–Lets go at once.

Casa Boronda belongs to the Monterey County Historical Society, and it is to the south of the city of San Jose, originally a cattle feeding region named *Rancho Del Rey*, in the present day city of Salinas.

When we made the appointment with Mrs. Godrel, thanks to the information given to us in Monterey, we never imagined what we were going see. We were shocked by the arsenal of original documents that took refuge there from the inclement passing of time.

In order to have access to them we had to go inside a large vault specially equipped to preserve and avoid the deterioration of the old documents. It was impressive.

When we got in, we noticed that the task was not going to be easy because the archives were arranged in a *sui generis* way in which the apparent disorder was very well organized by the unforgettable Mrs. Godrel whose sky-blue eyes flashed with joy every time a researcher, wearing the required white cloth gloves and showing extreme care in handling of the archives, presented her with some new discovery that revealed another piece of the history written in the annals that she so carefully guarded, as Saint Peter does the doors of Heaven.

Jean Jacques Vioget, pictured during the last days of his life.

It was there where we worked searching for countless hours, until we finally found documents of the first Californios, invaluable papers that withhold so much truth and that are the pieces of the puzzle of man's his-

View of the document vault of the Monterey County Historical Society.

tory, of California and of the world, all seemingly weaved by a diligent spider, that entangle lives and the ancestral past of a group of people, that apparently does not have too much past, but whose identity goes back not only to the Old Continent, but to the history of pre-Columbian America: grape, wine, pisco, Andean medicine...

–Brenda look , here are the archives of Bandini and Malarin and of the first Californios too!

–Let me see, love –she said to me, while reviewing the documents that I showed her, sounding very interested. I don't know how to thank her for spending all her spare time with me on this whim that has become an obsession for me. And to think that we met thanks to soccer. When I saw her for the first time and found out that she was from Uruguay, where everybody loves soccer and the fan base is strongly divided between two or three clubs, I could not come up with a better strategy than to approach her asking: "Are you a fan of Peñarol?." To my great surprise and good fortune, she was.

Archive of manuscripts from the first Californios, showing a requisition signed by Juan Malarin in 1833. (Courtesy Monterey County Historical Society)

–In their own writing, in their own writing, honey –explaining to her what it was all about– it states here everything that Malarin and Bandini owned, their estate, and it was not small.

–For Heaven's sake! –Mrs. Godrel exclaimed repeatedly sounding moved– that's good, but please handle everything very carefully, these papers are like children to me.

–Don't worry, we will do so with our utmost care –I replied to Mrs. Godrel while I touched the documents.

–Happy Independence Day! To our health!

–Thanks Mr. Bandini for inviting us to your house in celebration of the first dance in California in honor of the Independence Day of the United States of America. This foretells a good future.

–I wish so, General Stockton, I have worked very hard so this event comes out the way it should be.

–I know that for you, my friend Bandini, the situation may not appear to be absolutely pleasant, it must be difficult to get used to these times of change.

–General, the most important thing for me is the development of California.[41] I already said on one occasion that there must be substantial changes. I fought for that goal in the General Assembly of Mexico, where I represented California. As you will see, I have little interest to go back to the old ways if the changes bring our people well-being.

–Mr. Bandini, you should understand that California now belongs to the United States and that there are new rules in the game, it is no longer as when you arrived a long time ago. The Californios are not an elite anymore, they are just American citizens as all those that share this table with us today.

–I am not opposed, General, I only want all things to be done the way they should. I was in favor of the secularization of the missions to integrate into an homogeneous state, where many radical changes are needed; in the Presidios for example, where there are so many weak points and as many holes as in swiss cheese.

–Everything will be done at its proper time, you must be assured of that.

–Look General, since I arrived in this land from Peru, I realized the amazing potential California had for being a great country. For that reason my ten children were born here, I already have buried my dead under this ground, I grow my vineyards here, I have given my life to the development of this land, and in return, it has given me prosperity and happiness and I have seen all my dreams fulfilled, but I have the sad vision of an uncertain future coming from the hands of inappropriate people.

41. Juan Bandini was the author of a report about the social, political and financial status of California in the 1830s, where he suggested several recommendations for its future colonization and development.
(J. Bandini, 1830, R.M. Beebe, R. M. Senkewicz, 2001)

Today a man's word is not worth as much as it was before.

–Father! Come, the dance is going to start!

–Excuse me, General, but duty calls. This daughter of mine is one of my most appraised treasures, and she dances the fandango, the waltz and the *zamacueca* with such grace that not even cherubs can stop admiring her. Pardon me.

–Please go.

–Good, I'll be right back to continue with our conversation.

Bandini danced extremely well, indeed. A few minutes later, when the musicians finished playing the music and the people exploded in a fervent applause, Bandini returned to his chair next to General Stockton.

–Ok, I'm back to continue with our talk.

–You really dance very well, Mr. Bandini. It seems that you have all the qualities a man needs for being admired, now I know why you have such an excellent reputation.

–Please stop, the whole credit belongs to Margarita. She is the youngest of my daughters, she inherited the good ear and the grace of her mother. Josefa and Arcadia are seated right there. Do you see them? Each one is accompanied by her respective husband; the other ones, because I have five women and five men, are taking care of the guests.

–This is an excellent celebration, Mr. Bandini. By the way, what a fine liquor.

–It is pisco, brought from Peru. Always the best for my guests.

–Have you seen all the information that is in here about Bandini, Guillermo? This man was very rich and distinguished –Brenda said to me while reviewing the drawers of old documents describing the history of this

Californio who died believing in his ideals.

–Yes, but at the end of his days, and very unfortunately, he could not adapt to the change –I said to her with sadness, while I continued reading his story–. He had to see with his own eyes the eclipse that shadowed his vision and his era, plus the treason of those whom he helped when they were in need.

–A totally different situation than with Malarin, right? –Brenda pointed out while holding the documents of Juan Malarin in her hands.

–Oh, yes, because Juan Malarin was a visionary. He quickly figured out what was the best for him and he adapted to it. Bandini was betrayed by his own ideals. He became a politician, and this turned out to be bad for him; he was concerned with the progress of the whole State, whereas Malarin mostly envisioned what was the most appropriate for the future of his children, I don't judge him, I would have done the same thing. That was the reason why he forced his son Mariano to study English at the school of William Hartnell, this being the same man that arrived from Peru bringing cargo from the English company of John Begg & Co. It seems that Hartnell's school was the first of higher education in the history of California. Later in 1838, Mariano was sent to Peru to study law at the University of San Marcos of Lima, which was the most important in the west of the Americas.

–Guillermo! You won't believe this. Did you know Juan Malarin made jerky? Beef jerky. Look at this, it's amazing, jerky is nothing else than Peruvian *charqui*.[42]

–Yes, I knew that. In 1824, Malarin joined David Spence and formed a company that produced beef jerky locally, bringing people from Peru for its elaboration. But, the most important legacy left by Malarin to the United States are the legal precedents in the judicial system of rural land properties. Mariano taught law in Peru for a few years and returned to California after learning

42. *Charqui* or salted dry meat, is a technique for the preservation of meat created by the Incas. With the passing of time, *charqui* becomes part of the English language as the word "jerky."

of his father's death in 1849. As soon as he arrived he had to litigate with the United States government for the recognition of his family's land, which added up to more than ninety thousand acres, many of which were questioned because the previous Mexican government's documents were inaccurate, and some land was invaded by third parties over the years. All his land came from his father's estate and his association with Spence, in addition to the land inherited by his wife, Isidora Pacheco. Mariano moves to a farm in Santa Clara, and initiates a battle against the system. Finally, he makes his rights prevail and his family keeps possession of the majority of the land they inherited. It was forty years of hard legal confrontation against the government, at which time, perseverance and a little pisco, were accomplices for the successful ending of his task. The Malarin family expired with the death of Paula Fatjo in 1992. She was the grand daughter of Paula Malarin, Mariano's daughter. Sadly, the Malarin family name expired but it survives forever: Paula donated her forty eight thousand acre ranch named San Luis Gonzaga to the State of California before her passing, and now it is a State Park.

Suddenly Mrs. Godrel, our friendly host, appeared.

–Did you find what you were looking for? –she asked smiling.

–Well, yes there is some quite significant information here –I responded to her showing my excitement.

–But, what is your research about –she asked.

–To tell you the truth it is about Pisco Punch. We want to decipher it's history and what's behind it, how pisco arrives in San Francisco, where does the original recipe come from –I said to her.

–Look, I know very little about Pisco Punch, but if you came all the way down here, it must be worth it. I'll tell you what I know. Pisco is what was once called Peruvian brandy or from a place called Pisco? Right? –she said leaning slowly on the table that we were working at.

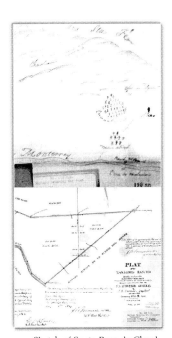

Sketch of Santa Rosa de Chualar (top), one of the properties of Juan Malarin in 1833, located a close distance from the present city of Salinas. Legal document of 1862 (bottom), where the property of that area is legally credited to the state of Mariano Malarin. (Courtesy Monterey County Historical Society)

—That's it —I responded with my eyes starting to shine and my mind eager to obtain any information.

—In 1843 —she said with her eyes looking up and far away—, a family named Torres arrived in Northern California from the northern part of Peru. The daughter had married a Yankee captain named Stephen Smith. In his cargo, Smith brings with the Torres —because in addition to his wife, he also brought his brother-in-law and his mother-in-law— the first steam mill in the history of California. Smith and the young Torres, his brother-in-law, became partners and were granted a huge amount of land in the areas that are now the city of Bodega and Fort Ross. I will summarize the story by saying that Smith and Torres built a large ranch named Rancho Bodega. They also purchased from Jean Vioget, the first barman in San Francisco, a parcel of land close to his tavern. The important point to make here is that Smith's mother-in-law, Maria or Manonga Torres, was very well-known for being an excellent nurse and healer and had brought back a large amount of secrets of the medicinal folklore of Peru in which milk punch was one of the most accepted. It was used as a tonic and contained pisco. But she also lavished her guests with a refreshing drink called *las once*, in which she mixed pisco, water, sugar and lime.

A Californio wearing typical clothing. Watercolor by Mauricio Rugendas, Mexico, ca. 1845.

43. "*Geographic-Historical Dictionary of the West Indies or America,*" 1789. Annex, Pg. 149: "PINEAPPLE: One of the best fruits in the world, native to America, and very common among the continent;... The taste of this fruit has something of muscat grape and pear of Good Christian, eaten with red wine and sugar it has the taste of strawberries. ...after fermenting its rinds in water for 24 hours a very tasteful type of cyder is obtained, they call it *Chicha of* pineapple, which is extremely fresh and sweet, and it is the one that is served as a gift at eleven in the morning..." [Textual translation] (Alcedo, 1789)

In Lima of the 1850s, a "tonic" was served mixing pisco with water, sugar and lime.
(S. Zapata A., 2001)

Doña Maria "Manonga" Torres, Peruvian nurse, arrives at Bodega, California in 1843, with her children, Manuel and Manuela, and her son-in-law, Captain Stephen Smith.

Once in a while she added some pieces of pineapple, sometimes pineapple *chicha*: a maceration made from the peals of that fruit.[43] If you are interested, there is a book that is called *History of Sonoma County* by J.P. Munro-Fraser, maybe you'll find something more there.

–What you have told us is more valuable than gold, I think we have the real spinal cord of the matter here. This is very impressive, thank you very much Mrs. Godrel –I said to her holding her hand.

–Please, don't worry, I am here to assist in as much as I can. If researchers like ourselves don't lend each other a helping hand, then what would we do? –she laughed holding my hand as well.

I looked for the book in a hurry, and while I opened it a very cheerful music started to surround me...

–Everybody is present here! Health to the Smiths!

–We didn't forget to invite anyone to this remarkable event. It could not have been any other way. Are you pleased, my dear Manuela? You know I'll do anything for you, my beloved wife.

–I really thank you, husband of mine. This is more than I could have ever imagined. Now please allow me to go and tend to our guests.

–Let me congratulate you, Smith, it is an event for all people of Yerba Buena to see. The operation of this majestic work of modern engineering: the first steam mill of California.

–Mr. Mayor, let me introduce you to my wife Manuela and her mother, Doña Maria Torres.

–Are you the one that prepares those magnificent punches of pisco, Mrs. Torres?

–Yes I am the one Mr. Mayor, I will oblige whenever you please.

–Then I congratulate you, even Juan Vioget is stunned with your punches.

The Smith-Torres' Rancho Bodega, where the first steam mill of California is inaugurated in 1844.

–Mr. Mayor, let me offer you some bread just baked in the oven, and whose flour was just made by the steam mill and by the prodigious hands of my daughter.

–Thank you very much, but I am concerned with General Vallejo[44] not moving away from the pisco jars. If we look the other way there will be nothing left there soon, ha, ha, ha, ha.

–No need to worry, Major. We have more than enough.

Suddenly, the jingle of some familiar bells interrupted my celebration at the Smith's ranch. Before I realized it, Brenda was handing the cellular phone to me.

–Matt wants to talk to you –she said.

–Thanks, honey. But tell me, are you ever going to take those bracelets off? We are going to have a hard time when we travel. How many are they, twenty? Aren't they too heavy for you?

–Go, talk to Matt, he is waiting for you –Brenda said to me somewhat annoyed.

–Hello Matt, what's going on? –I said while holding the telephone, but looking at Brenda out of the corner of my eye.

44. The Californio Don Mariano Guadalupe Vallejo was the military commander of Northern Alta California before and during the transition of governments between Mexico and the United States. Vallejo accepted the geopolitical change with open arms and adapted successfully to the new order. For this reason the cities of Vallejo and Benicia take his name and that of his wife's first name. General Vallejo was present during the great celebration of the inauguration of the steam mill of the Smith-Torres family, along with all the important inhabitants of the region and of Yerba Buena (San Francisco). (J.P. Munro-Fraser, 1880)

–I would like to invite you both to my house tomorrow night. I am going to have a party –Matt said through the earpiece.

–Brendita, Matt invited us to his house tomorrow night, he is having a party. How about if we take some pisco? –I said to her, sounding like I had my tail between my legs.

–Yes, whatever you say –she answered bluntly but not angry.

–Please don't get angry with me for mentioning your bracelets. I was not serious, the bells always distract me –I explained to her.

–That's fine, it never bothers me –she answered a bit hurt.

–Also... You know what? –I insisted– in fact I love the sound, it is relaxing to me, just as...

–That's enough, Guillermo. I forgive you, you do not need to say anything else –she said to me with a sad smile.

–Are you sure you are not angry, Brenda? If you are, I'll buy you another bracelet right now, with a lot of charms –I said to her trying to make her really smile.

–Everything is better than good –she said smiling– and no, I do not want another bracelet, I want you, I love you.

–And I love you too. Are you still a fan of Peñarol?

–Of course!

–So then, let me invite you to have a drink.

–Lets leave it for later, I start to work in one hour.

–Ok. Then –I told her giving her a kiss– I am going to look around the place to see if I can find something else and then we'll go...

–Ridley, I know where you got your punch recipes from –I told him right off the bat.

–What the hell are you talking about? –he said giving me such a penetrating look that made my knees freeze.

–Does the name Maria Torres ring a bell? –I continued.

–What do you have in mind? What is all this about, foreigner?

–I need to know –I said to him very distressed.

–Is this some type of blackmail? I know how to deal very well with people of your kind –he warned me while his hand went to his belt.

–No man! All I want is to find out a little more information so that the story can be unravelled –I said trying to calm him down.

–What story? What is it all about, Boy! –Ridley was becoming impatient.

–I had hoped that you were the one to answer that. It is you that appeared in my visions, you give me clues, riddles, and what I don't know. It is you that will help me compile the information, I need to find all the pieces that will solve this puzzle, otherwise why are you here? You know what I am looking for, it seems you are playing with me. Why? For what reason? –I asked putting my cards on the table.

–Well –he said to me uncovering an invisible mask from his face– I never imagined you were going to go so fast. I was hoping for an act of faith, you didn't need to research so deeply, you just had to follow the path I was giving to you. That was the way you were supposed to get to the Pisco Punch, the history before it and even the history of pisco in San Francisco, since it's beginning here and when it arrived. I was even going to tell you who drank it first in these California lands, but now you are confronting me, you are trying to divulge the secrets of my concoctions. No! I should not be on your list of non-trustworthy people. If this is all about knowing how Pisco Punch came to be, then it is right for you to know thanks to whom it came to be. Because

45. The first historical reference of a 'punch' found by the author dates from the year 1709 in the island of Santa Helena, a British colony off the coast of west Africa, when it is mentioned that by order of the governor of the island, the punch-houses must sell it at a price no more than two schillings: "a bowl of punch made with a pint of arrack, and with a suitable amount of sugar and lemon." (T.H. Brooke, 1806)

In Peru, the first mention of a punch found by the author dates from 1791. It is of a potent "punche" prepared with aguardiente (pisco) and was sold at the bleachers of the Acho bull-ring in Lima.
(J. Emilio A. Calmell, 1939, quoting José Rossi and Rubi, 1791)

you must know, my friend, that this is a chain of favors. Vioget had tried pisco as far back as the time he was in Lima. Then I came into the scene and bought his bar, which was the first bar of California, that should become clear to you; the beginning of Pisco Punch is here, with me. History cannot praise some and forget others, especially if those "others" are the pioneers, the precursors.

–But from all the choices you had, why did you choose pisco –I insisted–, how did you come up with the idea for a punch and why with milk.

–A punch exists forever, it is timeless and nobody can be attributed to be its creator.[45] But if you really want to know, I was looking for a drink that could equal old gin and when I stumbled upon pisco I did not have another option than to fall in deep love with its flavor and its versatility to obtain the perfect balance when making contact with any external agent, it is a drink of the Gods, an ambrosia with spice, with pretty extraordinary side-effects –he conferred to me–. The milk comes as an addition, my political family has the monopoly for the sale of milk in all Yerba Buena. Ask for the Miranda-Briones family.

–Please stop –I said to him– I know you are familiar with the milk punches that Mrs. Maria, or Manonga Torres, prepared, if not from her directly, you had it from Vioget.

–But, what is your point! If I had knowledge of it, it is my problem, all my secrets remain with me.

–It is too late for backing up, you put yourself in the middle of all this matter and you are up to your nose in it, if you start singing a song you should finish it. Those are the rules –I stated with the authority that the time and that my invested heart immersed in this research gave me the right to.

–You do not understand anything. If you keep pushing me around I will not come back –he threatened looking at me as nobody had ever done before.

–There's not much left. Give me another clue, please –I begged–. I need to end this research. Don't go away, I need to ask you...

Telephonic Revelations

I arrived at my house late that afternoon, I was very tired. I drew the living room curtains and enjoyed watching the squirrels that ran freely across the balcony, nature at its best. Each quack of the geese and the sound of the water spurts falling slowly in the lagoon relax and calm my soul, I feel very peaceful. It is almost hypnotizing to see the movement of the water in and the wake the ducks make when landing in the lagoon while I approach them to give them something to eat. Brenda buys special food for them and it must be very tasty because even the squirrels and the little birds perform acrobatics to reach some pellets before they fall in the water. Anyway, every one gets its own delicacy. I never realized how pleasant it was to be here, that's why Brenda doesn't want to move to a bigger place, this place is great. This week's long vacation is bringing me more satisfaction than I had planned... but I must disconnect that annoying telephone that interrupts the harmony with its ringing squeaky sound. Damn! It doesn't stop ringing, I should program the answering machine to pick up the call at the first ring.

–Hello, this call is for Guillermo de la Moscorra. I am a friend from San Carlos and I would like to talk to you about Pisco Punch –said a voice on my answering machine.

–It can not be! –I said running towards the telephone, hoping to answer it before he hang up–. Wait, wait don't hang up!

What should I do, I thought as I ran stumbling and jumping over the obstacles, is to put a telephone on the terrace or to clear the way of so much clutter. I must clean this terrace, but there will be an opportunity some other time.

–Wait please –I shouted as if the person on the telephone could hear me–. Don't hang up I'm right here... Hello! –I answered anxiously.

–Mister de la Moscorra? –a man exclaimed from the other end of the telephone.

–Yes. Tell me –I asked him excitedly–: are you EJP from Milli Robbins' column?

–No sir, I am his son. I know you have been looking for us. But you sound very excited, maybe it would be better that I call at another time –he responded to me understandingly.

–No! No, please. It was running to the telephone from the balcony where I was feeding the... Oh don't worry, but tell me, what is this all about? –I asked again, in a calm voice.

–Maybe we could get together tonight at my house, if you can, and talk about what you are looking for.

–Definitively, let's see, tell me your address and I'll be there later for sure...

With this person I was approaching a new horizon in my investigations.

I returned somewhat late from the meeting with E. J.P.'s son and forgot to pick up Brenda from work. I just couldn't come out of the trance, I couldn't believe what had just happened to me.

–Where were you, Guillermo? –Brenda asked with a worried look on her face, she had arrived home before I did–. I thought you would pick me up from work. I waited for you for a long time, and I had to come by myself. Your telephone was off. What happened to you?!

I couldn't hold it in anymore, I embraced her, lifted her from the floor, and spinned her around the room.

–Put me down, Guillermo, I am going to get dizzy! –she said laughing and somewhat surprised– What's going on, why are you so happy?

–Look at what I have here, look! It's what we have been looking for so long! The original recipe of Pisco Punch! –I shouted, kissing the old sheets of paper I had in my hand.

–Where did you get it? Wait, don't answer yet, let me find my glasses, they went flying off when you carried me. Here they are –and while looking around she added–: don't you think we must clean this terrace? I know: "there will be an opportunity later" –and then she returned to the subject–. Well, good, let me see it... But, where did it come from? Who gave it to you? –Brenda asked, without breathing.

–Remember when we were in the library and we found Milli Robbins' newspaper column, where there was this man who wrote about Duncan Nicol and Pisco Punch. This man wrote to Milli that he was a very good friend of Nicol, to the point that he had been at his side on his deathbed. Do you remember that he said that Nicol prepared Pisco Punch during the prohibition days in private parties and that he had trusted the recipe to him, but that for respect to Nicol he was not going to give the complete recipe away, or at least, not with some ingredients, but he would give her a method for making the Pisco Punch; not like the one at the Bank Exchange, because that one would be impossible to reproduce the reason being different factors: such as the shortage of the aforesaid ingredients and respecting Nicol's wishes of keeping the recipe secret. Then now it is my turn to be the guardian and honorary member of the fraternity of the most looked for recipe of our era!

–Oh my God! Let me see the recipe.

–I can't –I said to her seriously.

–What?!

–Not before you pass your initiation for belonging to the brotherhood –I said laughing.

–What are you talking about, Guillermo?

–You have been sharing with me each piece of history and painfully searching through the meanders of this intricated puzzle. How can I deny you this? It was a joke. It's just that I am very happy. Do you know what this means to me and how delicate this matter is, but nobody deserves it more than you do.

–Please explain it to me, I don't understand what it says: are these formulas or something, why is this line completely scratched out? –Brenda asked me, while reviewing the manuscript that she had in her hands.

–I don't know, but the rest looks intact. I can't believe how everything came to me. It was the fate of destiny, something was meant to happen. Everything appeared in such a strange way that it is very hard to explain. I don't know why the son of this man has conferred the recipe to me, I don't even know how I began with this, I only know that now that we have it, we cannot back up.

–Alright, love, but I can't decipher what is written here. I don't understand it.

–Come, let me explain it to you –I said to her while I taught her the recipe.

–I know what you are saying, but don't leave me with honey on my lips. Go and prepare me one right now –Brenda said, confused

–I can't, it takes more or less a week to make the ingredients, as far as I understand. Lets prepare it for Karen's Thanksgiving dinner and we will be making history by bringing the original Pisco Punch of San Francisco. We will look like kings, we will make history. But, the first thing we must do is to get gum arabic.

–Ok then, let me go to the grocery store and get the gum arabic. Are there several types,? –Brenda offered to go and asked me in a very happy voice, she had completely forgotten that I didn't pick her up from work a few hours before.

–No, it's unique, it's gum arabic and nothing else. I don't understand the reason for this ingredient, because sugar syrup or simple syrup should be enough, but well, if we do it we do it right.

–Ok, I'll be back soon, why don't you rest in the meantime, you look really tired – Brenda said, and left without being able to erase the excitement from her face.

–All right –I said, then went to serve myself a glass of pisco and closed my eyes...

–Hey! Sleeping again with a glass of pisco in your hand?! What's going on with you, boy, don't make me doubt your participation in this legacy. By the way: good job! –I heard Duncan Nicol say while I opened my eyes.

–Hello! Thanks. I searched everywhere for you after our last interview –I said to him still sleepy.

–Yes, I have been following your steps ever since then. You are a good hound, boy, I like your style and your attention to detail. Everything must be rigorously formatted, you are the perfect instrument for my plans, you have the perfect dose of rigidity and enthusiasm, in addition to being a good drinker, and a lover of pisco, of course. I'll explain the main secret of Pisco Punch in just two words: exact measures. Neither more nor less, the recipe goes as it is, and nobody can add or remove anything from it, neither the mixing procedure, that now you have in your hands and I hope you'll know how to use, remember the recipe you have is real, I wrote it, do you understand? About the erased ingredient, I'm sure you'll find why. I know times have changed, they changed at the end of my days, what was well accepted back then could now seem bad, so, well, everything is left to personal criteria. Come, follow me for a moment, please. But before, serve me a bit of that pisco that smells so good. And serve yourself one too. This cellar was my working place. It is here where I spent hours mixing ingredients trying to obtain Pisco Punch. And you cannot complain! It has more light than your living room and its way more organized than your terrace. I don't allow smoking here because it would contaminate the air, and this work requires optimal conditions. By the way, congratulations, I see you don't smoke anymore.

–Thanks, I am meeting goals –I said to him sounding impressed.

–Well, lets continue: these are my tools and measuring devices; remember, the volumes must be exact for the punch to be perfect. You must prepare the gum arabic overnight and then let it rest one more day, at the end you must boil it with the sugar syrup while taking away all impurities. The gum is very important, it is one of the decisive factors for obtaining the necessary effects.

–Why? –I asked intrigued, but he did not answer what I wanted to hear.

–That's your homework, I am not going to serve you everything on a platter. Well, lets continue, I don't have too much time. Lets go.

–Where do we go now?

–I want you to know how the Bank Exchange operated from the inside, I want you to see how, since it opened its doors in 1853, when it belonged to P.D. Kilduff & Co until I took it over, everything was maintained pretty much the same. The marble floors and the mahogany-made dinning room tables, bar and counter, where timeless players lay down twenty dollar bets, gambling dice and playing bil-

liards with gold coins. The mirrors, the glass shelves and the glasses, the oil paintings of scenes from the French revolution and that one of Samson and Delilah, all very expensive and brought through Cape Horn, many witnessed the turn of the century, then the earthquake and the fire that reduced to rubbish almost everything else. But the Bank Exchange continued imposed in the fate of time and its changes. Even though after Kearney street was broadened and Columbus street was built, transforming forever San Francisco's social and entertainment center, this caused the closing and bankruptcy of several famous establishments symbols of the San Franciscan Bohemian culture, such as Maguire's Opera House and the Snug bar. The Bank Exchange continued its steady pace until it became a bohemian temple and a banner of the glorious past of all pioneers and men of good standing. It was the most important and best reputed meeting place in this part of the world. My name and that one of the Bank Exchange resounded here just as much as it did at the other side of the Atlantic.

Interior of the Bank Exchange bar showing Duncan Nicol or "Pisco John," at the left, and regular customers.

–They sounded as Duncan Nicol and the Bank Exchange, but they resounded more as Pisco John and Pisco John's. Are you Pisco John? –I asked intrigued.

–Yes I am. It resulted from the use of the telephone. In 1903 we already had that service, and the number of the Bank Exchange was John 3246, that is to say, the first part of the number was verbal. Then, if somebody wanted to communicate with another person using the telephone he had to call the central telephone exchange office and say the name, for example: John, Main, Chuck, Black, Polk or anyone of about thirty groups. The Bank Exchange and I had the prefix John, then, if somebody wanted to communicate with me I had to answer: "here is John 3246." And if I called somebody I had to begin saying "this is John 3246." There were many that could not remember the exact telephone number and they asked the operator: "please with John of the pisco," which soon was simply reduced to: "with Pisco John, please" and my acknowledgement to "yes this is Pisco John." [46]

–That explains it... –I finally realized they did not call him Pisco John because of himself, but because of his telephone number.

Felt bells jingling inside my head, I heard the front door closing slowly and then Brenda's voice.

–Hi love, did you have a good rest? If you didn't, then keep resting, because today will not be the night you'll be preparing Pisco Punch –Brenda said–. I could not find the darn gum arabic anywhere. Somebody told me it has not been in the market for some time. And much less now, after the World Trade Center attack, since the Laden's family has a great part of the monopoly of this product. The only way is to order it on-line.

46. Pisco John's and Pisco John were the historical nicknames given to the Bank Exchange and its owner. Since both Duncan Nicol and the Bank Exchange shared the same telephone number, John 3246, two nicknames were necessary for obtaining a correct telephone identification in 1903.

1903 Telephone Directory of San Francisco shows the telephone number of Duncan Nicol and of the Bank Exchange as being "John 3246."

INSTRUCTIONS FOR USING TELEPHONE.—
To call Central Office, take the hand telephone from the hook, place to your ear, and operator will say, " Number ? "
When operator receives exchange name and number of subscriber wanted, she will repeat them to you in order to avoid mistakes.

HOW TO ANSWER A TELEPHONE CALL.—Remove the hand telephone from the hook and say : " Here is Main 297 " (or whatever your number may be). The party calling should say : " This is Main 298 " (or whatever the number may be).

Photomontage showing the Central Telephone Exchange building of San Francisco. The instructions to make and receive calls are shown below. San Francisco was the first city in the world to deploy a city-wide telephone interchange system using operators. In 1903, the service was still relatively new and most of the people were not yet used to memorize numbers. A young woman operator, such as the one shown in this photo, was instrumental in the popularization of the nicknames "Pisco John" and "Pisco John's."

–I can't believe it! –I said desperately, now complete-ly awake–. How can that be? I am going to look for it right now on the Internet –and I started searching right away.

I found several suppliers in a flash, but doubts en-tered my mind and I had to consult with my favorite bells.

–Look, here's one. What should I do, honey? Do I place an order or not? What if they make a connection between us and that terrorist? It just happened two months ago –remembering September 11th shook us up.

–Don't worry. You are buying it from another sup-plier. In addition you have sufficient evidence you don't have anything to do with those fellows.

–You are right, I don't have anything to hide, and as they say in my country "you can search me anytime you want." Ah! by the way, now I know why Nicol was nick-named Pisco John. I'll explain it to you...

After explaining it to her, another subject came to my mind.

–Ooops! Darned, I completely forgot. Tomorrow I need to go to the Peruvian Consulate to renew my pass-port. Remember, we will be traveling soon and I do not want last minute hurry ups.

–I have mine in order –Brenda clarified.

–Like everything you do, honey, you are so well orga-nized. Good, lets go to sleep –I was really tired.

–Remember, love, Matt's party is tomorrow evening –Bren reminded me.

–Isn't it a shame that we won't have Pisco Punch ready? Well, we can take pisco and prepare Pisco Sour. Then we can improvise some other drinks with pisco and take advantage that Matt is there to help –I said.

–Oh no! I forgot, tomorrow morning we must go to Sacramento. Don't you remember that we promised your kids we would take them to lunch? –Brenda said, a little ashamed for not remembering before.

–That's right, with all this commotion I had forgotten it completely, like this passport thing. It is Ok, it will be an excellent opportunity for me to relax from of all this, I'll go to the consulate in the evening then.

When we arrived in Sacramento we went directly to pick up the boys. I am so happy when we go out together, it is incredible how a human being can be so happy through his children. To see them laugh makes my soul smile, and hearing their experiences bring me the capability of being astonished, which I often feel I have lost. It is so wonderful being a father and so complex, because I feel that they are a part of me but at the same time they are completely different and independent people. One has all the obligations, but not all the rights. It gives me a little nostalgia to see them so grown up, although I know that they are always going to need me. At least that is what I want to believe. We had lunch next to the Sacramento river and later went for a nice walk around Old Town.

–Look, Guillermo, have you seen the photo that is hanging on that wall? It's a photo of the Bank Exchange –Brenda said to me, as she pointed at it.

–What?! In Sacramento? Did it have branches or something? –I said, sounding totally out of tune.

–I don't know, Guillermo. Now I understand less than I did before, we must find out.

–Yes, but later, now we are with the boys –I said, taking a deep breath. I knew the answer would come soon.

I went to the consulate that afternoon, I was in a hurry, because the time was becoming short and I could not delay the passport procedures any further. While climbing the stairs to the consul's office, images and ideas did not stop bombarding my head. The most intriguing thing was to find another Bank Exchange in

Text of the commemorative plaque of the Bank Exchange of Sacramento (top) and old photograph of the place (bottom).

Bank Exchange and Union Hotel

The photographs to the right provide an example of the metamorphosis of the buildings known as the Bank Exchange and Union Hotel. The restored buildings to your left at the corner of K and 2nd Streets.

An 1856 advertisement proclaimed:

"The Bank Exchange sells, Most Choice Liquors & Cigars," while the Union Hotel brags about its sleeping apartments 'with a view to comfort.' The visitor is provided with the best restaurant by a Mr. T. Fogg, and the Billiard Saloon is declared as 'the best lighted in the State.'"

Sacramento. I had to clean up my hard disk and all my research. I was thinking I would not give up for anything in the world, everything was becoming too strange and too formidable, when suddenly I tripped over a man.

–Sir! Please watch your step... Tell me, you are Peruvian, right? –a very distinguished gentleman said to me.

–Yes, excuse me... –I said surprised, and watching carefully–: How do you know?

–Peruvians are unmistakable to me. By the way, let me introduce myself: I am Charles Polhemus, Peruvian Consul in San Francisco.

–Nice too meet you, I am Guillermo de la Moscorra, I am here to renew my passport... Polhemus, you said? –I watched more carefully and asked–: Excuse me, what year are we in?

–Excuse me, what did you say? –the man answered, taking a very long glance at me, but not as long as the glance I took of him.

He was Charles B. Polhemus, a pharmacist by education, who was Consul of the United States in the Peruvian port of Paita, where Manonga Torres was from. He later became consul of Peru in San Francisco. I must talk to him, but what excuses would I make up to interview him? I thought of the most logical one.

–Pardon me, I was a little distracted. In reality I am a reporter, I write for *El Cometa*, and I came here to interview you –I told him with my best smile.

–Is that so! That's good, then let me buy you a drink at a bar that opened just a few months ago, it is in the Montgomery Block. It's a luxurious place, you'll see. In fact it is a bank exchange, but it also is a billiard saloon. It belongs to a friend of mine. The place is excellent, you'll like it and they serve

The Montgomery Block a few days after its inauguration. The Bank Exchange is located in the left corner of the building, behind the carriage. Illustration of 1854.

Peruvian pisco, which is considered an expensive deluxe liquor in this area.

–But what do you mean it's a "bank exchange" –I asked–: Is it a money exchange house?

–Oh! my friend, you have not been around too much have you? A bank exchange is a saloon where important people meet to do all types of business transactions.

–Ah! The most select of society, the *creme-de-la-creme*, as we say in Peru.

–Of course my dear reporter, one can find all San Francisco there and the other half of the world too.

–You mean the most powerful and wealthy men of the city get together at the bank exchanges –I specified, to remove all doubts from my mind.

–Something like that, the most important deals are closed in these places and the future of the society is defined there –he answered, making the concept of a bank exchange clear.

–So there are many bank exchanges –I insisted clarifying the idea.

–One in each city, more or less. But this one, in particular, gives me the impression, and I don't know why, that it is going to make history. Maybe due to the fact that this bank exchange is in San Francisco –he explained, pointing at the elegant surroundings which we had just entered, which I already visited several times, and that will keep a name of its own in years too come.

After entering the Bank Exchange I saw everything exactly as it was when I was there with Torrence. The same marble floors, that would begin counting the steps of history on its tiles, the same mahogany bar counter that would wear away its coating with the elbows of time and the drop of dice, rolling and smiling at the luck of who was there, all sponsored by quarrelsome cherubs flying over the billiard tables.

–I find it amusing –I said, as if beginning with the interview– that a pharmacist as you are ends up being the consul of a country that is not your own.

–I am the representative of your country because I resided there for a long time. Let me tell you, I worked in the port of Paita for several years and, believe me, I learned things about medicine and the power of nature that I could not have learned in a thousand years studying chemistry in a university.

–What do you mean? –I asked, sensing the answer would bring something good.

–I discovered wonderful healing powers of plants as simple as *matico* or *sabila*. I discovered certain properties of tree sap molasses that not even the most elaborate drug could obtain. Since then, I've been experimenting with different ingredients to develop important medicines, but what is working better for me –he said in a whisper tone of a church confession– are tester drinks. I have managed to create a time bomb, it is pretty dangerous because is highly deceiving, although the principle is fascinating.

–What is in it? –I asked, intrigued.

–Have you heard of gum arabic? I don't know if you know but the gum does not dissolve in alcohol. Well, one mixes a gum arabic solution with other components in a punch, although I am still experimenting on which precise liquor to use... At first sight, inside the glass, everything looks liquid, uniform in appearance, but at the time of entering the organism the gum settles down in the stomach coating it with the gum mucilage. It's like a layer of paint, one doesn't feel the effect of the alcohol until the organism assimilates the gum all at once. The rest, my friend, is history.

Then that is the property of the gum arabic, I said to myself. And when I was going to ask Consul Polhemus how he prepared it, a man touched my shoulder taking me away from the trance I was in and brought me back to the consulate.

–Excuse me sir, it was not my intention. Do you feel alright? –the consulate employee asked me with a worried look on his face.

–No, don't worry, I was distracted. One question, is the consul's office the next door to the right? –I said to him.

–Yes it is, do you have an appointment? –he responded politely.

–Yes, I am here to renew my passport.

–Are you Mr. de la Moscorra? Come in, please, we were waiting for you. I am going to take care of you –and I thanked him.

–I see that you will travel to Peru soon. For business or to visit family?

–I am going to visit my parents. But I do not know

exactly for how long because I am finishing my research...

–If I don't intrude what is it about? –he asked.

–About the history of Peruvian pisco in San Francisco, about Pisco Punch.

–I've heard something about Pisco Punch, how interesting, are you going to write a book?

I told him that that was my intention, then he said to let him know when it was finished. As I agreed about that plan, an idea filtered within my head.

–Excuse me, I am curious, was this the first consulate in San Francisco? –I asked, looking at the old pictures in the room.

–It was one of the first in the world –he answered–, and the first one of a South American country. This consulate was founded in March of 1849, when the brigantine of war *Gamarra* anchored in these San Franciscans coasts, sent by Peruvian president Ramon Castilla to protect the interests of our countrymen during the Gold Rush.

–How interesting. That was the time when Latin Americans were harassed by The Hounds, is that right? But if one analyzes The Hounds phenomenon it is easy to draw conclusions. Because they were a group of frustrated ex–soldiers of the American army and ex-convicted Australians who did not find a better way to justify their frustrations than blaming the successful miners who managed to obtain some wealth during the so ambiguous Gold Rush.

The Peruvian brigantine of war *Gamarra*, which travels to San Francisco in 1849 to protect the rights of Peruvian merchants and to bring the first consul of the city from a South American country.

–What I see happened during that time is that information had been distorted and manipulated, and for this reason, many people arrived here looking for fortune in the rivers and mountains of Coloma not having the slightest idea about mining. At the end, they found themselves with their back against a wall of reality when they realized that the task was not as easy as just blowing glass to make bottles, but it involved extremely hard work for being poorly rewarded –said the well versed

Illustration of 1854 of the attack of The Hounds to the San Francisco Hispanic community in July, 1849. The Peruvian Vicente del Campo was shot in the leg during the confrontation.

employee, whose name I fail to remember.

–There were vested interests –I said to him– that benefited a few, because when, in 1848, the *New York Herald* published that the gold findings in California were only comparable to the ones of the Viceroys of Peru and Mexico, they did not tell people that Pizarro and Cortes enslaved thousands of natives experts in mining, who brought the gold to their feet. None of the Conquistadors got their fortune in mining, but by exploiting native miners.

–The subject was, to give it a name, more than chaotic. Come to think of it, Guillermo; the population of San Francisco increased at an alarming rate, people arrived from all parts of the country and the world too. The shortage of basic products made San Francisco an extremely expensive city to live in. Excuse me, allow me to answer that call –he said while going to answer the telephone.

MARINE JOURNAL,
Port of San Francisco.

ARRIVALS.

March 29. Per brig of War Gen. Gammara, Rodriguez commander, from Caliao.

SAILED.

May 12. Per. brig of war Gen. Gamarra

Newspaper ads showing the arrival and the departure dates of the brigantine *Gamarra* in San Francisco. During its stay, the military crew of the ship assisted with the maintenance of public order after a request made by the mayor, since at that time the city did not yet have an organized police department. Unfortunately, the war ship returned to Peru just a few days before the attack of The Hounds to the city's Hispanic quarters and could not protect it.

–Can I get you a drink? –the barman asked me and continued without waiting for my response– You are not from around here are you? I have never seen you before.

–Are you... John Brown? –I asked, amazed, I could not believe my eyes.

–That's right, I can see I am famous. What can I serve you, my friend? –he asked again.

–A shot of pisco, please –I said to him, still bewildered.

–Italia? –he asked.

–Yes, the pisco made from aromatic grapes! –I answered excitedly.

–Good, I sense that you are one of ours. Are you also in transit? –he asked in a friendly tone.

Section of the *Alta California* newspaper from February of 1849, showing announcements advertising the City Hotel of John Brown, offering a large selection of liquors among other amenities; of Finley & Johnson, announcing "Italia" (pisco type Italia) coming from the cargo of the Peruvian brigantine *Calderon*; and of Robert Ridley renting one of his ranchos.

–No, I am doing some research.

–Things now are no longer how they used to be, man –he complained–. People have changed. Here's your shot. Wait, let me serve myself a glass too. To your health!

–To yours! Good pisco, Brown! Where do you get it? –I asked surprised by the good quality.

–It is from Peru. Now it is easier to get it than before, although it still is a bit scarce and expensive. They bring it in ships that arrive transporting miners and supplies from the East Coast, because they touch port in Peru on their way around the Horn. Will there be a shorter route some day?

–I am sure of that. So many people are coming here, ha? –I answered, continuing with my quest without mentioning about the Panama Canal.

Actual "Around the Horn" voyage chart of the American ship *Apollo* which transported miners from the East Coast of the United States to San Francisco during early 1849. It had a layover in the port of Callao, Peru.

–I don't know what is going to happen with this city, the people that come are stranger every day. The men are not that friendly nor do they care about the life of the others. In my days, times were not easy either, it was a violent era, but not as much as it is now. Listen my friend, when I took over of this place, during the Bear Flag Revolt which started a sort of witch hunt, Bob Ridley, the old owner of this bar was imprisoned for he was accused of being a Mexican official. Soon thereafter, when the Americans took over, they freed him. Then Ridley, who was very stubborn, decided to enter politics and ran for mayor of San Francisco. Since he did not win, he relocated to the area of Mission Dolores, assimilated in the Hispanic community, and legally left the bar in my hands, I bought it from him –Brown related–. But even so, with all the changes in government that followed as fast as lunar phases, the situation was not like it is now, not even when the Gold Rush started: the people that were here in the beginning days, were very different types of people, compared to those in the present. For the people of my time, money was of little value and everybody was willing to help their neighbor sincerely from the heart and with helping hands.

–What are you talking about, Brown, don't live in the past, that turns you into a loser, an old loser, don't be bitter –a man who was seated at the bar sincerely suggested.

–You are a witness, Sam, you have been here with me since the beginning, and who would have said that our tired eyes would have to witness the degradation of a city that once was the center of friendship and good manners. What happened with the Californios, with the pioneers, with the people who worried about the people around them and that grew while letting his fellows grow –Brown said turning to the person at the bar who was questioning his comments.

–That's right, foreigner, I have been here with John since the old days, seeing how times were changing... –and then he asked Brown–: Talking about that, can you serve me one of those milk punches with pisco, they take me back to the good times, they continue serving them at the Mansion House.

–I also want to try one of those punches, please. Tell me something while Brown serves us the punches, how was Ridley's Mansion House? –I asked.

–The Mansion House right now is one of the most popular establishment in all San Francisco, it surpasses this one which was Ridley's first and the first tavern of California when Vioget had it. The Mansion

The bar Mansion House, where Robert Ridley served his nutritious milk punches. Mission Dolores, founded in 1776, is shown to the left.

House is not that close, it is next to Mission Dolores. Still it is a success, people arrive from everywhere and it is the meeting center of the Hispanic community. Its hot milk punch has become very famous, so much, that there is no one that arrives in San Francisco that has not tried it at least once. Ah! And on top of that, bullfights and bull and bear fights are celebrated in front of the Mansion House every Sunday, as the Acho's festivities in Lima. Did you know? –he ask me at the end.

–Yes, I did –I answered, I had read about it.

–Here you have your punches, Ridley's style –Brown said to us giving us the glasses.

–John, are you still following the tradition of pisco and its punches, or what? –I wanted to know.

–Of course. I don't know if you are aware of it, but when the Yankees arrived here to take a hold of this land, the whole crew of the *Portsmouth* came to visit me and they were pretty thirsty. I squelched their thirst serving these punches of milk and other liquors, but pisco was one of their favorites, definitively –Brown answered.

Illustration of a bullfight in front of Mission Dolores, in 1842.

–So much so, that no crew member could miss their daily visit here, as with any other regulation, so that our friend Brown could oblige them with his utmost care –the other man at the bar intervened.

–Don't make me laugh, Sam. You are an old wolf, you never miss anything! –Brown said to him.

–Wait a moment! What's that small box I see there? –I asked, looking at a peculiar wooden box laying on the floor.

–It is a ballot box, foreigner, a historical box, from the first ever democratic election celebrated in California, the one that Ridley lost. Originally, it packed lime syrup bottles, bought by Robert Ridley from Captain Stephen Smith, who by the way, was married to a Peruvian whose last name was Torres –he informed me.

–Yes, I know who they are very well. Furthermore, Smith's mother-in-law used to prepare milk punches which Ridley later made famous –I answered.

Illustration of 1775 of the magnificent bullring of Acho, Lima. The first punches with pisco were prepared there.

47. "Silver Sour: lemon juice, 1 teaspoon; unsweetened gin, 1 wine glass; egg white, 1; sugar, 1 teaspoon; crushed ice. Put the egg white in a tumbler, beat it slightly, then add the lemon juice, gin, sugar and a table spoon of ice. Cover and shake well until cold, then strain into a small glass and serve." (Hopkins, 1910)

If you replace the gin indicated in that recipe from the late 1800s with pisco, you obtain a basic Pisco Sour. It must be pointed out that egg white contains albumen, a mucous protein similar in texture to gum arabic.

Silver Sour.

Lemon juice, 1 dessertspoonful; unsweetened gin, 1 wineglassful; egg, white of 1; castor sugar, 1 teaspoonful; crushed ice. Put the white of an egg into a tumbler, beat it slightly, then add the lemon juice, gin, sugar, and a heaped table-spoonful of crushed ice. Cover, and shake well until sufficiently cooled, then strain into a small glass, and serve.

Silver Fizz.

Gin, 1 wineglassful; juice of ½ lemon; white of 1 egg; icing sugar, 1 teaspoonful; carbonate of soda, a pinch; pounded ice. Fill a tumbler 3 parts full with pounded ice, pour over this the gin and lemon juice, then add the white of egg, beaten to a stiff froth. Shake well, then strain into another tumbler containing the icing sugar and carbonate of soda, and serve at once.

Reproduction of recipes of Silver Sour and Silver Fizz, published in 1910. Victor Morris, the creator of Pisco Sour, and resident of San Francisco until the beginning of the 1920s, offered both drinks at his bar in Lima. He renamed the Silver Sour as Gin Sour, and the one made with pisco: Pisco Sour. At that time, "silver" indicated the drink contained egg white, "golden", egg yolk and "fizz", soda water.

–Is that true... and how do you know that? –Brown asked intrigued.

–That doesn't matter, the important thing here is that lime syrup was already available during the very early days –I said putting into account what was happening in front of my eyes.

–That's right, we have been preparing punches with it, and pisco punches too –Brown insisted.

–Then, you already are holding half of the recipe of Pisco Punch... and that of Pisco Sour as well.

–Pisco Sour? –Brown asked surprised–. I don't know that one. But I do know another very good sour, it's called Silver Sour, it contains egg whites. And come to think about it, it would be great preparing it with pisco instead of gin. We have never tried it...

–Does it have egg whites? –I interrupted– But, then, the Pisco Sour comes from the Silver Sour! The recipe is almost exact, there's only one difference: it has gin instead of pisco.[47]

–I beg your pardon? –Brown said without understanding my pondering.

–Nothing, I was thinking out loud –I answered without stopping to think of what I have just discovered.

–Acts the same as everyone who passes through. Why don't you say what you are really thinking, boy –Sam said without accepting my answer and looking me straight in the eyes.

–Don't be like that, Sam. Man! the boy doesn't have bad intentions, you can tell from afar, he is not a miner either, he is just a journalist –Brown defended me and continued–. All miners behave like that, nobody ever has a first nor a last name, they are all unknown people with their own intentions, taking good care of their backs because they know that at any time any neighbor can take advantage of anything, as they themselves would do to somebody else. That is true, my foreigner friend, the discovery of gold has radically changed the history of this place. The peaceful time of the countryside life, the daily siesta, the no concern for borrowed money, are all in the past for ever. A new type of people have turned this city into an heterogeneous mass of several cultures, races, creeds and business methods never seen before in this land.

–That was the downfall of the people like Bandini –Sam noted.

–Exactly, Sam –Brown ratified–. Bandini never managed to understand the new monetary system, he could not get himself to fully accept the subject of credits and interest rates.

–The matter is... John, please serve me another punch please. Do you want another one? –he asked me, to which I consented–. Ok, two –and he continued–. The matter is, boy, that the men that come here, don't behave the way they do back home, they change because nobody here has a past nor a future, everybody is anonymous, there is no neighborhood, nobody wants the obligation of worrying about their fellow man. It is easier to come here, make some money and just go back home with a well washed and shaved face and without any worries on their backs.

–Here you have your punches. To your health! –Brown said taking part in the conversation–. Well, but I cannot deny that the saloon business is a remarkable success, because San Francisco is the mandatory stop for thousands of gold prospectors on their way to the mines. Also, it is in the saloons where all the sacrificed miners arrive to celebrate their triumphs or to cry their failures. In fact all service businesses have been the beneficiaries of this phenomenon: the City Hotel and the Parker

House are, in fact, living proof of what I am saying. And if we stay on that subject, I cannot complain, because I have made good money with it. Eh! Look who just arrived: Maguire –he said, turning towards the man who was approaching–. This is one of the men who came here attracted by the Gold Rush, but unlike many, he is a professional bartender from New York, and as you could understand, I could not let him go that easy. He is an extremely tenacious man; although illiterate, he has a taste for the art and the theater as the most illustrious. Maguire has become my right hand so much so that I have made him a partner with Parker at the Parker House. It is because of him really that the Parker House has risen three times from the burning ashes, as a phoenix.

Everything was making more sense than I could have ever imagined, things were fitting better. Ridley was right, everything comes from that time, in addition, Maria Torres gives a considerable twist to the story, taking into account the strategic proximity that she maintained with Ridley, to the point that he asks Smith for a box of lime syrup which Maria, Smith's mother-in-law, used to prepare punches. History entangles destinies and provides tracks of hidden events, that otherwise would not have had any connection whatsoever. Because, by chance, the first U.S. elections held in California in which Ridley participates and loses, took place in an improvised ballot box taken right out of Ridley's bar. This box is nothing else than the package of the lime syrup bottles that Smith gives Ridley. But, the most important issue here and the key to this lock comes later, after the bond between these two key individuals is established, and here comes the best part, Maria, Manonga Torres, used to *hacer las once*, which according to historians of the era was a Peruvian tradition of visiting friends at around eleven in the morning to have a refreshment prepared with pineapple rind, to which at a later date they added some pisco and pieces of other macerated fruit. For that reason, the meaning of doing *las once* derived from the eleven letters of the word "aguardiente" which was the generic word for brandy in Spanish. Manonga, as any other well educated Peruvian of her time, continued with the ancestral tradition, it was part of the luggage that she had brought from Peru, and she was used to inviting people that came to visit her in mid-morning, as she was used to doing in her native land.

Then, the roots of Pisco Punch were deciphered, the point now is to find the nexus between these characters and Duncan Nicol.

–Excuse me, Guillermo, this protocol hassle seems never ending –the consulate employee apologized, hanging up the telephone.

–Don't worry. I won't take more of your time, I must go, I am in a hurry –I said to him, impatiently.

–Here is your new passport –the man said while handing the document to me.

–Thank you. See you later –I shook his hand.

While I was leaving, I could not stop thinking about everything that had happened, suddenly a strange breeze hit my face...

–Hey, Guillermo, I was looking for you, I lost you –A voice which I recognized said to me, it was the Consul.

–Tell me, Mr. Polhemus –I replied.

–You, journalists, I do not know why, but you are always in a hurry or maybe you are all rude –he reproached.

–Sorry, I did not say good bye before. But I am

not impolite, I just can't explain it –I excused myself, I really just couldn't explain it.

–Don't waste your time, De la Moscorra, I like you anyway. I was looking for you for another reason. I needed information about the commercial situation of the Peruvian guano and since you come from there...

–Guano? Do you mean, guano from the Chincha Islands? –I asked, trying to locate the subject in the back of my mind.

–Man! What world are you living in? What other thing could I be talking about? I have some businesses in Peru, and I have managed to make some good money in the guano trading –he told me proudly.

–That's right! At the end of 1830s, guano fertilizer caused a world-wide revolution in agriculture. The famous guano boom! –I shouted happily as I remember it.

–Dear God! Please tell me something new! –Polhemus said, disappointed at my reaction–. Don't know if you know, but I am also the representative of Alsop & Co. This firm has its roots in Peru since the days of Viceroy Abascal. Well, Alsop & Co. and I have a small trade monopoly with the United Kingdom, Ireland and other countries in Europe.

–With guano? –I wanted to know.

–Of course –he emphasized–. Just so you have an idea, last year, in fifty three –1853, I thought–

Section of the Consul Directory of San Francisco of 1854 showing Charles B. Polhemus, representative of the firm Alsop & Co., as Consul of Peru (top). Alsop & Co. advertisement announcing the availability of guano from the Peruvian islands of Chincha in 1853 (bottom).

PERU—CHAS. B. POLHEMUS. (Alsop & Co.,)
California street, between Sansome and Leidesdorff.

☞ Guano Charters.—The undersigned are authorized to charter vessels to load guano at the Islands of Chincha for ports in the United Kingdom of Great Britain, Ireland, and on the Continent.   ALSOP & Co
San Francisco, Oct. 14, 1853.   f1

there was more cargo loaded from San Francisco to the guano Chincha Islands than all the cargo shipped from the city of Philadelphia, and more than a third of San Francisco's shipping permits were destined to Peruvian ports.

–Oh my God! I got it, with guano trading it's also how pisco comes to San Francisco –I said, connecting the dots.

–Obviously, when our ships unload tallow and load guano we have the chance to load up the exquisite brandy of Peru, which by the way, comes in really fascinating earthenware jars.

This new information was bringing my research to a full circle.

–And who exports it? I mean, the pisco, who's the supplier? –I asked.

–Domingo Elias; I am surprised you didn't know that –the Consul answered.

–That's right! Domingo Elias had... I mean, has the Peruvian monopoly for exporting all the guano of the Chincha Islands and in addition he was... is the founder of the modern pisco industry –I digressed.[48]

–Mister de la Moscorra, are you feeling ok? –the Consul asked worried.

–Are you asking me "are you drunk" diplomatically? –I asked him.

–Something like that. But since I am not a diplomat by profession I am not used to the language of protocol so I am not good at disguising something crude or disagreeable with something amiable. I am not insulting or judging you at all, after all I was the one that paid for your drinks at the Bank Exchange, but you look somewhat confused, as if you were in another time zone.

–Nothing like that –I said to him–, I am not even slightly buzzed. But when I arrived I had a blow to

48. In 1860, Domingo Elias produced in the valley of Ica, Peru, 70,000 *botijas* of "a distinguished brandy" which he commercialized with the name of "pisco" due to the port from where it was exported. (Werlich, 1978)

Don Domingo Elias, the first non-military President of Peru (albeit self-appointed), founder of the republican-era industry of pisco, exclusive contractor for the operation of the guano islands of Chincha, and owner of almost all the vineyards of the valley of Ica, in the 1850s.

the head of which I am not recovered completely, don't worry I am Ok, within reason. So please continue.

–No, Guillermo, you do not understand. I need somebody that can provide me with strategic information that I can use in my commercial endeavors I just mentioned to you.

–Ok, let me see... 1854, eh? –I said to him, trying to remember.

–Excuse me? – I must really be confusing the poor man with the subject of time.

–Nothing, Mister Consul. I was thinking out loud. But, yes, they are about to cancel Elias' guano concession and this is the reason he is going to organize a revolution in Ica very soon. He will take control and then nominate General Ramon Castilla for President. Since Elias is the owner of almost all of the Ica territory, he must have over 300 men under his command, whom surely must have been trained for combat expecting the forthcoming events. Well, at least those are the rumors that are circulating around the newspaper editorials. I also have very good sources –I said, bragging about my good memory.

–Very impressive, De la Moscorra. Man! You have the talent of a statesman! –he said to me, fascinated.

–It's nothing really, with a good journalistic smell and with a little help of history books, I can predict the future –I honestly laughed.

–You keep confusing me more every time, Guillermo. Doesn't matter, please send me a copy of the newspaper when your article is published; surely it will be interesting –the Consul requested.

–I'll do what I can –I answered, although I knew it was impossible.

The ring of the cellular phone shook me violently back to reality scaring Polhemus away. It was Brenda.

–Guillermo, are you ready for Matt's party? Hurry up, we must be there in one hour, you have to pick me up from work and we must change our clothes.

–I am still in the consulate, Brenda, but I am leaving right now. I'll be there as fast as I can.

–Perfect, how did it go?

–Better than I could have imagined, honey. I'll tell you everything on the way, kisses.

When we arrived at Matt's house everybody was waiting for us and for pisco tasting, very few of them had tried it before. That gave us points in our favor.

–Hello everybody! –Matt greeted us–. Before we officially start this get together I would like you to meet my friends Brenda and Guillermo, they are going to teach us a bit of history with the drinks they will have us try. In case somebody didn't know it, this is pisco, a brandy from Peru. Cheers and enjoy... –then he remembered–: Ah! And be aware this is not a party, it's a work meeting, so after tasting each drink, take your pencil and paper and write down your notes. So, go to work!

It was then that we began to prepare typical drinks with pisco, that soon triggered a fever of mixes and concoctions that flew over the blandest of all imaginations. Matt was fascinated with the versatility of the liquor. At one time he asked me intrigued if the substance was legal and if it was some kind of prohibited hallucinogenic drink, I assured him everything was perfectly legal.

We began with Pisco Sour. The guests were stunned. The party was beginning to get loud while we were experimenting with all the combinations that we could possibly imagine in the kitchen. Before serving the first round, I played a video on the TV with photographic sequences about the history of pisco and Pisco Punch, it

Bodega's Wine *

1 1/4 oz. pisco
1 oz. merlot wine
3/4 oz. cranberry juice
1/2 oz. sweet & sour **

Pour the pisco and the wine in a 4 oz. glass., add the cranberry juice and the sweet & sour. Serve with ice, very cold.

Mariano's Comfort *

1 oz. pisco
1/2 oz. vodka
1/2 oz. Captain Morgan rum
2 oz. pineapple juice
1/2 oz. simple syrup
lime

Pour the pisco, the vodka and the rum in a 4 oz. glass, add the pineapple juice, the simple syrup and lime to taste. Serve with ice, very cold.

Manonga's Tonic *

1 oz. pisco
1 oz. cherry brandy
1/2 oz. granadine syrup
sweet & sour **

Pour the pisco and the cherry brandy in a tall glass, add a lot of ice, the granadine syrup and fill the glass with sweet & sour.

* (Matt Dullaghan, 2001)

** Mix two parts of gum arabic syrup with one of lime juice.

Domingo's Delight

1 oz. pisco
1 oz. frangelico
1/2 oz. tuaca
hot coffee
whipped cream

Pour the pisco, frangelico and tuaca in a 4 oz. glass, fill the glass with hot coffee and add one spoon of whipped cream. A very special and relaxing drink, excellent after a hard day's work.
(Matt Dullaghan, 2001)

Ross' Pisco Punch, ca. 1937

1 1/2 oz. pisco
1 oz. granadine syrup
1/2 oz. lime
2 oz. water and ice

Mix all the ingredients in a shaker and serve in an 8 oz. glass.

This is a recipe of a supposed Pisco Punch found in a letter from Harold Ross, founder of the *The New Yorker* magazine, written in 1937 to Dave Chasen, owner of one of the most luxurious restaurants in Hollywood. Several famous movie stars of the time, such as Clark Gable and Elizabeth Taylor, used to visit that restaurant.
(Harold Ross, 1937)

was accompanied by a selection of specially chosen songs for the occasion. It began with Afro-Peruvian music which was followed by typical tunes from the Gold Rush and the golden age of San Francisco.

–It is amusing to be a barman, Matt –I mentioned while we were preparing the drinks.

–As long as you enjoy the drinks you are preparing –Matt said–. I think, Guillermo, this is your second vocation, because us barmen have a little of mathematicians inside and know some chemistry. I believe that we are in between the engineer and the alcoholic, I don't know which side we lean towards more, but the proportion goes according to the product, which is never altered by which factor comes first, right?

–Then, if what you say is true, I am... an Alcoholic Engineer? No, I am the one that is enjoying this, first class, cheers! –I toasted buoyantly. Then shouted to Brenda–: Honey! Come here, I feel like jumping on the table and dancing, like that day at the bar... –but when I saw her face, I added–: No, I won't! It was a joke, I am just very happy.

–We all are, love, everybody is happy –Brenda replied

cheerfully and then added–: Matt, congratulations, this party was a success.

–No. You were the success –Matt specified–. Pisco was a success, you have no idea how anxious I am to try Pisco Punch.

–Good, my dear Matt, I have news for you, as in the day when we first met: I already have the original recipe and if I tell you the story you won't believe it –I said to him.

–But then, why didn't we prepare it today?

–Because it takes almost a week to prepare the ingredients for the mix –I explained.

–That's great, you must tell me everything –he asked insisting.

Matt's party was a lot of fun, to say the least.

We were sleeping when the telephone rang.

–God, who can call at this late time? It's official, I am going to disconnect the phone –I had to answer it, since that night we had forgotten to set the answering machine–: Hello?!

–Guillermo, this is Matt, I could not sleep thinking... Listen, you must write a book, you must tell this story;

Milk Punch, ca. 1800

1/2 cup of pisco
2 cups of milk
1 cinnamon bark
1 egg
sugar to taste
cinnamon powder

Pour the pisco in a tall glass. Boil the milk with the sugar and the cinnamon bark. In a deep container, beat the white of one egg and then add the yolk. Remove the cinnamon bark and pour the boiled milk slowly always continuously beating the mix. Add the mix to the glass with pisco and sprinkle with cinnamon powder to taste. (Traditional recipe)

De la Moscorra's Pisco Sour

1 1/2 oz. pisco
1 1/2 oz. sweet & sour *
1/4 egg white
2 oz. ice
angostura bitters

Pour the pisco, sweet & sour, egg white and the ice in a blender. Blend at high speed for one minute. Serve in 8 oz. glasses and sprinkle a few drops of angostura bitters.
(Guillermo Toro-Lira, 2001)

* Mix two parts of gum arabic syrup with one of lime juice.

you cannot be selfish, somebody that has tasted pisco cannot be that selfish.

–That's what I always say –I replied, understandingly, although almost dead tired.

–You can do it! If you need my help I'll support you, although I don't know how, but you have my total moral support.

I could no longer sleep after Matt's call, my brain had begun to spin at one thousand RPMs, each piece of history was beginning to fit more clearly.

That was some good pisco! I thought while I was taking a shower, I do not have any hangover nor discomfort, but I was very fatigued anyway. Cold water! I began to write everything that I had compiled, watching the pond, the ducks and the squirrels playing on my disorganized balcony. I stopped writing for a while and somewhat cleaned the terrace, grabbed the broom and began, as I had never seen myself do, to sweep the balcony. Everything was cleaned up now. It took me less time than I thought. I then continued with my writing.

–Ok, I cleaned the terrace –I said to myself–, I stopped smoking, the only thing left to do is to clean up my library and... –the telephone rang–: Disconnect the telephone! Hello?!

–Mister De la Moscorra? –a very calm and pleasant voice said.

–Yes, who is looking for him! –I replied somewhat altered.

–Andrew Canepa –that's all he said.

–The historian? –I asked ashamed, lowering my stance and moderating my voice–. Hi, how are you. I have been trying to get in touch with you for a long time, but we always seem to miss each other.

–That's why I am returning your call. Your research is about Peruvian pisco in San Francisco is that right? –he asked slowly.

–Yes, basically it is –I replied.

—Well, I have a few interesting facts for you —he exclaimed—. Nicholas Larco, an Italian from Liguria who lived in Peru for many years, was one of the main importers of pisco in San Francisco until 1864, when his shipment of pisco was seized...

—Hell! They have seized Mr. Larcos' cargo of pisco. What are we going to do? —a voice exclaimed anxiously.[49]

—I don't know, but pisco is one of the most popular liquors and we cannot fail our customers —the other one answered.

—What if we serve something else? You know, we can make twisted drinks, and nobody will be able to tell the difference, I have an instruction manual that tells how to make wine from rum and it comes out perfect —a third man proposed.

—What are you whispering, you three loafers! The Bank Exchange has never, you hear, never served adulterated liquors, never!

—No, Mr. Parker, Mister George, sir. We don't have pisco, our supplier has had a mishap —one of them replied.

—What happened to Larco? —George Parker asked.

—They seized his cargo claiming problems with the containers. They say at the Customs House that they don't fulfill the official measurements, because they are not the same as the others, they are earthenware vessels that come from Peru, the ones they call *piscos* or *pisquitos*.

—But what kind of nonsense is that, Larco has imported pisco in exactly the same containers since 1849 and nobody ever said anything. That's silly! It must be a dirty trick from a competitor. What the heck! We will have to buy from Polhemus. Go, buy everything that is needed, we cannot open the bar

49. *Daily Alta California*, Jan. 6, 1864,:
SAN FRANCISCO WED., JAN. 6
CITY ITEMS
CUSTOM HOUSE SEIZURE - The Custom House authorities have seized and confiscated 200 jars of Pisco and libelled the Peruvian bark *Mandarina* for an alleged violation of the act of March 2d. 1799 and 1827 and February 27 1830 which states that 'No brandy can be brought into the United States except in liquor vessels of a capacity not less than fifteen gallons with measure and upwards [...] etc.' This action of the officials has created considerable comment in commerce circles, especially as Pisco has been imported in this port since 1849, and no question has arisen before of a violation of law. The liquor is made in Pisco, Peru, of grape, and is placed in earthen jars containing from 2 1/2 to 3 gallons each, the jar being made tapering to facilitate transportation in Peru, the custom being to sling three jars on each side of a mule. The liquor in question came consigned to Mr. N. Larco, who, on the 4th of December last, paid duty on some fifty odd jars, when no questions were raised . It does seem strange that custom, for so many years, having permitted its importation in its original packages, that at the late day, the law, if it does affect it, should be enforced. We have always been under the impression that the Custom House laws were framed for the protection of commerce and the honest merchants as well as to

SAN FRANCISCO, WEDNESDAY, JAN. 6.

☞ *See Third and Fourth Pages.*

CITY ITEMS.

CUSTOM HOUSE SEIZURE.—The Custom House authorities have seized and confiscated 200 jars of Pisco, and libelled the Peruvian bark *Mandarina* for an alleged violation of the act of March 2d, 1799, and 1827, and February 27, 1830, which states that "No brandy can be brought into the United States, except in casks or vessels of a capacity not less than fifteen gallons wine measure, nor any other distilled spirits, (arrack and sweet cordials excepted,) except in casks or vessels of the capacity of ninety gallons wine measure, and upwards, etc." This action of the officials has created considerable comment in commercial circles, especially as Pisco has been imported into this port since 1849, and no question has arisen before of a violation of law. The liquor is made in Pisco, Peru, of grape, and is placed in earthen jars containing from 2½ to 3 gallons each, the jar being made tapering to facilitate transportation in Peru, the custom being to sling three jars on each side of a mule. The liquor in question came consigned to Mr. N. Larco, who, on the 4th of December last, paid duty on some fifty odd jars, when no questions were raised. It does

Section of the 1864 newspaper article discussing the seizure of N. Larco's cargo of pisco.

without pisco. How about the other liquors? –the bar's owner asked.

–Everything is in order, sir.

–Perfect, then go to work! –Parker ordered, and when he saw me standing there he approached me. –Hey you, we are not opened yet.

–Something happened with the pisco, as I have just heard –I said to him.

–What's your problem man? –he sounded upset– Are you a spy or something like that?

–No, no, take it easy –I said, nervously, trying to make up a good excuse– I am... the, the... –stuttering, I did not know what to say.

–The what?! Somebody call the police right now! And don't move from there, you are going to explain to me who you are and what you want from me.

–Don't behave this way, calm down, I will explain it to you. I am... –then I remembered my identity with Polhemus–. Ah yes! I am a reporter from a Peruvian newspaper and I want to interview you because you are the owner of one of the most important saloons of San Francisco and one that serves pisco.

–Oh! Excuse me then. Just the way that you burst into my premises was not gentleman-like, you appeared so suddenly as if you were a ghost. It frightened me a little, you understand –he said to me in a much calmer voice–: But, please sit down and tell me what you are looking for... Enough! You guys go to work, everything has just been a misunderstanding! Ok, sorry. I am listening –Parker added.

–I wanted a little information about this saloon. I know it opened its doors for the first time in 1853 –I informed him, seeming very interested.

–That's right, at that time the place belonged to Kilduff & Co. Then my father, Thomas Parker, and his partner, John Torrence, acquired the business, it is from that time that pisco became an important liquor on our list of drinks. Torrence had this strong attachment for pisco, so much that he had to announce it in each and every advertisement he published.[50] He even got to list it as a renowned spirit, when back then it was not known so much, at least that's what my father thought. But, in reality, Torrence's biggest passion was the theater, he was involved with Tom Maguire, they even built a theater together.

–Excuse me –I interrupted–: Tom Maguire? The same one that was John Brown's partner at Parker House? He owned the Maguire´s Opera House and worked with Torrence.

–Exactly man, he was also the one who gave Torrence ideas of making punches of pisco. Maguire used to prepare them when he was a bartender at John Brown's place, who learned them from Bob Ridley.

–But do you also serve punches with pisco or don't you any longer? –I asked.

–Of course! That is one of the most important legacies that Torrence has left us, putting aside any personal differences he may have had with my father, I recognize he made valuable contributions; and the most important, in my opinion, is the list of punches of pisco which has put us at the level in which we are. Do you want to try one? We are a little bit short of pisco because of Larco's problem, but I have my personal reserve. It's first class –he offered.

–Thank you very much! –I thanked him sincerely–. I'd kill to the able to taste one of the famous San Franciscan punches, Mr. Parker.

–Eh, boy! Serve one punch of pisco to this gentleman... –and turning towards me he said:– excuse me you haven't told me your name.

50. John Torrence and Thomas Parker publish what may be the first advertising of the sale of pisco in the world (see following page). In 1858, the Bank Exchange publishes an advertisement in the city of San Francisco, offering billiard articles and the wholesale and retail sale of several liquors such as "Old London Dock Brandies, Port Wines, Sherries, Champagne, Apple Jack, Pisco, Arrac[k], Cordials, and Liquors." Pisco is advertised at the level of Apple Jack, a liquor made from apple juice (cyder), very popular in the Northern East Coast of the United States at that time, and of arrack a Hindi liquor, made of rice, and the basis for the first punch in the world. The word "punch" derives from the Hindu word "panch" that means five, the number of the original ingredients: arrack, sugar, lemon, tea and water.

BANK EXCHANGE

—— AND ——

BILLIARD SALOON,

CORNER OF

Washington and Montgomery Streets

SAN FRANCISCO.

TORRENCE & PARKER,

DEALERS IN

Billiard Balls, Cloths, Leathers,

CUES, CUE WAX, POOL BALLS, RONDO BALLS, ETC.

JOHN TORRENCE.  THOMAS B. PARKER.

ALSO, ON HAND AND FOR SALE,

OLD LONDON DOCK BRANDIES,

CUTTER'S OLD BOURBON WHISKY.

PORT WINES, SHERRIES,

AND ALL THE CHOICEST BRANDS OF

CHAMPAGNE,

Apple Jack, Pisco, Arrac, Cordials, Liquors,

ETC. ETC. ETC.

COPIES OF PHELAN'S GAME OF BILLIARDS.

BALLS TURNED AND COLORED.

Reconstruction of an advertisement published by the Bank Exchange in 1858 by John Torrence and Thomas B. Parker where pisco is announced for the first time (fourth line from the bottom, between Apple Jack and Arrac [sic]).

–Guillermo de la Moscorra –I replied.

–Please to meet you, George Parker –he said extending his hand.

–I know –I replied.

–Of course! You came to interview me. Excuse me, but this issue of Larco's pisco cargo seizure has left me a little stunned.

Suddenly, the young person with the punches arrived. I will finally get to taste it.

–Thanks, boy! –Parker said to the young man and then turned towards me–: Here it is, this drink has a little pineapple rind juice, pineapple is a fruit that you must know very well. It is native to South America.[51] Pineapple gives the drink much more class. At the same level of the drinks preferred by the stars of the theater and the intellectuals. This is another one of Torrence's legacies.[52] Since he was involved with the theater, the most selected celebrities from the Bohemian and artistic part of the society used to come to the Bank Exchange. The "Gods of the Theater" frequented this place and they continue doing so until today. But after marrying Mrs. Judah, the actress. You do know her right? –he assumed–. How come you don't? She is very famous. Well, after marrying her they had a son, John S., and soon thereafter he broke with his Bank Exchange business ties and dedicated himself completely to the theater. He still comes here once in a while, has a few drinks and then leaves.

–Guillermo, are you there, hello? –Andrew Canepa asked over the phone, making me come back from the astral trip to the Bank Exchange of George Parker.

–Yes, yes, sorry –I excused myself ashamed but feeling joy, because I had just found the missing link of my story–: it was Tom Maguire who brought the pisco legacy from John Brown to John Torrence.

51. Pineapple is of South American origin, native of Brazil, Paraguay, Bolivia and Peru. The Hawaiian pineapple industry begins in 1880, when Captain John Kidwel introduces the variety "Smooth Cayenne" into the islands. Pineapple is named "halakahihi" in Hawaiian which means "foreign fruit."

52. In 1910, almost thirty years after the death of John Torrence, it was published that the liquor arrack marinated with pineapple "acquires a much delicious flavor and it is thought to be unrivaled for making nectarial punch." (Hopkins, 1910)
Nevertheless, it is necessary to note that there are older historical references that relate pineapple being prepared in drinks offered at "eleven in the morning" (las once) in 18th century Peru.

Pineapple was an exotic and expensive fruit in San Francisco in the 1800s. This illustration was drawn in the diary of a visitor to the city, where he describes the scarcity of the fruit mentioning that "a Peruvian or Panamanian black woman" becomes surprised and shows nostalgia when she sees one of the fruits "of her country," for sale in a street of San Francisco. (Albert S. Evans / Ernest Narjot, 1873)

–I thought you had hung up on me –the historian mentioned.

–Oh, no –I assured him– I got a bit distracted, it's that... well, it doesn't matter, but tell me if we can get together to talk about Larco, I know you wrote a biographical article in the quarterly of the California Historical Society.

–Yes, the story is a bit long and very interesting –he informed, showing his interest in helping me.

–I also have some information on the matter that I would like to share with you –I anticipated to make sure a meeting was arranged–. In Miraflores, Lima, Peru, we have a Larco Avenue, and the famous singer of Peruvian Creole Music, Chabuca Granda, was the great-great-grand-daughter of a brother of the same Larco that came here, and he is the uncle of the same man that the avenue is named after.

–Interesting, I didn't know that –he said showing enthusiasm–. What about getting together tonight here at my house? I have some valuable information we can exchange. By the way, my wife is also Peruvian and we are both very interested in meeting you: would you like to come to... are you married? –I answered yes, and he extended the invitation to my wife–: Would you like to come to dinner to my house at seven thirty?

View of San Francisco, from the luxurious residence of Nicholas Larco, in the 1850s.

—Of course! —I exclaimed—. Terrific! We'll bring the pisco.

—Ok then —he said, and with an amiable good bye he hung up.

It was not even ten minutes after seven and we were already parked in front of the garage of the house at the address I had written down on a piece of paper. I did not have to look around too much, the Italian warmth in the surroundings was telling me we were in the right place. We wanted to wait awhile and arrive at the exact time, because as my father always said: "the time is at the time, it is not before nor later." And since we Peruvians consider the agreed upon meeting time as being just a gross indicator which can be off as much as hours, we decided to wait for a few minutes and make a good impression. I did not know why, but something was telling me this new friendship was going to mean much to me, so I wanted to start it on the right foot. Without letting a next thought come to me, the door at the entrance opened generously and let us perceive the shadow of our hosts' silhouettes.

We got out of the car immediately and climbed up the stairs that led us to the entrance where a man waited showing a white head and a blue smile. Next to him appeared a pair of innocently mischievous eyes, full of love and definitively Peruvian, who extended her open arms to embrace and to welcome us.

—But come in, please. It's a pleasure to have you in my house —Mrs. Canepa greeted showing us in.

—Thank you very much, the pleasure is mine, believe me —I said—. This is my wife, Brenda.

—Very good —the voice from the telephone said, very calm, almost as smooth as a velvet. A voice of wisdom forged by years and solidified by experience—. How are you? I hope you'll feel right at home. Miriam —he said, facing his wife— my love, can you please serve us something to drink.

–Oh! Excuse me –I said–, here is the pisco I promised, we also took the liberty of bringing some prosciutto with asiago cheese.

–That's wonderful! They are so nice, no Andy? –Mrs. Canepa said affectionately. Then she addressed herself to Brenda setting all type of protocol aside–: Are you also Peruvian?

–No, I am Uruguayan, but same as if I were, with Guillermo we spend more time speaking about Peru than even about ourselves.

–That's what happens, dear, when you marry an historian. You don't need to tell me! Look, I know which is the most typical dance of Genoa, but I doubt if Andy knows which is my favorite song –Miriam said laughing.

–Well, Miriam, should we ladies go in the kitchen and make Pisco Sour? –Brenda proposed.

–Sure! Come this way –Mrs. Canepa said, showing her the way to the kitchen.

–What a pretty house you have, Miriam –Brenda said, while she squeezed a lime for the Pisco Sour.

–Thanks –she replied–. We inherited this house from Andy's parents. Ever since we got it we've tried to keep it the same way my in-laws had it.

–But, it's so big, do you take care of it alone? –Brenda asked astonished.

–Yes, of course –Miriam replied amused.

–You keep it as if a house cleaning battalion had worked over time.

–Don't exaggerate! –Miriam laughed–. Well, how about we try a little sambuca while we prepare the Pisco Sour, it's a great Italian anisette that I have over here. My father-in-law used to say that every Italian must have a bottle of sambuca in his house. Here, take it, put this coffee bean inside.

–Delicious! –Brenda exclaimed, tasting the drink little by little.

–I add a little water to lighten it a bit, but I tell you

that our ninety year old Italian lady neighbor still looks like she is fifty thanks to her sambuca. That 's what she says: a glass every day –Miriam pointed out.

After a delicious dinner, Miriam and Brenda began to chat. While Andrew and I interchanged a couple of ideas, he suggested to me that I write an article for the bulletin of the California Historical Society using all the information that I had discovered about the story of pisco in San Francisco. I was not totally sure if that was the way to proceed, but it convinced me that I was going to write something anyway. It was too rich a story to leave it locked inside my head, I must expose it. Suddenly, Andrew stood up and asked me to follow him. We went inside his den, which was a dream come true for any reading aficionado. The walls were upholstered with all types of books, historical and fictional, the most sublime information and so perversely objective that not even Pinocchio's fairy would venture to bring her magic wand in for fear of tumbling down into the disillusion of boring reality.

–Here are all the historical references that exist in the city of San Francisco about the famous Pisco Punch. I hope you find it useful. I classified it all morning –Andrew said showing me a pile of books.

–How can I thank you, Andy! –I was moved.

–Listen, if you want you can take them with you, you can borrow them, but I don't know why I get the impression that you want to browse through them right away. Is that right?

–Yes, Andy, yes, please –I begged.

–Well. I'll leave you alone and I'll go back to the ladies. It's not good to leave them alone for so long, we can't afford such a high level of impoliteness –he smiled closing the door behind him.

My God! I said to myself, while reviewing each book, magazine and pamphlet that Andy had left me. I was so excited I did not know where to begin. I took a long sip of the Pisco Sour that Miriam so majestically prepared with Brenda's valuable assistance, which gives me the courage to begin the task ahead, it was far from easy. After glancing at all the information, I realized that the material was not really that much, at least for me, in fact it was almost twenty pages of data distributed between hundreds of publications. It was going to take time to put all this together. I was seriously thinking of calling Pinocchio's fairy, but I thought she may not want to help me. Suddenly, some celestial bells sounded in my ears, first I thought it was the fairy queen that had listened to me, but it was better than that, it was Brenda, always rescuing my destitute heart.

–Love, Andy and Miriam went to bed. They said to tell you good night. They didn't want to interrupt. They have been so nice to us, even offered us one of the guest rooms in their home, not to distract you from the research –Brenda said, while she looked at the books laying around me.

–Great! I need your help, please sit down.

Then, Brenda took her small glasses out of her purse, cleaned them using one of the tissue papers she uses for her allergy, and began to work. She took the first book and soon thereafter, the second. She is a fierce researcher.

–Look at this, Guillermo! –she shouted.

–What? –I asked scared.

–This one shows a Pisco Punch recipe from a John Lannes, written in a letter by a lawyer in 1941.[53]

–Let me see that... This Lannes, what a loafer –I said smiling–, he was close, but no cigar. He couldn't take it away from Nicol. Old fox. He was able to discover something, he mentions the gum syrup and the pineapple, but, the measures are mistaken! and they are not exact, as they should be. Nicol would have had a heart attack if he read this recipe.

–How do you know that, Guillermo? –Brenda asked intrigued.

53. The article "Secrets of Pisco Punch Revealed," written by W. Bronson, in 1973, revealed a Pisco Punch recipe written by a barman named John Lannes in 1941.

The Pisco Punch as prepared with Lannes' recipe can hardly be defined as tasting like "lemonade," as several historical references describe.
(O'Brien, 1948)
(Ross, 1937, 2001)

–Forget it, dear. Lannes doesn't mention lime and there are no indications of any secret ingredient.

–Guillermo, wait, maybe Lannes had the original recipe but he modified it a bit so as not to seem untrustworthy in Nicol's confidence.

–I don't think so –I replied convinced–, after all I have researched on this subject, there was no way Nicol could have given the recipe to Lannes, not for anything in the world.

–Look –she pointed out–, it also says that the previous owners to Nicol were: John Torrence and a certain Orrin Dorman, and that they were the ones that gave the recipe to Duncan Nicol. It also mentions that the Bank Exchange was called "Pisco John's" in honor of an old owner of the bar, which by using a simple association of names one can conclude is John Torrence.

–What a mess –I said as I stretched my body–. I think those names are mistaken; but who is this Dorman? Write his name down, it can be useful later.

Suddenly a book with a greenish cover and written in 1951 fell in my hand, it was called *Ark of Empire, San Francisco's Montgomery Block*, I opened it. Luckily it had an index. I hate books without an index.

–What?! Look, Brenda. This book mentions that John Torrence and George Parker founded the Bank Exchange together in... 1853! No way, and nothing about Kilduff. Aha! This seems to be the source of the first mistake. I mean, everything appears Ok, but there are several errors, the data was not cross-referenced using other sources. What could have happened to these researchers to be so mistaken on this point? They were not as picky as I am, I guess.

It was four o'clock in the morning when we finished studying all the information at hand. In summary, we found there was a basic agreement that Pisco John was John Torrence, that nobody could agree on who were the owners of the Bank Exchange before Duncan Nicol's time, nor who had invented the recipe.

–Honey... –I said to Brenda in a tone of voice that suggested that I was going to ask her something difficult.

–What? –she replied, in a fearful stance.

–Don't get angry for what I'm going to ask you –I said to her, almost begging.

–Oh no! –she closed her eyes, sensing my request.

–Tomorrow we must go back to the San Francisco Public Library to look through city directories.

–No! –she said devastated–: Of what years?

–From 1853 to 1921.

–What?! Almost seventy years! –she exclaimed in a whisper, then she leaned over a book shelf.

–Yes, let's go to sleep, tomorrow will be a hard day –I said showing an apologetic look on my face.

–You have to reward me for this one, eh? –she giggled.

–Of course! –I exclaimed without thinking twice.

The next morning we had breakfast with the Canepas, we thanked them for their hospitality and promised to meet again. Then we left for the library, our second home, with knowledge of cause and with all the precautions of the case. As my mother used to say: "take a leak before taking a long trip," because we didn't want to face the surreal environment of that bathroom again. We arrived with lots of time to spare, and while we submerged ourselves in old directories and duplicated microfilms all worn out by use, we discovered very interesting things that brought light into this dark tunnel I have gotten into when I decided for the first time to discover the true history of Pisco Punch, of Duncan Nicol and the Bank Exchange. Tired, but satisfied, we decided to return back home, but not without first taking photos of all the documents that interested us. We had all the necessary historical data and now we had to organize it in a logical way. I also took pictures of very interesting old advertisements, such as that of Coca Cola, of Vin Mariani... Those days were so different, I thought... Suddenly, it all appeared clear to me.

–I think I know what the crossed-out ingredient in EJP's manuscript was... –I said to Brenda, while I organized the panorama in my mind–. Think about it, at that time it was quite fashionable, and even Freud had praised its qualities...

–Do you think so? –Brenda asked me doubtfully.

–Of course I do –I replied immediately–. What other thing could be so secret, eh?

–I think you are right –Brenda answered and after a while added–: What are we going to do with those two hundred photos you took, Guillermo? Do we print them? –Brenda suggested.

–Yes I think so –I replied calmly and enthusiastically and feeling sure of having discovered the best kept secret–, then we'll arrange and classify all dates with the names, addresses, news and advertisements.

–That is going to be a tough job. Wouldn't it be great if we could enter all the data in the computer and then just ask for the answers? –Brenda fantasied.

–Like Star Trek!: "Computer: who invented Pisco Punch?" –I said, continuing with Brenda's fantasy.

–It would be terrific, no? –Brenda said laughing– But we are not there yet. So lets get to work.

The first thing we did was to make print-outs off the directories and newspaper advertisements from the time when the Bank Exchange was in operation. At least, this would be the pattern that would give us a continuity over time. This time we literally plunged inside the information and documents.

–Everything is making sense now, Brenda. John Lannes was the manager of the Bank Exchange from the end of 1919 until January of 1920, when the bar closed its doors because of the prohibition act of Volstead. But, the most important part is here: Lannes appears as owner of the Bank Saloon, a competitor of the Bank Exchange. This bar was located on 527 Clay street, and Lannes administered it since 1903. Do you know what I am saying: Lannes worked less than a year in the Bank Exchange. Do you think Nicol would have entrusted him with the recipe?

–In my opinion, no. Why should he? For what reason? Didn't he say that he would not give the recipe even to Volstead himself? –Brenda said sounding very convincing.

–That's true –I said without any doubt–. But lets review all the data to make everything clearer.

–How about if we serve ourselves a couple of drinks just to lighten the tension. Remember what your idol Manuel Atanasio Fuentes said about the effects of moderated drinking –Brenda suggested.

–That's right, lets stimulate ourselves with a bit of determination. Do you want pisco or wine? –I offered.

–Wine is ok, from the bottle I opened yesterday, please, it must have breathed enough by now –Brenda joked.

Advertisement of the *Daily Alta California* announcing the inauguration of the Bank Exchange on Friday, December 23rd of 1853, at 6 o'clock in the afternoon. Notice that the proprietors are P.D. Kelduff [sic] & Co.

–Yes, I'm sure it has. I am going to serve myself my mosto verde, which is good enough to win a gold award –I said while I took one bottle out of the box.

–Cheers!

–Cheers! Humm, that's good –I said savoring the drink and sitting down to continue–. Listen to this, all is clear: Kilduff & Co. are the founders and the first managers of the Bank Exchange, here's the newspaper advertisement that invites clients to the inauguration of the bar. This society is the one that started everything yet without any idea of what they were originating, Kilduff and his partner did not have any relation with the masters from the past.[54] It was John Torrence that retook the legacy that Tom Maguire left him, who learned it from John Brown, and he from Bob Ridley, and him from Jean Vioget; and he passed it to the ones that followed. That's the reason why many mistakenly assumed John Torrence was Pisco John.

–That's right, love –Brenda confirmed–. Then Torrence made a partnership with the Parkers, first with Thomas B. Parker, from 1856 to the beginning of 1859, and then with George F. Parker until 1861.

–Then –I added–, in 1862 George Parker remains as the sole owner until 1874. But, in 1875 the Bank Exchange does not appear listed in any directory.

–It must be the same time –Brenda commented– when Columbus Street was created, the bar was auctioned and the famous painting of Samson and Delilah was sold.

–How do you know that, honey? –I was astonished.

–Oh, dear –she said bragging–, you are not the only one that read Pauline Jacobson's *A Fire-Defying Landmark*. And according to her, at that time the owners are a certain Brown and another one nicknamed Little Perkins.[55]

–That's right–I confirmed–. George A. Brown and George F. Perkins appear as proprietors until 1878. Then

54. Contrary to what has been written in all modern articles about Pisco Punch, the Bank Exchange was founded by Patrick "Pat" Kilduff and John Meiggs.
(*S.F. Examiner,* Jan. 13, 1889).

John Meiggs and his brother Henry "Enrique" Meiggs emigrated to San Francisco in 1849 from New York. The Meiggs brothers held important public offices in the rising city of San Francisco. Nevertheless, in January of 1855, both untimely travel to South America. In 1868, Henry Meiggs went to Peru, where he died in 1877. He contributed with the demolition of the old walls surrounding Lima, which limited its urban expansion, and constructed 700 miles of railway in the coast and in the Andes of Peru.

55. "A Fire-Defying Landmark" is an article written by Pauline Jacobson. It was first published in *The Bulletin* of San Francisco, in May 4, 1912, Pg. 13. It was reprinted in a small book of the same name that the Bank Exchange gave to its customers. Years later, Pauline Jacobson writes a simplified version of this article and includes it as Chapter 2 in her posthumous book *City of The Golden Fifties.*

Advertisements published by the Bank Exchange from 1856 (top left) to 1862 (bottom right). In 1859, there is a transition of owners that goes from Thomas Parker & John Torrence, to both individually, to George Parker & John Torrence, and finally to George Parker alone. Pisco is shown advertised in 1858 to 1860 (three center ads), during the tenures of Thomas Parker and John Torrence. George Parker published similar advertisements until the end of the 1860s. No further Bank Exchange advertisements have been found after that date.

there is a name change, it changes from Bank Exchange to Brown & Perkins Liquor Saloon for seven consecutive years, but in 1885, after Perkins death, Brown, as sole owner, renames it again Bank Exchange, and without knowing it, starts the legend of what people would later call the "Temple of the Past," by hiring a young and capable bartender: Duncan Nicol. This happens in 1887, and from then on, until 1892, Nicol and Brown appear as co-owners.

–Love, since our quest has been now solved I am going to take a relaxing bath ok? –Brenda said stretching her arms satisfied.

–That's ok, you go... Then, in 1893 Nicol takes the last post alone, to become the creator of the legend that until today eats away at the soul of the eternal Bohemian spirits and serves as the inspiration for many essays and historical theorems that start without a beginning and finish without an ending...

An Eternal Goodbye

—Tthis is going to have a good ending —I heard the unmistakable voice of the inventor.

—I got it Duncan! I have discovered everything. I have it all and I don't know how —I exclaimed to him feeling moved.

—Yes you know it, now you have the fire. This time you did not fall asleep with the glass of pisco in your hand, I am proud of you, son —he congratulated me, giving me a pat on the back, which I did not feel.

—And now what? —I asked him with the nostalgia of a task fulfilled.

—You know what. Drink your whole glass in one gulp and go to work because the gum arabic just arrived.

—Guillermo open the door please, it has been ringing for a while and I am in the shower! Open it, please! —Brenda shouted from the bath.

—Ok, I'll get it...

—Who was it love? —Brenda asked still in the shower.

—The mailman... with the gum arabic package —I said, opening a box that contained bags of a white powder. Thinking finally, finally, finally, I will be able to solve the mystery.

–That is great! Lets start then –Brenda said, leaving the bath to take a look at the package.

–Honey, you are going to catch a cold, dry yourself, you are dripping wet –I said to her laughing.

–Can you imagine, we finally have everything here –she said while looking for a towel–, and now we only need to use our hands to go back in time. I am very excited, and happy for you!

–Go on, dry yourself while I tell you how it is going, and then help me prepare the punch. By the way, we need a pineapple. Can you also serve me a glass of pisco, honey? –I said to her from the kitchen, where I was preparing the gum arabic.

–Here. Ok Guillermo, I am going to buy the pineapple, so you can start to marinate. I'll be back soon –she gave me the pisco, and said while she looked for the keys.

–It must be sweet pineapple, it's called cayenne, although I do not know what they call it here.

–Ok, bye –she said as she was leaving.

–I'll wait for you, don't worry, I'll be here talking to myself. My God! it's a lot of work to prepare the gum syrup. Two whole days and then wait for one and a half more to marinate the pineapple. Mix, keep mixing, remove the impurities, well. Doesn't matter, it is worth it, that's the secret of success: at least one of the most important and crucial ones. Yes, thanks to the gum muci-

The magical potion of Duncan Nicol ready to render wings of cherubs to the thirsty.

lage the strength of the alcohol is disguised and the powerful drink seems a harmless pineapple refreshment, much like a lemonade, but after the fourth glass you'll feel the kick and then knocks you out! One moment... Then, it's true, these men gave these types of drinks to unsuspecting poor souls and then left them unconscious until they awaken in a ship sailing to Shanghai, or any far away place, like slaves, I don't know! Of course! All this happened during the splendor of the Bank Exchange, when Christopher Buckley became the head of the

Democratic Party of San Francisco after the suspicious death of Al Fritz, starting the dark era of lawless days in the city. Buckley was as corrupt as one of the worse kind, could it be that Nicol was involved in all this? The idea is not that preposterous, Buckley even had the judges on his payroll, he did and undid whatever he pleased in San Francisco with all the imaginable liberties. Could it be that Nicol was involved in all this? I sound crazy speaking to myself...

–Good, keep mixing carefully if not it will burn and become useless, you must make it reach its point. Now you have discovered the gum arabic secret. That's one of the Pisco Punch secrets of success, don't forget about the accuracy of the measures, there is nothing worse than a good drink badly prepared. Let me try it, humm... excellent! I was not mistaken in selecting you, now go and revive this lost spirit, bring its glory back, and don't pay attention to the dark side of the story, we all have our bad nights and our sins. Not everything is true. Not everything. Well, I believe it's time to say goodbye –Nicol said while fading away.

–Please don't go, I still have more things to discover –I begged, as I kept frantically mixing the gum arabic.

–Why are you like this? It is not good to put your foot where you have not been invited, curiosity killed the cat, you know –he said, while looking at the gum solution.

–Yes, but the cat died knowing, and I am dying to know –I replied, without giving up.

–You will never finish, it's a vicious circle, the more you learn the more you'll want to know. There are cracks that must never be filled, it's like a jig saw puzzle, it seems complete, but it never is, if not it would be a photo.

Duncan Nicol (second from the left) with his team of bartenders and assistants, posing behind the bar of the Bank Exchange in the 1910s.

–Please don't go away! At least tell me when I'll see you again –I begged.

–Every time you hold a glass of good pisco in your hand –he replied–. As for me, I believe I can now rest in peace. We have given Pisco Punch back to San Francisco and you guard the keys to the mystery, the legacy is now in your hands and I hope you know how to handle what has been entrusted to you. Handle the matter with wisdom. Then, like a good engineer, solve the equation and if there is any surplus according to any temporary or moral calculation coldly rule it out, after all, the wings of cherubs will continue existing in the souls of all good drinkers.

Duncan Nicol then extended his hand to me for the last time, and sealed with fire the mark of his finger on my immortalized pulse.

The End

Pisco Punch was first served, after almost a century, during the Thanksgiving dinner of 2001 in the home of Karen Verushka, in Sunnyvale, California. All the guests were impressed with the smoothness and the delicacy of the famous drink of San Francisco and they were all more than satisfied. It is needless to say we were the "masters" of this celebration.

Thanksgiving day of 2001 at Karen's house, after enjoying Duncan Nicol's Pisco Punch.

What you will read next is the original recipe, with one reservation: it lacks a secret ingredient. Suddenly, I heard Rudyard Kipling's voice saying...

–Go thither softly, treading on the tips of your toes, and ask him for one... the result is the highest and noblest products of the age. No man but one knows what is in it. I have a theory it is compounded of shavings of cherub's wings, the glory of a tropical dawn, the red clouds of sunset, and the fragments of lost epics by dead masters. But try you for yourselves, and pause a while to bless me, who am always mindful of the truest interests of the brethren.[56]

56. Written by Kipling in letters for the newspapers *Civil and Military Gazette* in Lahore, Pakistan and the *Pioneer* of Allahabad, India in 1889. (Asbury omits the first sentence and the word "shavings" in his 1933 book *Barbary Coast*.)

And since 2001, we have repeated the recipe of Pisco Punch for important events and, of course, every Thanksgiving day.

Pisco Punch

PISCO PUNCH

The real recipe, without the ingredient that nobody ever revealed, because Duncan Nicol took the secret with him.

Mix two ounces of Bottle #1 and two ounces of Bottle #2 in an eight ounce glass, fill the glass with ice and add a piece of the prepared pineapple.

Ingredients and their Preparation

All bottles are 750 ml.

Bottle #1
Italia [pisco type Italia]

Bottle #2
Mix one part of Bottle #3 with two parts of Bottle #4 and one part of fresh lime juice [originally from Acapulco, Mexico]. This mixture must be exact, for that reason it is recommended to prepare it in bottles. If the mentioned lime is not available read the final WARNING.

Bottle #3
Soak the rind of one pineapple in one liter (34 oz) of distilled water for 24 hours.

Strain well and store in a bottle, which must be used during the next the 24 hours.

Bottle #4

Macerate the pieces of the pineapple (without its residual juice) with the content of Bottle # 5 for 24 hours, then remove the pineapple and add the residual juice to the mixture.

Store in bottle and use during a period of 24 hours.

Use these pineapple pieces in the final presentation.

Bottle #5 – Gum Syrup

Mix the gum arabic solution with the simple syrup in a large pot. Bring to a boil for two minutes while mixing continuously. Strain with cheese cloth while the mixture is hot.

Store in well corked bottles in a fresh place for a maximum of three months.

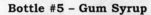

Gum Arabic Solution

Dissolve half a kilogram (1.1 lb) of first quality gum arabic powder in on liter (34 oz) of distilled water. Mix continuously, bring the solution almost to a boil and let it cool down. Skim the superficial impurities which are of white color.

Simple Syrup

Put two kilograms (4.4 lb) of sugar in a large pot. Add one liter (34 oz) of distilled water.

Beat the white of one egg until frothy. Add and mix well.

Take the pot to the fire having some cold water on hand. When the mixture begins to boil and the liquid raises, sprinkle a little of the cold water to keep the mixture from overflowing the pot. This process must be repeated THREE times before beginning to skim the impurities floating on the surface, which are of a white color. After the

FOURTH boiling remove the pot from the fire and skim all the impurities that float on the surface until the solution is very crystalline. Strain in cheese cloth while the mixture is hot and store in bottles.

Preparation of the Pineapple

Wash well one large Cayenne pineapple, not excessively ripe.

Remove the leaves and peel the rind. Set the rind aside, which will be used during the preparation of Bottle # 3.

Cut the pineapple in slices of approximately 2 cm (3/4 in) thick. Cut each slice in squares of 2 by 2 cm (3/4 by 3/4 in), disposing of the central core.

Place the pieces of pineapple in a flat tray that could allow the recollection of residual juices. Using a toothpick or fork puncture three or four holes in each piece of pineapple to reach half of its thickness, taking care not to perforate it.

Sprinkle the pieces of pineapple with a small amount of the content of the Bottle # 1, so that the holes tend to fill with the liquid.

Let rest for three hours. Strain the pineapple pieces and set the residual juice aside, both will be used during the preparation of Bottle # 4.

WARNING

Never prepare using the American yellow lemon. You can also use: key limes from Florida, Peruvian lemon or Chilean lemon "de pica." If these alternative lemons are used, the final flavor of the mixture in the Bottle #2 must be of a perfect balance between sweet and sour. None of these flavors must be preponderant.

Acknowledgments

The making of this book was not an easy task but it was made possible by the invaluable help of people and entities that believed in my research. The past five years, its days and nights, triumphs and defeats, findings and errors that seemed to be clearer as the perseverance and discipline put everything in place. The most important issue here is what I have gained: all the people that I met, the friendships that started and finally the lost recipe I recovered for the delight of the readers' palates.

First I want to acknowledge the staff of the various Public Libraries in the cities of Sunnyvale, San Jose and San Francisco, California. Also to the workers of the missions Carmel, Santa Clara, San Francisco (Dolores), San Juan Bautista, San Francisco Solano, San Diego, and Soledad. To the people at the Presidio Museum in San Francisco, the Italo-American Museum, the Old Customs House in Monterey, the California Historical Society, and the Society of California Pioneers. I thank every one of you.

My gratitude is to Sidney Lawrence a researcher that gave me the guidelines and points about his Ghirardelli family and that of James Lick; to Andrew Canepa for the valuable information he gave me about Nicholas Larco, Herman Melville and others, also for his input, his advice, moral support and invaluable friendship, one of the many benefits of this ordeal; to sir Richard Joséph Menn, Curator of the Carmel Mission; to Mona Gudgel Executive Director of the Monterey County Historical Society; to the "Los Californianos" society, especially to Lucille Corcel, Rudecinda Cindy Lo Buglio and their team of researchers; and to the Peruvian Institute of Genealogical Studies, mainly to Mela Bryce de Tubino and Miguel Ludowieg Ferrari, for the information regarding the Larco Family; and to cocktail historian Dave Wondrich for the information about Harold Ross.

Finally, I want to thank Matt Dullangham, first class bartender and friend, and to Karen Petraska for allowing me to prepare and serve Pisco Punch in their homes and to all the brave spirits that agreed to become tasters in the pisco tasting parties in all its different versions and in the form of Pisco Punch.

Bibliography

Appleton, Robert, *The Catholic Encyclopedia*, Archdiocese of Lima, Vol. IX, New York, 1910.

Asbury, Herbert, *The Barbary Coast*, Alfred A. Knopf Inc., New York, 1933, Pgs. 226-227.

Alcedo, Antonio, *Diccionario Geográfico-Histórico de las Indias Occidentales o América*, Madrid, 1789. Vol. 5, Vocabulario, Pg. 28: 'Botija,' Pg. 149: 'Piña.'

Bacari, Alessandro & Canepa, Andrew, "The Italians in San Francisco in 1865, G.B. Cerrutti's Report to the Ministry of Foreign Affairs," *California History*, Vol.LX, No. 4, Winter 1981/82, Pg. 350.

Balababova, Svetla, et. al., "First identification of drugs in Egyptian mummies," 1992, *Naturwissenschaften* 79:358.

Barry, Theodore A. & Patten, Benjamin A., *San Francisco in 1850*, foreword by J.A. Sullivan, 1947, Pg. 124.

Beebe, Rose Marie & Senkewicz, Robert M., *Lands of Promise and Despair*, Santa Clara University, Heyday Books, 2001. "1784 -The Death of..., Francisco Palóu," Pg. 226.; "1830 - A Secularization..., Juan Bandini," Pg. 375.

Beerman, Eric, "Manuel Quimper, un marino limeño en la costa oeste del Canadá." Article presented at the "Coloquio Internacional sobre Juan Francisco de la Bodega y Quadra," taken place in Lima, from the 17th to the 19th of August of 1994. Published in *Derroteros de la Mar del Sur*, Año 4, No. 4, 1994.

Benvenutto Murrieta, Pedro, *Quince Plazuelas, una alameda y un callejón*, Talleres de don Teodoro Scheuch, Lima, 1932, Pg. 301.

Blanchard, Peter, "The 'Transitional Man' in 19th-Century Latin America: the Case of Domingo Elias of Peru," *Bull. Latin Am. Res.*, Vol 15, No. 2, 1996, Pgs. 157-176.

Bronson, William, "Secrets of Pisco Punch Revealed," *California Historical Quarterly*, Fall 1973, Pg. 229-240.

Brooke, Thomas H., *A History of the Island of St. Helena, from its Discovery by the Portuguese to the Year 1806; to which is Added an Appendix*, Chapter V, From Year 1708..., Black, Parry, and Kingsbury, London, 1808.

Brown, John H., *Reminiscences and Incidents of 'The Early Days' of San Francisco, by John H. Brown, Actual experience of an eye-witness, from 1845 to 1850*, Mission Journal Publishing Co., San Francisco, California, Cap. VI, 1886.

Bryant Dakin, Susanna, *The Lives of William Hartnell*, Stanford University Press, Stanford, California, 1949.

Byrne, Henry L., "Life of James Lick," *Quarterly of The Society of California Pioneers*, Vol. 1, No. II, San Francisco, 1924.

Caballero, César A., *Peruanidad del Pisco*, Edit. Nueva Educación, Lima, Perú, 1972, Pg. 12.

Calmell, José Emilio A., *Historia Taurina del Perú, 1535-1935*, Taller Tipográfico de 'Perú Taurino' y 'Perla y Oros,' Lima, 1939, Pgs. 132, 172.

Cárdenas de la Peña, Enrique, "Juan Francisco de la Bodega y Quadra en San Blas de Nayarit." Article presented at the "Coloquio Internacional sobre Bodega y Quadra, Lima," August 1994, Published in *Derroteros de la Mar de Sur*, Año 4, No. 4, 1994.

Cieza de León, Pedro, *Crónica del Perú*, Pontificia Universidad Católica del Perú, Fondo Editorial, 1985, Lima, Pg. 91.

Cisneros, Carlos B, & García, Rómulo E., *Guía del Viajero Callao, Lima y sus Alrededores*, Imprenta del Estado, Lima, 1898, Pgs. 28, 42, 179, 187.

Clark, Donald Thomas, *Monterey County Place Names*, Krestel Press, Carmel Valley, California, 1991. Pg. 440: 'Rancho Chualar;' Pg. 448: 'Rancho Guadalupe y Llanitos de los Correos;' Pg. 469: 'Rancho Zanjones.'

Cook, William H., *The Physio-Medical Dispensatory: A Treatise on Therapeutics, Matteria Medica, and Pharmacy, in Accordance with the Principles of Physiological Medication*, Cincinnati, 1869. Pg. 32: 'Gum Arabic.'

Coroleu, José, *América, Historia de su Colonización*, Volume II, Montaner y Simón Editores, Barcelona, 1895, Pg. 179.

Daily Alta California, "Summary of ships in the port of San Francisco for the year 1853," December, 30, 1853.

Daily Alta California, "From Peru, Fifteen Days Later," February 4, 1854.

Daily Alta California, "City Items, Customs House Seizure," January 6, 1864.

Daily Alta California, "Twenty-three Gallons of Whiskey Converted into Forty Gallons - Seventh Edition," Henry Watter & Co., Publishers, July 2, 1854.

Davis, Keith A., *Landowners in Colonial Peru*, University of Texas Press, Austin, Texas, 1984, 'Andres Jimenez,' 'Miguel Cornejo': Pgs. 14, 18, 51, 52. Wine commerce routes: Pgs. 87, 91.

Davis, William H., *Seventy-five Years in San Francisco*, Edited by D. S. Watson, 1929, John Howell, San Francisco, Ch. 38: "Nathan Spear's Grist Mill; The First."

Fink, Augusta, *Monterey County - The Dramatic History of its Past*, Western Tanager Press, San Francisco, 2000, Pgs. 57-61.

Foote, Horace S., *Pen Pictures from the Garden of the World or Santa Clara County*, Chicago, The Lewis Publishing Company, 1888, Pg. 357.

Fuentes, Manuel A., *Estadística General de Lima*, Tipografía nacional de MN Corpancho, por J. Henrique del Campo, Lima, 1858, 'Andres Jimenez,' 'Miguel Cornejo,' Pg. 20.

Fuentes, Manuel A., *Elementos de Higiene Privada, extracto de diversos autores*, Tipografía nacional de MN Corpancho, por J. Henrique del Campo, Lima, 1859, Pgs. 222-224.

Fuentes, Manuel A., *Lima or Sketches Of The Capital of Peru*, London, 1866, Pg. 146.

Heyerdahl, Thor, et. al., *Pyramids of Túcume*, Thames and Hudson, Great Britain, 1995, Pgs. 9-37 y 134-141.

Holliday, J.S., *Rush for Riches, Gold fever and the making of Calfornia*, University of California Press, 1999, Pgs. 60-61.

Hopkins, Albert A., *The Scientific America Cyclopedia of Formulas*, Scientific America Publishing Co., New York, 1910, 'Beverages - Alcoholic:' 'Arrack,' Pg. 227; 'Silver Sour,' Pg. 243; 'Punch,' Pg. 244; 'Gum Arabic Mucilage,' Pg. 318.

Huertas Vallejos, Lorenzo, "Producción de Vinos y sus derivados en Ica, Siglos XVI y XVII, Lima, 1988." Archivo General de la Nación, Lima; Protocolos Notariales de Ica, Pr. Nº99 del notario Francisco Nieto, 30 de Abril de 1613.

Jacobson, Pauline, *A Fire-Defying Landmark*. Article first published in *The Bulletin*, San Francisco, on May 4, 1912, Pg. 13. Reprinted in a small pamphlet of the same name which the Bank Exchange distributed as a gift to customers and associates.

Jacobson, Pauline, *City of The Golden Fifties*, University of California Press, 1941, Pg. 4.

Jarcho, Saul, *Quinine's Predecessor: Francesco Torti and the Early History of Chinchona*, Baltimore, John Hopkins University Press, 1933, Pg. 280.

Jones, Idwal, *Ark of Empire, San Francisco's Montgomery Block*, Doubleday & Company, Garden City, New York, 1951, Pg. 200.

Kipling, Rudyard, *Kipling's Letters from San Francisco*, San Francisco Colt Press, 1949.

Kipling, Rudyard, *From Sea to Sea*, March-September, 1889, Cap. XXIV, 1899.

Knox, Thomas. W., *The Underground World: a Mirror of Life Below the Surface, with vivid descriptions of the Hidden Works of Nature and Art...*, J.B. Burr, Hartford, Connecticut, 1886. Pg. 253, cited by H. Asbury, 1933.

Lawrence, Sidney, "The Ghirardelli Story," *California History*, Vol. 81, No. 2, 2002, Pg. 90.

Lecaros Cavero, Fernando, *Los Aguardientes de Ica, Estudio sobre su elaboración, origen de su nombre, etc.*, Biblioteca de la Revista Vinícola, Lima, 1936, Pg. 4.

Leslie, Frank, "Rambles in California," *Bew Family Magazine*, 1859. This article makes reference to a certain Hutchings, a *CalMagazine* writer in 1858.

Lick, Rosemary, *The Generous Miser, The Story of James Lick of California*, The Ward Ritchie Press, 1967.

Melville, Herman, *Billy Budd, Sailor And Other Stories*, "The Encantadas, Sketch Eight, Norfolk Isle and The Chola Widow," Penguin Books, New York, 1986, Pg. 106-121.

Monaghan, Jay, *Chile, Peru, and the California Gold Rush of 1849*, University of California Press, 1973, Pgs. 91-92.

Milla, Carlos, *Génesis de la Cultura Andina*, Colegio de Arquitectos del Perú, Lima, 1983.

Mugaburu, Joséphe, *Diario de Lima (1640-1694)*, Vol. II, Biblioteca Nacional, Imp. C. Vasquez L., Lima, 1935, Pgs. 94, 171, 172.

Munro-Fraser, J.P., *History of Sonoma County of California*, Alley, Bowen & Co., San Francisco, California, 1880, Pg. 54.

O'Brien, Robert, *This is San Francisco*, Whittlesey House, New York, 1948, Pgs. 39, 40.

Odgen, Adele, "Captain Henry Fitch, San Diego Merchant, 1825_1849," *The Journal of San Diego History*, Fall 1981, Vol. 27, No. 4.

Osio, Antonio María, *The History of Alta California, A Memoir of Mexican California*, translated by R.M. Beebe & R.M. Senkewicz, The University of Wisconsin Press, 1996.

Olympic Park Associates Newsletter, "The Legendary Elwha Salmon," Vol. 2, No. 3, December 1994, Everett, Washington.

Osorio, Mario, *En El Nombre*, Impresión Tecnim S.A., Lima, 1991.

Osorio, Mario, *Estructuras y observación chaupín*, Mario Osorio, Edición Nicol S.A., Lima, 1988.

Osorio, Mario, "El otro lado de la cumbre, The other side of Machupicchu," Lima, 2001.

Osorio, Mario, "Pir Ua, estructuras de observación," Lima, 1990.

Pitt, Leonard, *The Decline of the Californios*, University of California Press, Berkeley, 1984, Pgs. 110-112.

Richards, Rand, *Historic Walks in San Francisco*, Heritage House, San Francisco, 2002, Pg. 179.

Rodecape, Lois Foster, "Tom Maguire, Napoleon of the Stage," *California Historical Society Quarterly*, 20:308.

Ross, Harold, *Letters from the Editor - The New Yorker's Harold Ross*, edited by T. Kunkel, The Modern Library, New York, 2001, Pgs. 117-118.

Rossi Rubi, José (aka Hesperióphylo) "Idea de las diversiones públicas de Lima," *Mercurio Peruano*, No. 4, January 13, 1791.

Ryal Miller, Robert, *A Yankee Smuggler*, Santa Barbara Trust for Historical Preservation, Santa Barbara, California, 2001.

San Francisco City Directory - 1854, Foreign Consuls in San Francisco, Pg. 228.

San Francisco City Directory, 1900-1916.

San Francisco Chronicle, "The Ladies Came in By a Special Door," Millie's Column, June 12, 1959.

San Francisco Chronicle, "Talk of Pisco Punch Brought Mail With a Punch," Millie's Column, June 24, 1959.

San Francisco Chronicle, "Happy Memories of Pisco Punch," Millie's Column, June 8, 1960.

San Francisco - Telephone Directory - February 1903, The Pacific States Telephone and Telegraph Company, General Information, Pg. iv; 'B,' Pg. 13; 'N,' Pg. 192.

Sarmiento de Gamboa, Pedro, *Relación y Derrotero del Viaje y Descubrimiento del Estrecho de la Madre de Dios antes llamado de Magallanes*, Buenos Aires, 1950, Vol. I, Pg. 18.

Señán, José, *The Letters of José Señán, O.F.M., Mission San Buenaventura, 1796-1823*, L. Byrd S., The Ventura County Historical Society, John Howell Books, 1962.

Schultz, Christian, *Manual for the Manufacture of Cordials, Liquors, Fancy Syrups, &c. &c.*, 1862, recipe 350: 'Sirop de Gomme,' Pg. 199.

Shutes, Milton H., "Henry Wager Halleck," *California Historical Society*, 16:199, 1937.

Shumate, Albert, *Mariano Malarin - The life that spanned two cultures*, California History Center De Anza Collegue, 1980.

Thomas, Jerry, *How to Mix Drinks or The Bon-Vivants Companion*, New York, recipe 217: 'Brandy and Gum,' Pg. 82.

Twain, Mark, *Territorial Enterprise*, June 17-23, 1864, Virginia City, Nevada; "Mark Twain in the Metrópolis." Reprinted in "The Works of Mark Twain; Early Tales & Sketchers," Vol. 2 1864-1865, University of California Press, 1981, Pgs. 10-12. Section of the last paragraph of one of his articles.

Ward, Geoffrey C., et. al., *Mark Twain, An Illustrated Biography*, Alfred A. Knopf, New York, 2001, Pg. 54.

Werlich, David P., *Peru, A Short Story*, Southern Illinois University Press, Carbondale, 1978. Pg. 100.

Witt, Heinrich, *Diario 1824-1890,* Vol. I *(1824-1842),* Banco Mercantil, Lima, 1992.

Young, Daniel, *Young's Demostrative Translation of Scientific Secrets; or A Collection of Above 500 Useful Receipts on a Variety of Subjects,* '48: Cider without Apples,' '71: Pure Wine,' '80: Brandy from Oil Cognac,' Rowsell Ellis, Toronto, 1861.

Zapata Acha, Sergio, "Alimentos Tradicionales de la Cocina Peruana," *Boletín de Lima*, Vol. XXIII, No. 124, 2001, 'Pisco,' Pg. 42.

Illustrations

All the photos and illustrations by the author, in the author's private collection, or as indicated below:

Pg. 11 ("Bonanza Kings," Louis Macouillard), –Published with permission of Wells Fargo Bank, N.A.

Pgs. 14 (left) (LC-USZ62-130410), 14-15 (center) (LC-USZ62-132171), 23 (HABS CAL,38-SANFRA,6), 27 (top) (LC-USZ62-28851), 53 (LC-USZC4-1578, partial view, numerated by the author), 151 (LC-USZ62-27048), 152 (HABS CAL,38-SANFRA,1-) –Courtesy of the Library of the Congress, Prints & Photographs Division.

Pgs. 24 (1905.17500,S1,SS1,V6:101, partial view), 29 (190 5.17500,S1,SS1,V2:100), 35/34 (1992.036,:51), 39 (bottom) (1963.002:0618), 64/65 (top) (1963.002:1473, partial view), 85 (1963.002:0145 –redigitized and relocated text), 115 ("Land Case Map E-905, Landscape Maps Collection"), 171 (1963:002:1464, partial view) –Courtesy of the Bancroft Library, University of California, Berkeley.

Pgs. 27 (bottom), 40 (top), 117 (top), 137, 139 (bottom) –Courtesy of the San Francisco History Center, San Francisco Public Library.

Pg. 32 ("Mariano Malarin," Leonardo Barbieri, 1852-1853, M. Roca collection) –Published with permission of de Saisset Museum, University of Santa Clara, California.

Pg. 61 ("'Trying out tallow,' pencil and watercolor, William Rich Hutton, ca. 1848, HM 43214 #61") –Courtesy of The Huntington Library, San Marino, California.

Pgs. 95, 106 (top and bottom) –Photo NASA.

Pg. 97 –Eduardo Herrán Producciones, © 1985.

Pgs. 117 (bottom), 118, 122 (top) –Photos by the author, published with permission of the Monterey County Historical Society.

Pg. 149 ("Chart of the Voyage of the Apollo, SFM/HDC29. F89-061/1849") –Courtesy of the San Francisco Maritime National Historical Park.

Pg. 65 (bottom) –Portolá Expedition Foundation, © 1971.

Pgs. 67 (top) (Paez, 1773) y 68 (Trousset, 1879) –Mission Carmel, California.

Pgs. 21 (top) y 70 –Museo Naval de Madrid.

Pg. 63 (Paret y Alcázar, 1770) –Museo del Prado, Madrid.

Index

Abascal, Viceroy of Peru 158

Acho, Lima, bullring 73, 128, 152, 153

Andean civilization 93, 94, 95, 96, 104

Alsop & Co. 158

Alta California, region 32, 60, 68, 72, 73, 125

Alvarado, Carmen 30

Alvarado, Dominga 30

Antúnez de Mayolo, Santiago 94, 98

Apollo, ship 149

Arawi, Andean human group 96

Arequipa
>   map *Corregimiento* of 105
>   and Moquehua wine 103, 104, 105, 106

Arica, port 105

Arrack, punch 128, 167, 168

Asbury, Herbert 14, 15, 21, 57, 191

Atahualpa, Inca 103

Ayllar, brothers 96, 99

Ballot box, San Francisco's first election 153, 156

Bandini, Juan 118, 119, 120, 121, 155

Bank Exchange 10, 11, 13, 14, 15, 20, 21, 22, 23, 24, 26,
>   28, 29, 31, 37, 47, 48, 53, 55, 74, 75, 82, 83, 84, 86,
>   133, 136, 137, 138, 139, 141, 142, 143, 159, 164, 165,
>   167, 169, 176, 177, 178, 179, 180, 181, 182, 183, 186
>   inauguration announcement 180

Bank Exchange (continued)
    advertisements 168, 182
    champagne cocktails 84
    definition 143
    of Sacramento 141
    site before it was built 53
Bank Saloon 179
Bear Flag Revolt 150
Behring, Vitus 63
Benicia, city 125
Bitters, drink 112
Blas Valera, chronicler 96, 104
Bodega
    Bay 20
    Rancho 123, 125
Bodega, city 123
Bodega y Quadra, port 71, 72
Bodega y Quadra, Francisco de la 20, 21, 62, 68, 70, 72
Boronda, Casa 62, 116
Botija perulera 102, 104
Brannan, Samuel 37, 38, 39, 40, 41, 53
    illustration of house 40, 53
Brown & Perkins Liquor Saloon 183
Brown, George A. 181, 183
Brown, John H. 46, 47, 48, 53, 148, 149, 150, 151, 152, 153, 154, 155, 167, 169, 181
    illustration City Hotel 48, 53
Buck & Breck, recipe 164
Buckley, Christopher 186, 187
Bull and bear fights 72, 73, 152

Cajamarca, city 100
Calderon, ship 148
California Star, newspaper 38, 40, 53
Californio(s) 32, 113, 117, 118, 119, 121, 123, 125, 150
Callao, port 60, 100, 103, 149, 166, 229
Canary Islands 50

Canepa, Andrew 30
Cañizares, José de 71
Caravantes, Marquis 50
Carmel, Mission 66, 67, 70, 71, 72
Castilla, Ramon 146, 160
Cavenecia, José 60
Charles III, King 62, 63
Charqui, (beef jerky) 121
Cherub's wings, shavings of 15, 191
Chicha 32, 92, 93, 101, 102, 104, 124
Chicha of pineapple 32, 124
Chincha, islands 106, 158, 159
Chinchon, Viceroy of Peru, Count of 110, 111
Chinchona, herb 110
Chinook (King salmon) 72
Chiuda, Stephen V. 84
Chiuda, Vladimir 84
Chola Hunilla 78, 79
Chullo, vicuña hat 61
Cieza de Leon, Pedro, chronicler 92
City Hotel 48, 53, 148, 155
Coca Cola 21, 178
Coloma, mountains of 146
Columbus Street, construction and change 137, 181
Cordova, port 71, 72
Cornejo, Miguel 103, 104
Cot, Juan José 60
Croix, Viceroy of Mexico, Marquis Françoise de la 63, 64
Croix, Viceroy of Peru, Federico de 71

Daniel O'Connell, ship 115, 116
Delmira, brigantine 116
Dorman, Orrin 176

Elias, Domingo 76, 159, 160
    illustration 159

Elwha, river 72

Field, Charles, doggerel 14
Finley & Johnson 148
Fitch, Captain Henry 115
Fort Ross 123
Fort Sutter, distillery 46, 47
Forty-niners 20
Fritz, Al 187
Fuca, Juan de, strait 70
Fuentes, Manuel Atanasio 72, 179

Galapagos, islands 79
Galen 110, 111
Gamarra, brigantine of war 146, 147
Ghirardelli, Domingo 30, 32, 33, 34, 35, 41, 53
    first house 34, 53
    chocolate factory photo 35
Ghirardelli, Domingo Jr. 35
Gold Street 38
    meaning 38
Gold Rush 20, 21, 30, 37, 38, 39, 40, 107, 146, 150, 156,
    sea route during 149
Granda, Chabuca 171
Grape
    different species of 50
    native to California 50
    first introduction to Peru 50
Guaman Poma de Ayala 93, 96
Guano 41, 49, 158, 159, 160
Gum arabic 134, 135, 136, 138, 145, 154, 161, 163, 164,
    185, 186, 187, 194
Gum syrup 175, 186, 194

Hacer las once 32, 123, 156, 157, 169
Halleck, Captain Henry 52, 54, 112, 113
Hartnell, William 60, 62, 121

Hotaling & Co. 14, 15
Hounds, attack of the 146, 147
Huancavelica, mercury mines 105
Huascar, ship 60
Huaynaputina, volcano explosion 106

Ica, production of wine region 49, 71, 102, 103, 106, 159
Inca Roca 92

Jackson Street 38, 39, 52
Jackson and Washington, alley between streets 52
Jacobson, Pauline 13, 21, 181
John Begg & Co. 58, 59, 60, 121
Judah, Mrs., actress 169

Kearney Street 31, 47, 137
Kilduff & Co. 136, 166, 176, 180, 181
Kipling, Rudyard 15, 191

Lannes, John 23, 25, 48, 49, 50, 175, 176, 178, 179
Larco Avenue 171
Larco, Nicholas 30, 34, 52, 53, 165, 166, 167, 169, 171
        pisco seizure 165, 166, 169
        office 34, 53
        San Francisco view from his mansion 171
Las once (see *hacer las once*)
Lasuen, Friar Fermin Francisco 68, 69, 70
Leonora, ship 115
Lick, James 30, 32, 33, 37, 38, 39, 40, 41, 42, 43, 44, 53
        adobe house 53
        astronomic observatory 42, 44
        buying lots in San Francisco 38
        mansion photo 43
        mill photo 43
Lima 30, 32, 33, 35, 58, 60, 67, 73, 104, 107, 108, 112, 116,
        121, 124, 128, 152, 153, 154, 171, 181
        capital of South America in the 17th century 107

Lima (continued)
    City of the Kings 107, 108
    poets and writters of the 17th century 107
    wealth in the 17th century 107
Lime 53, 84, 85, 123, 124, 153, 154, 156, 161, 162, 163, 164, 173, 176. 193, 195
Lime syrup 153, 154, 156

Maguire, Tom 28, 29, 137, 156, 167, 169, 181
    Opera House 28, 29, 137, 167
Malarin, Juan 32, 33, 41, 118, 121, 122
Malarin, Mariano 32, 122
    portrait painting 32
Malarin, Paula 122
Mandarina, ship 165
Mansion House 151, 152
Mark Twain 26, 27, 28, 29
Matt recipes 161, 162, 163, 164
Mazeppa, ship 30
McCulloch & Hartnell 60
McCulloch, John 60
Meiggs, Henry 181
Meiggs, John 181
Melville, Herman 78, 79
Miranda-Briones, family 128
Mission Dolores 150, 151, 152
    photo 151
    illustration of bullfight 152
Monterey 32, 57, 58, 59, 64, 68, 72, 117
    Customs House , photo 58
    Customs House , illustration 59
    bay, illustration 64, 65
    Presidio of 72
    simplification of Spanish name 58
Monterey County Historical Society 116, 117, 118
Montgomery, Captain John 45, 46

Montgomery Street 15, 21, 22, 38, 39, 45, 51, 53, 75, 84
        bordering the coast 53
        intersection with Washington Street 22, 75
Montgomery Block 14, 15, 23, 25, 28, 37, 39, 52, 53, 142,
        143, 176
        commemorative plaque 37
Morris, Victor 48, 49, 50, 86, 154
Murcilla, Captain Andres 115

Napoleon III 76
Niantic, ship 18, 21
Nicol, deaf-mute helper 15, 49, 75
Nicol, Duncan 15, 21, 23, 24, 25, 48, 55, 56, 57, 75, 80, 82,
        83, 84, 85, 88, 133, 135, 137, 138, 139, 140, 157, 175,
        176, 177, 179, 183, 185, 186, 187, 188, 189, 191, 193
        photo 24, 137, 188
Nicol, Mary 49
Nootka, island 70

O'Brien, Robert 20, 21
Olympic, peninsula 72
Once (see *hacer las once*)
Osorio, Mario 96, 97, 98
Oyagüe, Captain José María 60

Pacheco, Isidora 122
Paez, José, painter 67
Paita, port 21, 79, 115, 142, 144
Panama Canal 149
Parker, George F. 28, 165, 166, 167, 169, 176, 181, 182
Parker, Thomas B. 166, 167, 168, 181, 182
Parker House 156, 167
Pearl Harbor, discovery 72, 73
Pedro Manuel *El Griego*, first producer of pisco 49, 106
Pedrorena, Miguel de la 60, 116
Perez, Juan 70

Perkins, George F. 181, 182

Peru 20, 30, 32, 33, 37, 41, 46, 49, 50, 58, 60, 61, 71, 72,
      86, 91, 98, 100, 102, 103, 104, 107, 110, 112, 114,
      115, 116, 119, 120, 121, 122, 123, 128, 142, 143, 145,
      147, 149, 157, 158, 159, 161, 165, 169, 171, 173, 181
      name definition 104

Peruvian Bark 110, 111, 112, 116

Phillip II, King 50

Pineapple 25, 32, 124, 157, 169, 170, 175, 186, 193, 194, 195
      chicha (see *chicha* of pineapple)
      in San Francisco 170
      origin 169

Pines, bay of 64, 65, 68

Pisco, port 102, 103

Pisco, valley 106

Pisco
      advertisements of sale 31, 148, 168
      effects when drinking 72, 73
      Bank Exchange advertisements of 168, 182
      first manufacturing 49
      Italia type 115, 148, 193
      saving a live 78, 79
      versatility of 86, 161

Pisco John 16, 20, 23, 48, 75, 83, 84, 85, 137, 138, 139,
      140, 176, 181, 191
      reason of nickname 138

Pisco Punch 14, 15, 17, 19, 20, 21, 22, 23, 25, 27, 49, 55,
      56, 57, 74, 75, 76, 77, 82, 83, 84, 85, 86, 101, 112,
      122, 127, 128, 131, 133, 134, 135, 136, 138, 140, 146,
      154, 157, 161, 162, 163, 174, 175, 177, 178, 181, 187,
      189, 191, 193,
      effect when drinking 17, 20, 25
      popularity in San Francisco 57, 75
      recipe 193

Pisco Sour 19, 86, 140, 154, 161, 163, 173, 175
      de la Moscorra's, recipe 16
      origin 154

Pisko container 102, 104

Pizarro, Francisco 103, 147

Pizarro, Pedro, chronicler 100

Polhemus, Charles, Peruvian Consul 142, 145, 157, 158,
        161, 165, 166

Ponchos, imported from Peru 115

Portolá, Gaspar de la 64, 65

Portsmouth, brigantine of war 152

Portsmouth Square 45, 46, 47, 53

Potosi, silver mines 104, 105

Port of the Kings 65

Presidios of Alta California 72, 73, 119

Princess Royal, ship 70

Punch

        origin 128

        milk 53, 128, 151, 152, 153, 163

        milk, recipe 163

Quimper, Captain Manuel 62, 68, 69, 70, 72, 73

Quina, tree 111, 116

Quipucamalloc 96

Rancho del Rey 116

Ridley, Robert 53, 54, 113, 114, 126, 127, 148, 150, 151, 152,
        153, 156, 167, 181

Ross, Harold 162

Saccsaywaman 99

Sacramento, city 140, 141, 142

Sacramento, gold in rivers of 41

Salinas, city 116, 122

San Blas, port 70

San Carlos Borromeo del Río Carmelo, Mission 66

San Carlos, ship 71

San Diego, city 64, 71, 115

San Diego de Alcalá, Mission 64

San Francisco
 discovery of the bay 65
 earthquake and fire of 1906 13, 14, 15
 first map of the bay 20
 first map of streets 115
 illustration of old coast 18, 53
 Public Library 81, 82, 85, 115, 133, 177
San Marcos University, Lima 32, 41, 121
Samson and Delilah, painting 26, 137, 181
Santa Rosa de Chualar, rancho 122
Santa Rosa of Lima, painting 67
Sarmiento y Gamboa, Pedro 102, 103
Serra, Friar Junípero 64, 66, 67, 68, 69, 71, 82
Silver Sour 154
Simple syrup 135
Smith, Captain Stephen 53, 123, 124, 125, 153, 156
Smith-Torres, rancho 125
Snug, bar 137
Sonora, ship 20
Spence, David 121, 122
Stidger, Oliver Perry 23, 25
 saving Montgomery Block 25
Stockton, General 118
Sugar syrup 135, 136

Tallow 59, 60, 61, 69, 115, 159
 commerce 60
 illustration collecting 61
Telegraph Hill 14
Tiabaya and Socabaya, vineyards 103
Tiahuanaco 99
Tom Sawyer 28, 30
Torrence, John 27, 29, 30, 144, 166, 167, 168, 169, 176, 181, 182
Torres, family 123
Torres, Manuela 124, 125, 153
Torres, María "Manonga" 123, 125, 127, 128, 142, 156

Transamerica Pyramid, building 21, 22, 34, 37, 48

Vallejo, city 125
Vallejo, General Mariano Guadalupe 125
Vancouver, Captain George 70, 72
Vancouver
        city 72
        island 70, 71
Vicuña hats 61, 115
Vin Mariani 178
Vioget, Captain Jean Jacques 53, 113, 115, 116, 117, 123,
        126, 151, 181
        bar 116, 151
        illustration of house 53
        photo 117
Vizcaíno, Navigator Sebastían 64, 65
Volstead, Act 21, 86, 179

Washington Street 21, 22, 31, 39, 47, 48, 52, 75
Washington and Kearney, street intersection 31, 47
Wine, 16th century commercial routes of 104, 105

Yerba Buena (San Francisco), El Paraje de la 113, 114,
        115, 116, 124, 128

Addendum

Revisiting San Francisco's Pisco Punch - An Essay

Foreword

Ever since I wrote the first manuscript based on my research about Pisco Punch, I was encouraged by many to write a paper for one of the California historical societies. After a long set of trials and tribulations –that lasted more than three years– instead I made the decision of publishing it in the form of a fantasious pseudo-fictional historical novel, based as accurately as possible in factual historical evidence. I thought that presenting it in that way could result in the most entertaining reading, better suited for any casual person not familiar with the history of San Francisco's famous punch. Having published it in that form in the Spanish edition of *Wings of Cherubs* and now in its English version, I feel it is appropriate to present the most important aspects of my research in a way that could be regarded perhaps as being more erudite. The target audience will be those readers and cocktail history researchers that are familiar with the currently accepted notions about the history of Pisco Punch and those who are curious enough to spend more time reading something that is somewhat less entertaining. I have decided to include here, as an addendum to the English version of *Wings of Cherubs*, an essay that highlights what I feel are my most important historical discoveries and conclusions about San Francisco's mysterious concoction. This essay has been, finally, presented to a Californian historical society for publication in a summarized version.

Introduction

Being a Peruvian-born, long time resident of the great Bay Area and a longer time fan of pisco, it is no wonder I became so interested in the famous legend of the Pisco Punch of San Francisco. For six years, I have been investigating trying to answer the questions that could explain why the centuries-old Peruvian pisco brandy was so well liked in these far away shores. As I immersed myself deeper into the research, and much to my surprise, something became very evident. I found that many of the well reputed historical sources that were published about Pisco Punch did not agree and sometimes presented significant contradictions regarding, for example, who had invented the recipe; who were the original founders of the Bank Exchange and Billiard Saloon –the celebrated bar founded in 1853 where the famous concoction was served until 1919; who were its owners prior to Duncan Nicol, the last link in a long chain of succession of owners. Because of the confusion, I decided to take a different approach and prepared myself to start from zero and as it is said, to pick the matter with a very fine tooth comb. I present this article showing the results of my findings that, in my opinion, are surprising in many respects.

The Bank Exchange and Billiard Saloon

A thorough research of old San Francisco newspapers, city directories and other sources revealed that Idwal Jones was mistaken when he wrote in 1951 that the founding proprietors of the Bank Exchange were George Parker and John Torrence. In his colorful book *Ark of Empire*, Jones places these two men tending at the Bank Exchange during the opening night of the Montgomery Block on December 23, 1853.[1] My research revealed that the original owners of the Bank Exchange was a partnership named P.D. Kilduff & Co., as posted in an advertisement published in the *Daily Alta* of Monday, on December 19, 1853 (see page 180).

This discovery, which I believed was significant, was later corroborated in the addendum of the San Francisco City Directory of 1853 which listed *Kilduff P D, Bank Exchange, 162 Montgomery, h 34 Virginia street* and by the directory of 1854 in the 'Appendix – Directory of Buildings, Montgomery Block' section as *No. 166 Bank Exchange, P.D. KILLDUFF & Co., Proprietors.* A newspaper article titled "Cocktail Years Ago" published by the *San Francisco Examiner* in January 13, 1889, mentions that the Bank Exchange *was opened by John Meiggs and Pat Kilduff* giving light to the name of the other partner.

Further research showed that P.D. Killduff arrived in San Francisco from New York around the Horn on board the *SS Tennessee* on April 14, 1850. He also appears on a list of passengers arriving in San Francisco aboard the *SS California* on October 4, 1857. He was a member of San Francisco's Fire Department Sansome Hook and Ladder Co. No. 3 in 1855 and 1856. The San Francisco City Directory of 1875 lists a Killduff P.D. as a keeper of a saloon living at 1016 Market street. It is not known what was Killduff's influence and legacy in the future legend of the Bank Exchange and Pisco Punch, but his existence certainly raises questions about the accuracy of the currently accepted sources of the history of the bar.

John Meiggs was City Controller of San Francisco in 1854 but he is probably better known for being the brother of Henry "Honest Harry" Meiggs.[2] Both arrived from Catskill, New York, in 1849, and traded in the lumber business. On October 6, 1854, both men and their families sailed suddenly and without notice to South America. Henry Meiggs had just finished building a wharf –today known as Fisherman's Wharf– according to many using questionable financing practices. Stellman writes in 1922: *'Honest Harry' Meiggs and his brother, the newly-elected City Controller, had sailed away on the yacht American, leaving behind them an unpaid-for 2000-foot wharf and close to a million in debts; forged city warrants and promissory notes were held by practically every large business house in San Francisco.*[3] Henry Meiggs died in 1877 in Lima, Peru, a wealthy man, after being contracted by the Peruvian Government to build more than 700 miles of railroad tracks in the Andes, among other enterprises. No further records have been found of John Meiggs, but some information states that a John G. Meiggs built railroads in Argentina during the late 1880s.

After the Meiggs' sailed to South America during early October of 1854, the partnership of Kilduff and Co. is dissolved and the Bank Exchange is sold. Pauline Jacobson gives an insight of who becomes one of its owners after John Meiggs departure. She writes that soon after October 24, 1854: *Jerry Bryant, who had struck up a boon companionship with Orrin Dorman, one of the proprietors of the Bank Exchange saloon, induced Dorman to sell out his interest to John Torrence...*[1] Dorman, a career actor, also held other theatrical interests with Torrence, one being the San Francisco Minstrels which eventually became the famous Maguire's Opera House. In addition to Jacobson's assertion that John Torrence was not an original founder of the Bank Exchange, there is also another strong reason to believe so. On December 24, 1853, just the next day after the opening of the Bank Exchange, the Metropolitan Theater was inaugurated. John Torrence was one of its proprietors. Undoubtedly, it is the readiness of what was the largest and most elegant theater in the State what must have taken all of Torrence's energy and attention.[5] Torrence keeps his interest in the theater until January 1864 when he sells his share to a William H. Lyon.[6]

Jones' error and several other contradictions written by other authors concerning the early and later proprietors of the Bank Exchange led me to do a more detailed research. Several sources, such as the *Daily Alta* and *Bulletin* newspapers as well as San Francisco city directories spanning from 1854 to 1921, were patiently reviewed. It became clear that Jacobson's findings of 1912 to 1916 were the most accurate of all the historical sources that are available. That is not surprising, since she was a contemporary of Duncan Nicol and had the chance to interview him and other people that frequented the Bank Exchange. I also discovered a couple of things Jacobson did not report, one being the complete name of the *man named Brown* who she wrote was one of the last owners of the Bank Exchange prior to Duncan Nicol.[7]

The table in the next page shows the results of my findings and lists the names of all the proprietors of the Bank Exchange since its inauguration in 1853 through its closing in

Bank Exchange Proprietors	Years	
Kilduff & Co. (1)	1853 - 1854	n/a
John Torrence & Thomas B. Parker	1855(?) - 1859	a, b, c
Thomas B. Parker & Co. (2)	1859	d
John Torrence	1860	e
John Torrence & George F. Parker	1861	f
George F. Parker	1862 - 1875	g, h
George A. Brown & George F. Perkins (3)	1876 - 1885	n/a
George A. Brown	1886	n/a
George A. Brown & Duncan Nicol (4)	1887 - 1892	n/a
Duncan Nicol	1893 - 1919	n/a
John Lannes (5)	1920	n/a

(1) According to Pauline Jacobson, Orrin Dorman is part owner until the end of 1854 when he transfers his share to John Torrence.

(2) As shown in an advertisement published in the *1859 San Francisco Almanac*. The *San Francisco City Directory* for the same year lists and advertises *Thomas B. Parker & John Torrence* as owners (see Figure 2c and 2d).

(3) Bank Exchange is not listed in the San Francisco city directories from 1879 to 1885. But the locale is listed as *Brown & Perkins, Liquor Saloon* for that period.

(4) Bank Exchange owners listed as *Brown & Duncan* in 1887 and in 1888. Duncan Nicol listed as *Nicol Duncan (Brown & Duncan), r. 1709 Jones* for those two years.

(5) Bank Exchange and Duncan Nicol not listed in the *1920 San Francisco City Directory*. John Lannes listed as *mgr Bank Ex.* Neither the Bank Exchange, Duncan Nicol nor John Lannes are listed in the *1921 San Francisco City Directory*.

BANK EXCHANGE AND BILLIARD SALOON,
Corner of Washington and Montgomery Sts., San Francisco.

We have constantly on hand and for sale, Billiard Balls, Cloths, Cues, Cue Wax, Cue Cutters, Cue Chalk, Cue Points, Fifteen Ball Pool, with Racks and Triangles, &c. Balls Turned and Colored.

☞ The BAR will be found at all times supplied with

THE MOST CHOICE WINES AND LIQUORS.

JOHN TORRENCE,
THOS. B. PARKER. |
TORRENCE & PARKER, *Proprietors.*

a

BANK EXCHANGE AND BILLIARD SALOON
Corner of Washington and Montgomery Sts., San Francisco

TORRENCE & PARKER,
DEALERS IN
Billiard Balls, Cloths, Leathers, Cues, Cue Wax, Pool Balls,
Rondo Balls, &c. Balls Turned and Colored. Also, Choice Wines and Liquors, Wholesale and Retail.
JOHN TORRENCE.
THOMAS B. PARKER.

b

BANK EXCHANGE
— AND —
BILLIARD SALOON,
CORNER OF
Washington and Montgomery Streets
SAN FRANCISCO.

TORRENCE & PARKER,
DEALERS IN
Billiard Balls, Cloths, Leathers,
CUES, CUE WAX, POOL BALLS, RONDO BALLS, ETC.

JOHN TORRENCE.  THOMAS B. PARKER.

ALSO, ON HAND AND FOR SALE.
OLD LONDON DOCK BRANDIES,
CUTTER'S OLD BOURBON WHISKY.
PORT WINES, SHERRIES,
AND ALL THE CHOICEST BRANDS OF
CHAMPAGNE,
Apple Jack, Pisco, Arrac, Cordials, Liquors,
ETC. ETC. ETC.

COPIES OF PHELAN'S GAME OF BILLIARDS.
BALLS TURNED AND COLORED.

c

BANK EXCHANGE,
Corner Montgomery and Washington streets
SAN FRANCISCO.

THOMAS B. PARKER & CO,
Have constantly on hand and for sale at Wholesale and Retail,
**Old London Dock Brandies, Port Wines
Sherries,**
And all the choicest brands
CHAMPAGNE, Apple Jack, Pisco, Arrac
Cordials, Liquors, etc., etc.
—ALSO—
Billiard Balls, Cloths, Cues, Cue Points, Cue Wax, Chalk, Pool
and Rondo Balls, Cue Cutters, Pool Bottles, &c.
COPIES OF
Phelan's Game of Billiards.

d

BANK EXCHANGE
— AND —
BILLIARD SALOON,
CORNER OF
Washington and Montgomery Streets
SAN FRANCISCO.

JOHN TORRENCE
DEALER IN
Billiard Balls, Cloths, Leathers
CUES, CUE-WAX, POOL BALLS, RONDO BALLS, ETC.
ALSO, ON HAND AND FOR SALE,
OLD LONDON DOCK BRANDIES
CUTTER'S OLD BOURBON WHISKY,
PORT WINES, SHERRIES,
APPLE JACK,
PISCO, ARRAC
CORDIALS,
LIQUORS,
Together with all the
Choicest Brands of
CHAMPAGNE,
ETC. ETC. ETC.
COPIES OF PHELAN'S GAME OF BILLIARDS
BALLS TURNED AND COLORED.

e

BANK EXCHANGE,
—BY—
TORRENCE & PARKER,
MONTGOMERY BLOCK,
S. E. Corner Montgomery and Washington Streets,

The BANK EXCHANGE contains a spacious and magnificently furnished

BILLIARD ROOM,
Phelan's Best Tables,
A BAR, at which the choicest
LIQUORS AND WINES
WHOLESALE WINE AND LIQUOR STORE,

☞ The Proprietors also beg a pleasure in stating that they are the
SOLE AGENTS FOR THE PACIFIC COAST
FOR THE CELEBRATED
J. H. Cutter's OLD BOURBON WHISKEY.
JOHN TORRENCE.
GEO. F. PARKER

f

BANK EXCHANGE
—BY—
GEORGE F. PARKER,
MONTGOMERY BLOCK,
S. E. Corner Montgomery and Washington Sts,
SAN FRANCISCO.

The BANK EXCHANGE contains a spacious and magnificently furnished

BILLIARD ROOM
Phelan's Best Tables,
A BAR, at which the choicest
LIQUORS AND WINES
WHOLESALE WINE AND LIQUOR STORE,

☞ The Proprietor also begs a pleasure in stating that he is the
SOLE AGENT FOR THE PACIFIC COAST FOR THE CELEBRATED
J. H. CUTTER'S OLD BOURBON WHISKY.
GEO. F. PARKER.

g

BANK EXCHANGE
—BY—
GEORGE F. PARKER,
MONTGOMERY BLOCK
cor. Montgomery and Washington Streets

The BANK EXCHANGE
Contains the most Magnificently Furnished and most Commodious
BILLIARD ROOM
IN THE UNITED STATES,
WHICH IS SUPPLIED WITH TEN OF
Phelan's Best Tables,
A BAR, at which the choicest
LIQUORS & WINES
WINE AND LIQUOR STORE,

☞ The Proprietor also feels a pleasure in stating that he is the
SOLE AGENT FOR THE PACIFIC COAST FOR THE CELEBRATED
J. H. CUTTER'S OLD BOURBON WHISKY,
GEO. F. PARKER.

h

January 1920. Unfortunately, it appears that San Francisco did not publish a city directory in 1855, thus the impossibility to verify the Bank Exchange ownership for that year. Facsimile copies of all the Bank Exchange advertisements published in the San Francisco city directories are shown on page 227. The letters shown in the last column of the table are used to correlate the advertisements published in those years. The letters 'n/a' indicate that I could not find any Bank Exchange advertisements for that period of time.

The reason for Jones' oversight may now become evident. He may have assumed the partnership of John Torrence and George Parker, shown in the 1861 San Francisco City Directory, occurred since the saloon's opening in 1853, when in reality Torrence's participation started late in 1854 or 1855 and with Thomas B. Parker instead.

The period between 1859 and 1861 marks an interesting transitional period in which the saloon's ownership is transferred from John Torrence & Thomas Parker, to John Torrence & George Parker, to eventually just George Parker. 1859-1860 is a curious period because according to the advertisements both John Torrence and Thomas Parker claim to be the sole proprietors of the saloon (advertisements d and e).

The total tenure of John Torrence as owner or co-owner of the Bank Exchange was six years, from late 1854 to 1861, and being the sole proprietor only in 1860. Again, Jones is mistaken when he writes that John Torrence managed the Bank Exchange *for long years*. At least relatively speaking, since Torrence's six year total tenure was very short as compared to George F. Parker's fifteen, George A. Brown's sixteen and Duncan Nicol's thirty two.

Herbert Asbury is also mistaken when in 1933 he writes that Duncan Nicol invented Pisco Punch and that it was the most popular drink of San Francisco in the 1870s.[8] As it turns out, Duncan Nicol worked at the Bank Exchange only since 1887. Furthermore, the famous Button Punch, which was served to Rudyard Kipling in 1889,[9] and the predecessor of Pisco Punch according to Idwal Jones, was rendered during the senior tenure of George A. Brown. Kipling's writings of 1889, where he describes his sensations when trying a Button Punch, mentions that the punch was served by a German bartender. Further research have failed to confirm if George A. Brown was German but some sources mention that Duncan Nicol was a native of Scotland.

Bronson, author of the landmark article "Secrets of Pisco Punch Revealed" published by the California Historical Society in 1973, mentions that the secret recipe of Pisco Punch was given to Duncan Nicol by John Torrence and Orrin Dorman and that both were the prior owners of the Bank Exchange.[10] This is also in error for several reasons, one being that the prior owners of the Bank Exchange before Duncan Nicol were George A. Brown and George F. Perkins, which together with the prior ownership of George F. Parker, lasted a long twenty five years. Secondly, John Torrence died in 1885, making it impossible for him to give Duncan Nicol the recipe during his tenure at the Bank

Exchange.[11] John Torrence was the owner of the Bank Exchange twenty six years before Duncan Nicol and Orrin Dorman was thirty three before, during his very short tenure. Transfer of any "secret recipe" after so many years, in such a hard drinking town as San Francisco was in those days is a highly unlikely possibility. Probably following Asbury's writings, Bronson also mentions that Duncan Nicol presided over the Bank Exchange since the 1870s which, as mentioned before, is not the case.

Pisco in San Francisco

Having clarified the historical sequence of owners of the Bank Exchange and the ownership tenures since 1853 to 1920, I will now turn to the history of pisco brandy's presence in San Francisco. But before, I will present a short description and history of the Peruvian brandy.

The European grape (Vitis vinifera) was first introduced by the Spanish Conquistadors in Peru in the mid 1500s. One of the most suitable places for its cultivation was found to be the Ica valley, 180 miles south of Lima. Ica wine production started shortly after and wine was distributed in great amounts along all Spanish possessions on the Pacific Coast. Pisco brandy was first distilled in the Ica valley in the early 1600s or possibly in the late 1500s. In 1614, King Phillip II, persuaded by Spanish wine producers, ordered the banning of wine production in all Peru. This order, which was only partially brought to practice, caused an increase in the efforts for producing brandy. Possibly for the purpose of speeding the manufacturing and the commercial process, pisco was distilled from the recently fermented musts of grape.

Strictly speaking pisco is not a brandy, which is distilled from wine. Pisco is distilled before the grape must has turned into wine and when it still contains a significant content of the grape sugar. Scholten writes in 1997 that pisco is: *a pommace brandy, produced from the residual grape skins, seeds, stems, and pulp remaining after fermented wine is pressed off...*[12] That is not correct, pisco is made with the same pure grape musts that wines and brandies are made of, being the only difference that it is distilled before the must has turned completely into wine.

Over the centuries, pisco brandy spread over South America, it was initially shipped from the port of Pisco in the region of Ica, Peru, thus the reason for its name. Today pisco is considered the national liquor of Peru and Chile, although they are manufactured differently.[13]

The first documented importation of pisco to California comes from San Diego merchant Henry Delano Fitch, who in July 21, 1830, brings on board his ship *Leonora* from Callao, Peru, great quantities of sugar and *piscos de aguardiente de Ica* [pisco brandy from Ica].[14]

IO41

Illustrations of the early 1600s by Guaman Poma de Ayala showing the city port of Pisco and the neighboring towns of Nazca and Ica in Peru. Notice the large amounts of grape vines and birds depicted ("pisko" means bird in the Quechua language). The descriptive Spanish text mentions the region of Ica as having *the best wine in the kingdom which is inexpensive and as abundant as water.*

The first historical record of pisco imported to San Francisco comes from the memoirs of one of its first residents, William Heath Davis, who writes: *In 1839, early in the year, the brig 'Daniel O'Connell,' an English vessel, arrived at Yerba Buena* [San Francisco] *from Payta, Peru, ... having on board a considerable quantity of pisco or italia a fine delicate liquor manufactured at a place called Pisco.*[15] In order to clarify the naming of the liquor as mentioned by Davis, in those days Peru produced two types of pisco: regular pisco and pisco type Italia, or simply called Italia, which was made from the aromatic Italia grape, also known in San Francisco as *La Rosa del Peru* (The Rose from Peru). Italia type pisco was contained in 3 gallons small clay jars called *pisquitos*, while regular pisco came in 15-25 gallons *botija perulera* or *pisko* (see figures in pages 102 and 104).[16] The latter was sometimes also transported in barrels.

The sale of pisco in San Francisco was advertised in early 1849, several months before the arrival of the first ship carrying gold miners from the East Coast. It was published by the firm of Wright & Owen in the *Alta California* several times between January and March of 1849 announcing the sale of several goods. Both types of pisco were advertised. They arrived in the cargo of the Peruvian ships *Susana* and *Calderon*. The pisco type Italia came in jars and was identified as *italian pisco*, suggesting an Italian origin of the brandy, which is not the case. Wright & Owen announced the sale of their products at their store *on the corner of Washington and Kearney streets, sign of the cigar factory*, one block away from where the Bank Exchange will be built five years later. On March 8, 1849, the advertisement was published in the front page of the *Alta California* (see page 31).

Another set of advertisements were found in the *Alta California*. They were published by the firm of Finley, Johnson & Co. in November 23, 1848 and January 9, 1849. This time the pisco was identified just as Italia, which as said before, was the name given in Peru in those days for pisco made of Italia grapes. The liquor came in the cargo of the Peruvian ships *Correo de Cobija* and *Calderon*. Pisco and Italia were very visible in San Francisco during the 1849 Gold Rush, to the extent that many a gold miner from the East Coast tried pisco for the very first time in a San Francisco saloon.[17]

NEW GOODS FOR SALE.

EX Coreo de Cobija. Prints, poncho cloth, blankets, flannels, silk bandas, cotton hdkfs, toweling, over coats, pants, vests, woolen shirts, regatta do, socks, boots and shoes, silk umbrellas, saddle cloths,

GROCERIES—

Beef, pork, bread, S. I. sugar, manilla do, coffee, molasses, ginger, syrup, rice, barley, oat meal, split peas, codfish, arrow root, tapioca, manilla segars, champagne, port, mosto and marsala wines, italia, absinthe, brandy in cases or casks, rum, stoughtons, elixirs.

SUNDRIES—

Jewelry assorted, knives and forks, chisels, riveting hammers, sheath knives, jack do, crockery ware, & &c. For sale by   FINLEY, JOHNSON, & CO.
Portsmouth House, Clay st.
San Francisco, Nov. 23d, 1848.   5-tt

NEW GOODS,

LANDING from Brigantine "Calderon," and for sale by the subscribers.

Champagne,	Prints,
Cognac,	H'dkfs, Silk,
Wine, ass'd in cases,	" Cotton,
do in pipes,	Clothing,
Cordials ass'd	Saddle Cloths,
Italia,	Shawls,
Am. Beef and Pork,	Medicines,
Cassimeres,	Shirts,
Brown and Bl'd Domestics,	Shoes,

Together with a large variety of desirable articles.
FINLEY JOHNSON & Co.
San Francisco, 9th Jan. 1849.   2-tf
NEW GOODS.

The partnership of Finley Johnson and Co., started trading in San Francisco in the early 1840s. During the Gold Rush, the firm had a store at the Portsmouth House at Clay Street which also housed the first saloon and billiard room of the Pacific Coast.[18] It was opened in the late 1830s by the Swiss Jean Jacques Vioget, captain of the Peruvian ship *Delmira*, who was a recipient of the first cargo of pisco mentioned by Davis in 1839. Vioget was also the first surveyor of San Francisco and designed the first street layout of the city. Finley & Johnson was one of the wealthiest firms of San Francisco in 1849.[19]

The partnership of Stephen A. Wright and John S. Owen was short lived, it lasted only a little over two months. Later, both men became involved in several important administrative roles of the city.[20]

Pisco was one of the preferred liquors of the elite of San Francisco and the most expensive spirit in 1849.[21] In 1858 the Bank Exchange, the most luxurious saloon to date, advertised for the first time the availability of pisco in its premises (see page 168).

One of the most avid importers of pisco was Nicholas Larco, an Italian born in the Liguria region and an ex-resident of Lima who came to San Francisco during the midst of the Gold Rush in August of 1849. Larco imported pisco at least once a year since his arrival in 1849 until the 1860s. It should be noted that during that decade Larco was considered *the greatest star of the Italian colony of San Francisco.*[22]

In 1864, 200 jars of Larco's pisco were seized by Customs House officials alluding to a violation in the volume of the earthenware jars where the liquor was transported. The seizure caused several concerns in San Francisco's commercial circles, as described in a front page editorial article published by the *Daily Alta California* in January 6, 1864 (see pages 165/166, note 49).[23] The pisco in question was auctioned a few days later and after a trial that lasted until the end of August, Larco was indemnified and financially compensated.[24]

This unexpected event curiously coincided with the nascent period of the American era California wine and brandy industry. Just two weeks before the seizure, the *Daily Morning Call* published an advertisement from Kohler & Prohling announcing that their California-made wines and brandies had received five premiums out of six at the Ohio State Fair held last September in Cleveland.[25] This announcement was soon followed with another advertisement titled "Analysis of California Wines," complaining that, as compared to foreign wine, California wine was *sixty odd percent more expensive to produce.*[26]

But regardless of any possible attempt designed to limit pisco importation, the consumption of the Peruvian liquor continued strong in San Francisco in the years to come. In 1870, a geologist named Thomas Knox is convinced that *San Francisco is a nice place to visit* after tasting pisco for the first time.[27] In 1888, Rudyard Kipling writes a vivid allegory about a drink containing pisco.[28] In 1912, Pauline Jacobson reports to San

Franciscans of the time that Duncan Nicol's Pisco Punch was based on pisco, *a Peruvian brandy made from the grapes which grow up in the High Andes of South America.*[29]

By the turn of the century, pisco was used as the base for many drinks prepared in several San Francisco saloons.[30]

Pisco John

San Francisco's lore tells that the bartender that served Pisco Punch was nicknamed Pisco John and the Bank Exchange Pisco John's. Jones is the first source that identifies Pisco John as being John Torrence. I have failed to find any historical evidence that suggests Torrence was ever nicknamed Pisco John. Did Jones make that assertion just because of Torrence's first name? It is unlikely in my opinion that Torrence was Pisco John. There is no evidence that supports that claim. The only indication that Torrence was ever related to pisco were the advertisements he published with Thomas Parker, but pisco was shown in a hardly prominent way. Where did the nicknames Pisco John and Pisco John's come about? How could a person named Patrick, Thomas, George or Duncan be nicknamed John?

I was ready to give up to the common accepted notion, although unverified by historical evidence, that during his relatively short tenure John Torrence was a sort of a "piscoman" that somehow deserved the nickname of Pisco John, when I stumbled upon the San Francisco Telephone Directory of 1903. To my surprise, I saw that both Duncan Nicol and the Bank Exchange shared the telephone number: John 3246 (see page 139, top).[31] In those years, the first part of the telephone "number" was verbal and was chosen from a group of about thirty names such as Polk, Main, Chuck, Black, John, etc. The suffix " John" assigned for both Duncan Nicol and the Bank Exchange sparked my curiosity and decided to dig a bit into the history of telephony in San Francisco.

The first commercial telephone system implemented in the United States was in New Haven, Connecticut, on January 28, 1878. It was for 50 subscribers communicating in a party line mode. On February 17, Western Union implements in San Francisco the first Telephone Exchange system in the United States where people could call any subscriber individually.[32] San Francisco was not only on the cutting edge of drinking as Carl Nolte wrote recently,[33] but it was on the leading edge of communication technology as well. These first attempts to commercialize telephones required speaking with an operator and identifying the party to call by its name. The operator had to memorize the names of all the subscribers. As the number of subscribers grew, the task of memorizing names became a practical impossibility and the telephone numbering system was born. It had two parts: an alphanumeric part that identified the particular Telephone Exchange and a number. The names and the numbers were chosen phonetically so that they could be quickly understood and minimize possible communication errors especially when considering the relatively very poor electroacoustic quality of the equipment in those days. Initially, there was an outcry when a person was suddenly identified not by their name, but instead by a meaningless string of arbitrary letters and numbers. The pioneer Chinese Telephone Company in San Francisco's Chinatown, founded in 1887, refused to implement the numbering system because the Chinese community felt it was rude to refer to people by numbers. In 1901, the Chinese Telephone Company required operators to memorize nearly 1500 names together with each subscriber place of residence in order to differentiate people with the same name.[34] The nascent telephone technology certainly had its growing pains, but none more evident than during the beginning of the 20th century. People were not used to associate numbers with names and committed so many mistakes that frustrated the telephone companies. Even as late as 1911, the San Francisco Telephone Directory published a "Rules for Good Service" instruction page, that among other curious demands, orders the subscribers always to use the directory and never try to remember a telephone number in order to minimize guessing and thus the possibility of wrong number calls that were slowing the system down.[35]

In 1903, the San Francisco telephone company instructed its subscribers to answer a telephone call by first acknowledging – in the case of Duncan Nicol – : "Here is John 3246" and to the calling party reply "This is John 3246" (in the case Nicol's receives the call). This logical procedure was requested to confirm that the party calling had indeed reached the required destination (see page 139, bottom). These telephone system rules brings us the first plausible popular association of the nickname "John" with Duncan Nicol. It is not difficult to imagine a turn of the century person trying to call Duncan Nicol just remembering the John part of the number and asking a young telephone operator, perhaps pretty well acquainted with the virtues of the punch, to connect him with "the John of the Pisco." Eventually, a patient operator after receiving many a call from technologically in-savvy souls, agreed to acknowledge Nicol's calls with "Pisco John" a highly mnemonic and phonetically differentiated sound. To distinguish the calls addressed to Duncan Nicol from the ones to the Bank Exchange itself, the wisdom of the passage of time thought it was necessary to create a second nickname: "Pisco John's" meaning "the place of Pisco John." Thus, it was Duncan Nicol himself the person originally nicknamed Pisco John, as all historical evidence points out he was, but not because of his name or of any other prior owner's, but because of his telephone number in 1903.

Pisco Punch Recipe

In 1973, Bronson published a John Lannes' recipe of Pisco Punch which he found in 1964 in a letter written by a lawyer in 1941. In the 1920 San Francisco City Directory

Lannes is listed as *mgr Bank Ex* which gave strong credibility for the recipe being Duncan Nicol's original. Lannes' recipe for Pisco Punch is the following:

1/2 pint (8 oz.) of gum syrup [pineapple flavored]
1 pint (16 oz.) distilled water
3/4 pint (10 oz.) lemon juice
1 bottle (24 oz.) Peruvian Pisco Brandy
Serve cold in 3 or 4 oz. punch glasses
Put one piece of pineapple marinated in gum syrup
Lemon juice or gum syrup may be added to taste

Bronson was convinced that the secret of Pisco Punch was the gum arabic contained in gum syrup. I decided to investigate his claim further. *The Scientific American Cyclopedia of Formulas* edited by Albert Hopkins, is an incredibly vast compilation of formulas and recipes, published in 1910, used in the preparation of products as diverse as paints, lubricants, alloys, soaps, ice creams and alcoholic and non-alcoholic beverages, among several other things.[36] In the section of punches, Hopkins defines a punch as being a beverage made of various liquors or wine, hot [or cold] water, the acid juice of fruits and sugar. Then adds: *It is considered to be very intoxicating, but this is probably because the spirit, being partly sheathed by the mucilaginous juice and the sugar, its strength does not appear to the taste so great as it really is.* Gum arabic is basically sap from the trunk of two sub-Saharan species of the acacia tree. The gum is produced by the trees as a way of resealing the plant's bark in the event of damage, a process called gummosis.[37] The gum is a perfectly edible combination of polysaccharides and glycoproteins and is considered to be one of the most concentrated forms of mucilage substances found on earth. Thus, according to Hopkins' definition and the extraordinary mucilaginous characteristics of gum arabic, the gum was used for the purpose of further "hiding" the alcohol present in Pisco Punch and key in creating its historically reported smoothness, as very well noticed by Bronson. It appears Pisco Punch was designed with the intention of providing maximum possible alcoholic potency in the most subtle possible way –probably to the point of purposely trying to deceive the drinker– using state-of-the-art bar-tending techniques of the day. The fruity bouquet of pisco was the perfect accomplice for Nicol's mischievous concoction. Hopkins also informs that punches were almost universally drunk by the middle classes in the 1850 and 1860s and that they had almost disappeared by 1910, being superseded by wine. Thus, Duncan Nicol might well have invented Pisco Punch as a reminiscence of the old days of San Francisco at his *Temple of the Past* as Jacobson wrote the Bank Exchange was in 1912.

In May 13, 1937, Harold Ross, founder of *The New Yorker* magazine, writes a letter to

Dave Chase in which he persuades him to sell Pisco Punch in a Los Angeles restaurant.[38] He sends him a recipe he had *recently discovered*. Ross lived part of his teenage days in San Francisco in the early 1900s and had first hand experience of the popularity of the concoction even witnessing, correctly, that pisco was imported in *little clay jugs*. Ross' recipe for Pisco Punch is the following:

> 1 part sour .... lime
> 2 parts sweet .... grenadine syrup or sugar
> Ross writes: *(I think syrup is the best probably)*
> 3 parts ....Pisco
> 4 parts water and ice. Mix in a cocktail shaker

Ross' recipe calls for grenadine syrup or sugar instead of gum syrup and for lime juice instead of lemon juice as in Lannes' formula. It has a 4-3-2-1 water-alcohol-sweet-sour part mixture. This ratio first appeared in the Shrub formula published in Toronto by Young in 1861.[39] It was offered as a Rum Shrub by John Maguire, the brother of the Opera magnate Tom Maguire, at his Snug bar in San Francisco. The Snug introduced Rum Shrub in 1856 as *a rather nectarish drink*.[40] A Rum Shrub was rum mixed with sugar and lemon or lime juice left to age for several weeks. Interestingly, and compatible with the Rum Shrub basic formula, Ross mentioned that Pisco Punch *used to taste like lemonade but had a kick like vodka, or worse*, similar to the description made in 1949 by O'Brien that it *tastes like lemonade but comes back with the kick of a roped steer*.[41]

More insight about Duncan Nicol's "lemonade" can be obtained from the *San Francisco Chronicle* writer Millie Robbins, who five years before Bronson's discovery of Lannes' recipe, writes a column about Pisco Punch, of its deceptive potency and that it was a favorite of the San Franciscan Ladies of the time.[42] Robbins requests readers to provide any information that may give insights about the mysterious lost recipe. To her surprise, Robbins receives a large amount of letters that *could be enough to publish a little bartender guide on our own*.[43] Robbins selects a letter claiming that its authenticity cannot be questioned. The letter was from an anonymous resident of San Carlos identified with the initials EJP who claimed he was at Nicol's bedside in February 1926 when he passed away *in that Sutter street hospital*. The point that convinces Robbins of the authenticity of the letter was EJP's comment about not even Nicol's wife knowing the punch recipe. EJP said that Nicol's wife being practically blind since childhood, and much time alone, was not a bit interested in either Pisco Punch or the Bank Exchange. Then adds: *The formula for the punch DID NOT DIE with Mr. Nicol. But out of my great respect for him I do not believe that his recipe, which he treasured so much, should be published. However, I am enclosing a formula which, although not an exact facsimile of the original (the main ingredients are not available in San Francisco anyway), is so close no one today could tell the difference.* As reported by Scholten, the formula of Pisco Punch given to Robbins is the following:

Cut up a pineapple and marinate it overnight in Pisco
Place cracked ice in a 6 oz. glass
Add 1 1/2 oz. of the Pisco
Add the juice of a lime
Add 1 oz. of pineapple juice or gum syrup
Add a piece of marinated pineapple
Fill glass with plain water

Very close to Lannes' recipe and, interestingly, also with the 4-3-2-1 formula ratio of the Rum Shrub and Ross' Pisco Punch. One difference is the use of lime (also in Ross' recipe) instead of lemon. Regarding this discrepancy, another of the letters sent to Robbins in 1959 provides what could be a deciding evidence. A Stephen V. Chiuda writes that his late father, Vladimir Chiuda, used to provide the Bank Exchange with *limes imported from Acapulco*, Mexico, and that in one occasion he delivered a cargo to the Bank Exchange and that Nicol rewarded him with one of his *famous champagne cocktails*.[44] I verified that from 1900 to 1905 the partnership of Vladimir Chiuda & Napoleon Botto had a wholesale produce store at 413 Montgomery, just a couple of blocks from the Bank Exchange. From 1906 to 1916 Vladimir Chiuda is listed with several other partners but still in the produce business.

Another clue in Ross' letter is his assertion that during the early 1900s: *All San Francisco bars used to sell them* [Pisco Punch]. John Lannes is listed in 1903 working at The Bank Saloon located at 527 Clay. That saloon, a competitor of the Bank Exchange, must certainly have had its own version of Pisco Punch. Was Lannes' recipe Nicol's original? Probably not for several reasons. As Bronson discovered, John Lannes is listed as being the manager of the Bank Exchange in the 1920 San Francisco City Directory. Prohibition closed the bar's door permanently on January of 1920. It appears that Nicol sold the Bank Exchange to Lannes late in 1919 because in the city directory of that year, Nicol is still listed as its sole proprietor. Only in the 1920 city directory Lannes is listed as manager of the Bank Exchange while Nicol is not. It seems very unlikely that Nicol had included the original recipe as part of the deal since, according to O'Brien, Nicol emphatically said that: *Not even Mr. Volstead can take the secret from me.* Could Lannes have used some type of industrial espionage as Bronson suggested? Maybe, but what could have been Lannes incentive for that? After all, Prohibition was just around the corner and he had his own recipe he served at his saloon.

Historical sources indicate that Nicol mixed each punch with almost religious care. It can not be better exemplified than in Jacobson's article where she quotes an old timer little barber as saying: *E-v-e-r-y one of them is mixed the same. I had nine of them punches and e-v-e-r-y one of them was mixed the same. If you came here for THIRTY-FIVE years e-v-e-r-y one would be mixed the same.* Lannes recipe call of *lemon juice or gum syrup may be added to taste* makes one wonder if his recipe was really Nicol's original.

Whoever has tried Lannes recipe at face value will notice that it results in a punch that is pretty uninspiring. A close examination of Lannes recipe reveals a break-up of bartending mixing rules, well exemplified by the Rum Shrub 4-3-2-1 water-liquor-sweet-sour ratio. The sweet and sour component proportions just don't seem right. Lannes recipe calls for 3 parts of pisco, 2 of distilled water, 1.25 of lemon juice and 1 of gum syrup. These proportions seem rather odd. Was this the Pisco Punch recipe served at The Bank Saloon? Did Lannes purposely give Crawford Green in 1941 the wrong proportions? As it may be, only after a considerable tweaking in the quantity of the components Pisco Punch's renowned *lemonade* flavor comes to light. It has almost the same absolute quantities as called for in the Lannes recipe but are applied differently to each ingredient, in addition of using lime juice instead of lemon's, as shown in the next Table.[45] The recipe calls for Italia type pisco, as Asbury indicates, verified in Ross' letter and in the trial documentation of Larco's pisco seizure. Italia type pisco makes a significant difference in the final aroma of the punch.

Ingredient	Lannes' Pisco Punch	Revisited Pisco Punch
Pisco	24 oz. (3)	24 oz. (3) (Italia type)
Pineapple gum syrup	8 oz. (1)	16 oz. (2)
Lemon/lime juice	10 oz. (lemon) (1.25)	8 oz. (lime) (1)
Distilled water and ice	16 oz. (2)	32 oz. (4)

This recipe matches closely the ratios of the Rum Shrub and both EJP's and Ross' Pisco Punch recipes. You can go and judge by yourself. At the first sip you will agree with all the people that have tried it. "It's smooth... tastes like lemonade... does it have alcohol?" Yes it does, but you will barely notice, at least at the beginning. The magical effect of the gum mucilage and the sweet and sour combination makes the strong and fruity Italia pisco brandy almost vanish to the taste and one will not notice its effects until it is probably too late.

In order to minimize waste and maximize potential benefits, it is almost certain that Nicol may have added a relatively small step during the preparation of his punch. One which could have further contributed to the punch renowned smoothness and overall appeal. Since the 1700s, in Peru, there was a popular drink called *chicha de piña*.[46] It was prepared by simply soaking the rind of a clean pineapple for 24 hours in water. It produced a refreshing drink that was very popular for its medicinal properties, especially related to the digestion. Nicol could have easily prepared the *chicha* by soaking the pineapple rind –which was a waste of his punch preparation process– in distilled water and use this as the water component of the punch (see recipe in page 193). During the late 1800s, pineapple wine (Zumo-Anana) was believed to have several digestive benefits (an excellent side benefit for any punch of the day) as shown in an advertisement published in a medical journal of 1895 and reproduced here as a reference.[47]

Was Pisco Punch a Doped Drink?

Jacobson described the effect of Pisco Punch as *floating the drinker in the region of bliss of hasheesh and absinthe* and that *it will make a gnat fight an elephant* (see page 17).[48] Bronson in 1973, attributed such descriptions as probably due to the *grain alcohol and fusel oil traces* found in pisco. Scholten in 1997, attributed the unusual effects of drinking Pisco Punch as probably being due to an exaggeration because the alcoholic content of Pisco Punch is not that much different from today's Martini or any similar drink. I was not totally convinced with any of these explanations and decided to research the subject further. Could Pisco Punch have been laced with some kind of drug? The mention of a *bliss of hasheesh* should not be taken lightly since no alcoholic drink can produce an effect similar to that drug.

My initial suspicion turned into a distinct possibility when I found an interesting article titled "Drinking High Toned and What Came of It" published by the *Daily Alta California* in January 28, 1864. The article describes a somewhat comic account of an anonymous visitor to the Bank Exchange that drinks a concoction named Buck and Breck, during George Parker's bar's tenure. Because of its importance for the subject, I will hereby include the complete and non edited reproduction of that article:

Daily Alta California, January 28, 1864
SAN FRANCISCO, THURSDAY, JAN. 28
CITY ITEMS

Drinking High Toned, and What Came of It
     One of the oldest subscribers to the ALTA and one, too, held in high esteem, not only by ourselves but by a lot of friends from Los Angeles to Siskiyou, sends us the following, the experience of taking a "high toned drink:"
     I met two friends; was asked how I felt? Said I did not feel well – was almost sick. They recommended me to come along with them, and take a drink. "It will set you up." "You'll feel better." Went into the Bank Exchange – my friends called for a "Buck and Breck" – did not know what kind of a drink that was, and besides didn't like the name. I'm an original Black Republican (voted for Fremont in fifty-six).[49] Waited to see the beverage concocted – barkeeper filled a tumbler one third brandy, then put in something that looked like a solution of verdigris added a bright crimson liquid, and then filled the glass with champagne. Suggested to the barkeeper that it must be a strong drink. He said: "Oh no! you may take twenty of them. It couldn't affect you a bit; they always take them to sober off on!" Friend said it was high toned – conceded to try one. It was bully! Pleasant to the taste and mild as a zephyr – began to feel better immediately. My headache, which had continued a week, left me instantly. My boots which had been compressing my corns fearfully all morning were as "easy as old shoes;" in fact, I was not standing in them, was floating around in the air, a foot from the floor!

THE EXHILARATING EFFECT
     Sailed out through the door without opening it: street was full of people; Stock Board had just adjourned; ran foul of my friend S; he said I was just the man he'd been looking for; Estralla del Monte could be bought for fifty dollars a share; thought he said Real del Monte; knew it was down; must go up again; and told him to pitch in and buy for me; handed him my pocket book, containing five hundred in greenbacks; told him to sell them and make an advance in his purchase; invited my broker to the Bank Exchange to

have a drink; insisted he should call up his friends, felt rich; had forgotten that I owe a dollar in the world; took another Buck and Breck; felt still better; it seemed to endow me with the strength of a Hercules; felt ineffable contempt for Samson struggling with the Philistine Fire Zouaves! [50] I could have stood them on their heads! No excuse for him that his hair was short; wasn't I as bald as a badger? and if they have piled on to me too thick, and I got licked, do you think I'd been the contemptible sneak that he was, and laid the blame all on my wife? [51] – no! took another high toned drink on that, and started for my office.

HE COLLIDES

Attempted to cross the half of Merchant street not occupied by the Bulletin office, heard a rushing sound and felt myself propelled through the air, turning innumerable summersaults, alighted on the end of my nose and balanced myself there, just long enough to hear "Why don't yer get out er the way, say?" Arose to my feet and discovered one half my coat and my pantaloons pocket "spitted" on the shaft of the butcher's cart.[52] Butcher boy had alighted, and was examining the cart to see if I'd chafed the paint. "Felt like sailing in!" and cleaning Washington Market out. Knew I was wrong though; what right has a person on foot to a street crossing anywhere in San Francisco? especially when they are "taking home der meat."

Went back and took another "Buck and Breck," and borrowed a Shanghae overcoat, to cover my tatters. Concluded to go home. This time took the other side of Montgomery street. Was in something of a hurry, my nose was swelling fast, and one eye felt very much as if it was turning black.

ADVENTURE WITH THE HOOPS

Overtook two ladies walking side and side, out of step and wearing enormous skirts (they occupied the side walk completely), they looked as if they had donned a Sibley tent, with nothing in sight but their heads poked through the top. One lady trailed a long shaving, the other an old bone; they stirred out the dust fearfully. Tried to pass them by an oblique movement to the right, then to the left; they immediately deployed and stopped me. While skirmishing around just six feet in their rear, waiting for a chance to pass, was jostled by a man behind me, and stepped on to one lady's tail; brought her up with a graceful bow backwards, relieving her of the bone and about two yards of trimming. Apologized strenuously; lady would not forgive me; said I was a brute. My pride was injured; resolved to move back to Siskiyou; had the reputation of being the politest man in Deadwood City. Stepped off the side-walk into the gutter, and proceed homeward.

REACHES HOME

Wife was in bad temper had waited dinner three hours took one look at me; thought I was intoxicated, and flew into a violent passion (I was as sober as I am this instant); said she knew how it would be when I got down here among these vile San Franciscans and you have been in a fight too! Tried to explain to her "'ow it hall'appened," would not hear a word; said she would get a divorce. A lucky thought struck me; told her if she attempted that I'd go to Squarza's, get drunk on his Anti-Divorce punch and "block the game." [53] She could not understand the threat, but it stopped the scolding and she heard my story, took pity on me and bath my eye. I was growing weaker every moment, could scarcely stand; the fearful jar from the butcher's cart was falling upon my nervous system and had also occasioned a rush of blood to the feat. Wife had to call assistance to put me in bed. I have been sick a week.

A careful reading of the article can bring into light what Buck and Breck contained. It had brandy, champagne and two unidentified mixes: a solution of verdigris and a bright crimson liquid. While it is impossible to identify the contents of these last two liquids, the general description of the drink as being "High Toned" strongly suggests it contained some type of tonic probably laced with a drug. After having the first drink, the person mentions his headache went away instantly and that he was floating around in the air, a foot above the floor. This effects can hardly be attributed solely to a mix of brandy and champagne. Then he goes on to an exhilarating effect period of euphoria with a total disregard of money, including an apparently superhuman feeling of strength and bravery combined with possible hallucinations centered around an oil painting of Samson and Delilah. During this period the person drinks two more, possibly showing signs of craving. Then he has a somewhat serious street accident to which he gives, strangely, relatively very little importance. Before deciding to walk back home, he has a fourth drink and then a funny encounter with two ladies walking on the street, one of whom he partially undresses. Finally, once at home, he begins to feel *weaker every moment*.

After reviewing the drug literature I found one drug that could explain several, if not all, of the symptoms felt by the drinker at the Bank Exchange. It is cocaine. Native Peruvians have used cocaine as contained in natural form in the leaves of the coca plant for at least 5,000 years. They had the belief that chewing the sacred leaf will promote contact with the spirit world. Before 1855 cocaine was only available in leaf form. In that year, a German scientist named Friedrich Gaedecke put coca leaves in alcohol and got a solution he named Erythroxylon. Four years later, a fellow German scientist named Albert Niemann made white crystals from coca leaves and called it cocaine. According to modern literature:Cocaine induces a *sense of exhilaration in the user primarily by blocking the re-uptake of the neurotransmitter dopamine in the mid-brain.*[54] Exhilaration was indeed the term used by the *Daily Alta California* to describe the actions of the drinker at the Bank Exchange. Cocaine was deemed as being a *phenomenal remedy* for the cure of headaches in those days, an effect also felt by the drinker.[55] The drug also provides a sense of physical and mental strength and a decrease in inhibitions which are followed by a long period of withdrawal and depression. All those symptoms are well accounted for in the article's story. The literature revealed that cocaine was first used freely in the 1860s and that people were using it as a recreational drug almost as soon as it was synthesized. It also revealed that just a few years after its synthesis, cocaine appeared in cigarettes, ointments, nasal sprays, and preparations sold as tonics. During the late 1800s, cocaine was available almost everywhere in the U.S. mainly infused in countless tonics and secretive patent medicines used as an antidote for neurasthenia, melancholia and other ailments.[56] These legal tonics were usually mixed with other substances and were sold in a liquid form and cured whatever ailed you, just as the friends that persuaded the anonymous drinker at the Bank Exchange said. Almost certainly the Buck and Breck, as served at the Bank Exchange in 1864, had coca in it and could thus have been one of the first concoctions of that type in the world.

The most popular cocaine laced drink at that time was Vin Mariani (Mariani Wine), first concocted by the Italian Angelo Mariani in France in 1863. Vin Mariani was Bordeaux wine infused with coca leaves. Nearly all popular personalities of the day used and endorsed it. These Vin Mariani lovers included: Queen Victoria, The Pope, Thomas Edison, and many others. The Figures in the next page show some popular advertisements of Vin Mariani of the late 1800s.

In 1886, and in response to the market success of Vin Mariani, Doctor John Pemberton of Georgia invented Coca Cola, a concoction that included coca, which was sold at his pharmacy in Atlanta. The following year Asa Chandler, a fellow Atlanta pharmacist and a business man, purchased the formula rights and turned Coca Cola into one of the most popular drinks in the U.S. by the 1890s and 1900s.

Unknowingly of the effort of Albert Niemann, an Italian scientist named Paolo Mantegazza extracted cocaine from coca leaves at the end of the 1850s. After witnessing the use of coca by the natives in Peru, he was able to isolate the active ingredient and tested it on himself in 1858. In a scientific medical paper that soon followed, he wrote: *I sneered at the poor mortals condemned to live in this valley of tears while I, carried on the wings of two leaves of coca, went flying through the spaces of 77,438 words... God is unjust because he made man incapable of sustaining the effect of coca all life long.* [57]

An equally euphoric and curiously similar allegory is recorded by Rudyard Kipling, after having a Button Punch at the Bank Exchange in 1889, during the bar's tenure of George Brown and Duncan Nicol (Kipling writes that the bartender was *a German with*

long blond locks and a crystalline eye.) Alluding to an unusual secrecy surrounding the drink and to the nature of its recipe, Kipling wrote: *Go thither softly, treading on the tips of your toes, and ask him for a Button Punch. It will take ten minutes to brew, but the result is the highest and noblest products of the age. No man but one knows what is in it. I have a theory it is compounded of shavings of cherub's wings, the glory of a tropical dawn, the red clouds of sunset, and fragments of lost epics by dead masters. But try you for yourselves, and pause a while to bless me, who am always mindful of the truest interests of the brethren.*[58]

It is interesting to note that both Mantegazza and Kipling use the term "wings" in their descriptions, while the anonymous drinker of Buck and Breck felt he was *floating around in the air.* Vin Mariani advertisements are also strongly influenced by wings and flight themes. Kipling also decides to use another very curious word in his allegory: "shavings," a word still commonly used today to describe cocaine that has been "shaved" out of its crystal form.[59] Button Punch could have been another coca laced drink, probably the successor of the Buck and Breck and possibly the predecessor of the Pisco Punch. Since the early 1800s in Peru, pisco was used as the base for several liquors made of coca leaves, cherry, peach, orange rind, celery, vanilla or quinine (Peruvian bark) and since the late 1870s or early 1880s Doctor Alzamora offered in his pharmacy store in Lima a popular bitter drink made of both coca and quinine.[60] By 1898, there was at least one firm in Lima dedicated exclusively to the export of coca leaves and two houses of pure cocaine, mainly owned by German immigrants.[61]

Did the original San Francisco's Pisco Punch contain coca? Possibly yes, for several reasons. First, the pisco and the coca were both made and imported from the same country. Easily, the pisco coming from Lima could have been already infused in coca leaves. Secondly, Nicol could have decided to maintain the Bank Exchange tradition of the highly successful Buck and Breck and later the Button Punch, when he invented the Pisco Punch. Finally, Jacobson's description that Pisco Punch floats the drinker into a *region of bliss of hasheesh* now becomes another strong evidence, instead of just a possible exaggeration. According to the literature, hasheesh is another drug whose effects could also be interpreted as producing the feeling of flight.

Duncan Nicol may have encountered a problem by the early 1900s. The detrimental effects of extensive use of cocaine were discovered by the medical community which led to its prohibition by the California Board of Pharmacy in 1907,[62] and later to its ban by the U.S. Congress with the Harrison Act of 1914.[63] Coca, initially universally accepted as being a wondrous cure-it-all alkaloid quickly became the pariah of society. Its days of widely spread and legal use came to a stop almost as fast as it had started. The Coca Cola Company decided in 1905 to remove the cocaine part from its beverage but maintained the caffeine.

Nicol may have decided to continue preparing Pisco Punch the same way as in the old days. This may explain the unequaled level of secrecy that surrounded the Pisco Punch recipe, which was so influential in the creation of its mysterious legend. It may well be that Nicol did not have another choice than to keep the formula a secret. In Nicol's favor one must highlight that he limited the drinking of only one Pisco Punch per person.[64] That limitation may have been not just a legend of lore designed to attract customers, as others have suggested, but because of real necessity. It could have been the best way Nicol could figure out how to limit the danger of abuse of the drug and also the risk of being exposed. But five years later Nicol could not keep beating the system. The Act of Volstead Act of 1919 permanently closed the doors of the Bank Exchange and of all the saloons in the U.S.[65] However, it has been reported that Nicol continued serving Pisco Punch in private parties during the Prohibition period until his death in 1926.[66]

During the depression of the 1930s, it was cocaine's turn to fade away. The consump-

View of San Francisco's Market Street during the end of the 1890s, at the peak of the world's coca craze. To the right "painless dental surgery" is being offered, one of the first medical applications of cocaine.

tion in the U.S. disappeared until the late 1960s.[67] But San Francisco always remained a pleasure-oriented city through the decades. Well exemplified during the prohibition "boot-leg" days at Half Moon Bay and during the days of extensive use of hasheesh in the Haight-Asbury district in the 1960s. San Franciscans have always been bohemian and adventurer people in nature, as they were during the Gold Rush days. Pisco Punch was just another chapter of that history. During the early 1900s, it was to the people of San Francisco as Vin Mariani or Absinthe were to the people in Paris. All these concoctions were mysterious and controversial, but well accepted by writers, poets, painters, actors, musicians and by anybody that deemed it appropriate to use the help of that extra kick for inspiration.

In 1933, the Golden State Beverage Co. manufactured a bottled version of Pisco Punch. One can only guess how similar to Nicol's original this version of Pisco Punch was.

NOTES AND REFERENCES

1. *Ark of Empire*, Idwal Jones, Doubleday & Company, Inc., Garden City, New York, 1951, Pgs. 79, 102-103.

2. *This is San Francisco*, Robert O'Brien, Whittlesey House, New York, 1948, Pg. 68.

3. *Port O'Gold*, Louis J. Stellman, 1922, Ch. XXXVI, Fevers of Finance; for more information about this subject refer to: Memoirs of General W.T. Sherman, William.T. Sherman, 2nd ed., D. Appleton & Co., 1913 (1889), Vol. 1, Ch. 4 and to "The Wharf that Transformed the Life of Henry Meiggs", San Francisco News Letter, December 5, 1925.

4. *City of the Golden Fifties*, Pauline Jacobson, University of California Press, Berkeley and Los Angeles, 1941, Pg. 277.

5. "City Items," *Daily Alta California*, December 31, 1853.

6. "Notice of Dissolution of Partnership," *Daily Alta California*, January 27, 1864.

7. *City of the Golden Fifties*, Pauline Jacobson, University of California Press, Berkeley and Los Angeles, 1941, Pg. 8; and "Playhouses of the Pioneers," Pauline Jacobson, The Bulletin, August 12, 1916.

8. *The Barbary Coast*, Herbert Asbury, Alfred A. Knopf Inc., 1933, Pg. 226.

9. *Kipling Letters from San Francisco*, Rudyard Kipling, San Francisco Colt Press, 1949.

10. "Secrets of Pisco Punch Revealed," William Bronson, *California Historical Quarterly*, Vol. LII, Fall 1973, No. 3, Pgs. 229-240.

11. *Lone Mountain The Most Revered of San Francisco's Hills*, Ann Clark Hart, The Pioneer Press, San Francisco, 1937, Chp. IV Writers and Artists.

12. "San Francisco's Wondrous Drink, Pisco Punch," Paul Scholten , *The Argonaut*, Vol. 8, No. 2, Fall 1997, San Francisco Historical Society, Pg 9.

13. Chilean pisco, as opposed to the Peruvian, is distilled from grape musts that have been fermented for longer periods of time, when many of the original sugar and other components are absent and more alcohol is present. This requires a lower amount of grapes per liter of pisco produced and usually the addition of water to reduce an initially higher alcoholic content.

14. Dictation of Mrs. Captain Henry D. Fitch : Healdsburg, Calif. : ms.S, 1875 Nov. 26, BANC MSS C-E 67-10 (Bneg 518:17), Pg. 154. The Bancroft Library, University of California, Berkeley

15. *Sixty Years in San Francisco*, William Heath Davis, A.J. Leary Publisher, San Francisco, 1889, Pgs. 249-250.

16. *The Barbary Coast*, H. Asbury, Alfred A. Knopf Inc., New York, 1933, Pg. 226. For names and volumes of pisco containers refer to *Guía del viajero - Callao, Lima y sus alrededores*, Carlos Cisneros y Rómulo García, Imprenta del Estado, Lima, 1898, Pg. 187, and note 31 on page 102.

17. *A Yankee trader in the Gold Rush; the letters of Franklin A. Buck*, Compiled by Katherine A. White, 30-29653. U.S. Library of Congress, A 28773. In a letter written in San Francisco by New Yorker Franklin Buck to his sister on August 22, 1849, he ends the letter with *...and I will drink [to] your health in a glass of Italia and go to bed.*

18. *Reminiscences and incidents of "the early days" of San Francisco actual experience of an eye-witness, from 1845 to 1850*, John H. Brown, Mission Journal Publishing Co., San Francisco, 1886.

19. *San Francisco*, sponsored by The City and Council of San Francisco, Hastings House, New York, 1940, Pgs. 97, 205, 206. *El Dorado or Adventures in the Path of Empire*, Bayard Taylor, University of Nebraska Press Lincoln and Lincoln, 1949.

20. Stephen A. Wright sells his share to Lambert B. Clements on April 24, 1849 ("Copartnership Notice," *Alta California*, February 8, 1849; Dissolution, April 24, 1849) a month before, he had received the largest amount of votes for the election of the District Legislature ("For District Legislature," *Alta California*, February, 22, 1849) and later opens the Miner's Bank with a capital of $200,000 (*San Francisco*, sponsored by The City and Council of San Francisco, Hastings House, New York, 1940, Pg. 115.)

John S. Owen is elected Treasurer of the city of San Francisco in 1849 ("The Election," *Alta California*, day/month unknown, 1849.)

21. Pisco Italia was sold in San Francisco at $22 per 3 gallon *pisquito* jar. As a comparison, gin was sold at $3 per gallon, rum at $4, whiskey at $3, and French brandy at $6. "Prices in San Francisco," *The Panama Star*, Vol. 1, No. 13, Pg. 3, June 10, 1849.

22. For Larco's pisco importation affairs see: "Seizure for Alleged Breach of the Customs Regulations," *Daily Evening Bulletin*, January 5, 1864. For Larco's involvement in the Italian community see: "The Italians of San Francisco in 1865: G.B. Cerruti's Report to the Ministry of Foreign Affairs," Alessandro Baccari and Andrew M. Canepa, *California History*, Vol. LX, Winter 1981/82, No. 4., Pgs. 350-369.

23. "City Items - Custom House Seizure," *Daily Alta California*, January 6, 1864.

24. Case 1380, The United States of America v. 200 Jars of Pisco; United States Common Law, Equity, and Admiralty Case Files, 1851-1903; United States District Court for the Northern District of California, San Francisco, CA; Record Group 21, Records of District Courts of the United States; National Archives and Records Administration-Pacific Region (San Francisco), San Bruno, California. The Statement of Facts of Judge Odgen Hoffman states (literal quote follows): *Pisco is a spirit manufactured in Perú from the Muscatel Grape and is sent to foreign countries and imported into the Port of San Francisco from Perú in earthen jars called Pisquitos*; while Larco states that he imported *200 jars of Pisco Italia, an article manufactured from the Muscatel grape in the Republic of Peru.*

25. "Grand Triumph of California Wines," *Daily Morning Call*, December 24, 1863.

26. "Analysis of California Wines," *Daily Morning Call*, April 4, 1864.

27. *The Barbary Coast*, Herbert Asbury, Alfred A. Knopf Inc., 1933, Pg. 227.

28. *Kipling's Letters from San Francisco*, Rudyard Kipling, San Francisco Colt Press, 1949. Originally written for the newspapers *Civil and Military Gazette*, in Lahore, Pakistan and for *The Pioneer* of Allahadad, India in 1889, later reproduced in Chap. XXIV of his work *From Sea to Sea*, 1889.

29. "A Fire-Defying Landmark," *The Bulletin*, Pauline Jacobson, May 4, 1912, Pg. 13.

30. *Letters from the Editor - The New Yorker's Harold Ross*, edited by T. Kunkel, The Modern Library, New York, 2001, Pg. 117.

31. *San Francisco Telephone Directory* - February 1903, The Pacific States Telephone and Telegraph Company.

32. "Early Work on Dial Telephone Systems," Bell Laboratories Record, R.B. Hill, Vol. XXXI, No. 1, January, 1953, Pg. 22.

33. "Days Before the Disaster," *San Francisco Chronicle*, Carl Nolte, Sunday, April 9, 2006, Pg. A10.

34. "The New Chinese Telephone Company," San Francisco Examiner, Sunday, November 17, 1901.

35. " Rules for Good Service," *San Francisco Telephone Directory - 1911*, The Pacific States Telephone and Telegraph Company.

36. *The Scientific American Cyclopedia of Formulas*, Edited by Albert A. Hopkins, Query Editor of The "Scientific American," Scientific American Publishing Company, New York, 1910.

37. "gum arabic," Wikipedia.com

38. *Letters from the Editor - The New Yorker's Harold Ross*, edited by T. Kunkel, The Modern Library, New York, 2001, Pgs. 117-118. The existence of this letter was brought to my attention by cocktail historian Dave Wondrich of *Esquire* magazine, writer of "To Be Drunk Slowly - 'It's That Propulsive': San Francisco's Mythical Pisco Punch," for which I am very grateful.

39. *Young's Demonstrative Translation of Scientific Secrets*, Rowsell Ellis, Toronto, 1861, 91. SCHRUB: Take of lemon juice 1 pint, white sugar 2 pints, rum 3 pints, water 4 pints; mix and colour ready for use.

40. "Adjoining Maguire's Opera House...," *Daily Alta California*, December 1, 1856.

41. *This is San Francisco*, Robert O'Brien, Whittlesey House, New York, 1948, Pgs. 39-40.

42. "The Ladies Came in By a Special Door," Millie's Column, *San Francisco Chronicle*, June 12, 1959.

43. "Talk of Pisco Punch Brought Mail With a Punch," Millie's Column, *San Francisco Chronicle*, June 24, 1959.

44. "Happy Memories of Pisco Punch," Millie's Column, *San Francisco Chronicle*, June 8, 1960.

45. Pineapple gum syrup is prepared by soaking overnight 2cm x 2cm pieces of a fresh pineapple in gum syrup for 24 hours. There are several ways to prepare gum syrup. One dating back to 1862 was published by Dr. Christian Schultz in *Manual for the Manufacture of Cordials, Liquors, Fancy Syrups, etc.* (see "Gum Arabic Solution" & "Sugar Syrup Preparation" in pages 194-195). Another way to prepare gum syrup, although relatively modern, is described by Bronson. A summarized version follows. Mix well one pound of gum arabic in powder with one pint of water, take almost to boil and let cool down. Remove all surface impurities while cooling down. Prepare a sugar syrup made of four pounds of refined sugar and one quart of water boiled to 220°F. Add the gum arabic solution. Boil for one minute and remove all impurities from the surface. Filter through cheese cloth while warm and store in corked bottles.

46. *Diccionario Geográfico-Histórico de las Indias Occidentales o América*, Antonio de Alcedo, Madrid, 1789, Anexo, Piña, Pg. 149.

47. *The Homoepathic News Monthly*, F. A. Luyties, Saint Louis, Mo., Vol. XXIV, No. 8, Aug. 1895, Pg. 301. Bromeline or bromelain, a natural digestive enzyme with anti-inflammatory properties, is found in peak concentration within the pineapple rind.

48. *A Fire-Defying Landmark*, a pamphlet distributed as a compliment by the Bank Exchange and reproduction of an article of the same title written by Pauline Jacobson and published in the *San Francisco Bulletin* on May 4, 1912.

49. Buck and Breck, the name of the drink, was very popular in San Francisco during the Presidential Elections of 1856. It alluded to the nicknames of James Buchanan and John Breckinridge, future President and Vice President of the U.S. (*The Spectacular San Franciscans,* J. Cooley Altorocchi, E.P. Dupont and Co., New York, 1949, Pg.103.)

50. Zouaves were colorful U.S. Civil War fighters that wore flamboyant uniforms.

51. The anonymous visitor to the Bank Exchange makes a somewhat euphoric reference to the famous painting of Samson and Delilah that hung at the bar. Mark Twain describes the painting in some detail when he visits the Bank Exchange the same year in an article published in the *Territorial Enterprise*, June 17-23, 1864, Virginia City, Nevada.

52. This curious accident took place on Merchant Street, in an area close to the offices of *The Bulletin* newspaper.

53. Victor Squarza was a famous punch manufacturer in San Francisco during the mid 1860s. He prepared several punches with curious names such as Anti-Divorce, Morning Comfort, Anti-Dyspeptic Appetizer, Lady's Tea and Cocoa, etc.

54. Refer to for example: http://www.cocaine.org - June, 2006.

55. *América*, José Coroleu, Montaner y Simón Editores, Madrid, 1895, Vol. 2, Pg. 208.

56. "Between Coca and Cocaine: A Century or More of U.S.-Peruvian Drug Paradoxes, 1860-1980," Paul Gootenberg, Latin American Program Working Papers, The Woodrow Wilson International Center, Washington D.C., 2001; an excellent description of the socio-economical history of cocaine in the U.S.

57. "Sulle virtù igieniche e medicinali della coca e sugli alimenti nervosi in generale," Paolo Mantegazza, 1858, Ann.Univ.Med., 167: 449-519.

58. *Kipling's Letters from San Francisco*, Rudyard Kipling, San Francisco Colt Press, 1949. Originally written for the newspapers *Civil and Military Gazette*, in Lahore, Pakistan and for *The Pioneer* of Allahadad, India in 1889, and reproduced in Chap. XXIV of his work *From Sea to Sea*, 1889.

59. See for example: *Choosing Not To Use: Alcohol, Tobacco, and Other Drugs*. EDC. Newton, Mass; Education Development Center, Inc./Rocky Mountain Center for Health Promotion 1996.

60. *Quince plazuelas, una alameda y un callejón,* Pedro Benvenutto Murrieta, Lima, 1932, Pgs. 300-301, 174-175.

61. *Guía del viajero - Callao, Lima y sus alrededores*, Carlos Cisneros y Rómulo García, Imprenta del Estado, Lima, 1898. Pgs. 179. C.M. Schröder & Co. exported coca leaves and A. Kitz & Co. and Pehovas hermanos & Co. exported cocaine.

62. "The Origins of Cannabis Prohibition in California," Dale H. Gieringer, Originally published as "The Forgotten Origins of Cannabis Prohibition in California," *Contemporary Drug Problems*, Vol 26 #2, Summer 1999, Revised by the author Feb 2000, Dec. 2002, Mar. 2005, *Contemporary Drug Problems*, Federal Legal Publications, New York 1999.

63. "Harrison Narcotics Tax Act of 1914," Historical Documents, www.historicaldocuments.com/HarrisonNarcoticsTaxAct.htm - June, 2006.

64. "House of Pisco Punch. Duncan Nichols' saloon in the Montgomery Block. Duncan Nichols on extreme left. Only one Pisco Punch was allowed per customer." :101, Roy D. Graves Pictorial Collection; The Bancroft Library, University of California, Berkeley. Annotation in photograph.

65. "The Volstead Act," Historical Documents, www.historicaldocuments.com/VolsteadAct.htm - June, 2006. Also known as the National Prohibition Act. It was later repelled in 1933.

66. "Talk of Pisco Punch Brought Mail With a Punch," Millie's Column, *San Francisco Chronicle*, June 24, 1959.

67. *Hooked: Illegal Drugs and How They Got that Way. Volume 2: Cocaine/LSD, Ecstasy and the Raves*, DVD Documentary, A&E Television Network, Cat. No. AAE-70807, The History Channel, 2000.

Guillermo Toro-Lira, the author, is a native of Lima who has lived near San Francisco for over two decades. Since the late 1990s, he began researching about the Peruvian relations in the history of California. *Wings of Cherubs* is the initial result of his research, which he plans to expand in future publications to present an historical overview of the social, cultural and commercial relationships between the territories of the Pacific. The Spanish version of *Wings of Cherubs* won a Gourmand World Cookbook Award 2007 as the Best Wine Literature Book of the World written in Spanish.

CPSIA information can be obtained at www.ICGtesting.com
Printed in the USA
BVOW032244110213

313010BV00001B/121/P